PENGUIN BOOKS
A Year with the Ladies of Llangollen

Elizabeth Mavor has written several novels (one of which was shortlisted for the Booker Prize), a biography of the Duchess of Kingston and *The Ladies of Llangollen* which is the Ladies' own story, also published by Penguin. She is married to the illustrator, Haro Hodson, has two sons and lives in Oxfordshire.

CW00952469

A YEAR WITH THE LADIES
OF LLANGOLLEN

Compiled and edited by Elizabeth Mavor

PENGUIN BOOKS

Penguin Books Ltd, Harmondsworth, Middlesex, England
Viking Penguin Inc., 40 West 23rd Street, New York, New York 10010, U.S.A.
Penguin Books Australia Ltd, Ringwood, Victoria, Australia
Penguin Books Canada Limited, 2801 John Street, Markham, Ontario, Canada L3R 1B4
Penguin Books (N.Z.) Ltd, 182–190 Wairau Road, Auckland 10, New Zealand

First published by Viking 1984
Published in Penguin Books 1986

This selection and foreword copyright © Elizabeth Mavor, 1984
All rights reserved

Made and printed in Great Britain by
Hazell Watson & Viney Limited,
Member of the BPCC Group,
Aylesbury, Bucks

Except in the United States of America,
this book is sold subject to the condition
that it shall not, by way of trade or otherwise,
be lent, re-sold, hired out or otherwise circulated
without the publisher's prior consent in any form of
binding or cover other than that in which it is
published and without a similar condition
including this condition being imposed
on the subsequent purchaser

Contents

The Ladies' Outings
in the 'Hand' Carriage.

ASTON
Seat of the Lloyddes.

BRYNKINALT
Seat of Lady Dungannon.

CHIRK CASTLE
Seat of the Myddeltons.

HALSTON
Seat of the Myttons.

PORKINGTON
Seat of the Owens.

WYNNSTAY
*Seat of the
Watkin Williams Wynns.*

Main Centres
WREXHAM
Where the Post came in.

OSWESTRY
*Where their friends
the Barretts lived.*

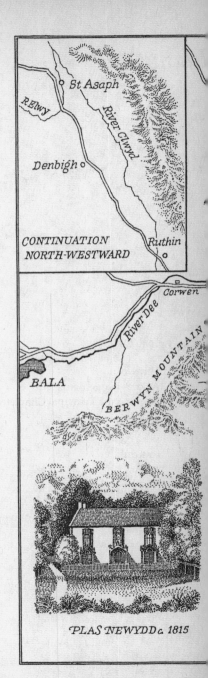

PLAS NEWYDD c. 1815

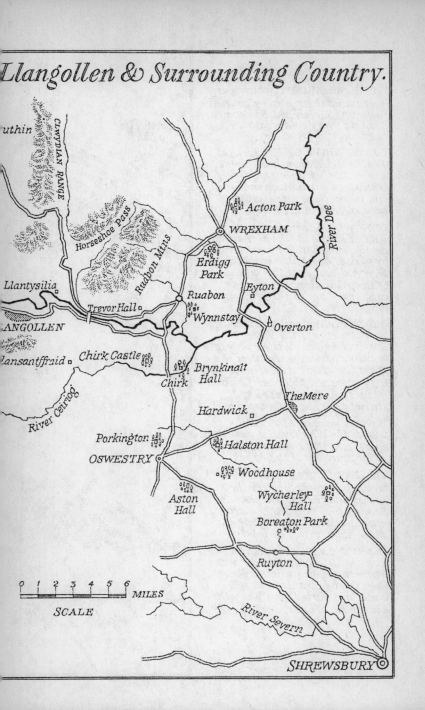

Llangollen & Surrounding Country.

Ruthin

CLWYDIAN RANGE

Horseshoe Pass

Ruabon Mtns.

Acton Park

WREXHAM

River Dee

Llantysilio

Erdigg Park

Eyton

Trevor Hall

Ruabon

LLANGOLLEN

Wynnstay

Overton

Llansantffraid

Chirk Castle

Brynkinalt Hall

Chirk

River Ceiriog

The Mere

Hardwick

Porkington

Halston Hall

OSWESTRY

Woodhouse

Aston Hall

Wycherley Hall

Boreaton Park

Ruyton

0 1 2 3 4 5 6   MILES

SCALE

River Severn

SHREWSBURY

THE HOME CIRCUIT, *which was just round their garden, potagere, fowl yard, melon bed. Sometimes, in rain or very cold weather, they ran it.*

TO THE WHITE GATE, *which led into the field before their cottage, where little Bishop attempted to exhibit an air balloon and failed, and where Nancy, the amiable bear, was exhibited.*

PENGWERN, *their favourite walk of all, led to the enchanting meadows under Pengwern Wood by way of the Mill near Plas Newydd and past the cottage of their landlord, often in the company of one of their favourite cows.*

BLAEN BACH, *another favourite walk, by way of the valley of the Cyfflymen. On their way to the little hamlet where they had spent their first winter in Wales they gathered holly berries for hedges, and primroses and strawberry plants for their banks.*

TOWER, *was rented by their friends the Whalleys - it was two miles from this cottage in the neighbourhood of the Abbey.*

VALLE CRUCIS ABBEY, *a favourite picnic place for the Ladies and their friends. Anna Seward had found this charming and unalarming spot 'grand, silent, impressive, awful'!*

LLANTYSILIO, *whose Church with 'the little cracked bell' was where the Ladies worshipped. Their friend Mrs Roberts of Dinbren is buried here beneath a large funeral urn.*

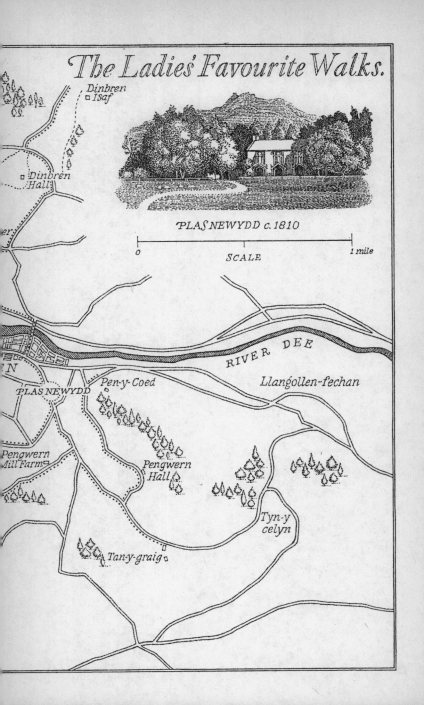

The Ladies' Favourite Walks.

PLAS NEWYDD c. 1810

0   SCALE   1 mile

Dinbren
Isaf

Dinbren
Hall

RIVER DEE

Pen-y-Coed

Llangollen-fechan

PLAS NEWYDD

Pengwern
Mill Farm

Pengwern
Hall

Tyn-y
celyn

Tan-y-graig

Foreword

It has been told elsewhere how in 1778, to the fury and consternation of their aristocratic Irish families, Eleanor Butler and Sarah Ponsonby eloped and fled to a cottage in North Wales. This book, taken from their Journal, is the story of their subsequent life together in the Vale of Llangollen.

Our changed attitude to the celebrated friendship of the Ladies of Llangollen serves only to show how the passage of time can sometimes bestow an amiable afterglow upon what has formerly been considered scandalous. The record of that once doubtfully regarded relationship was first brought to public notice by Mrs G. H. Bell with the publication of the charming *Hamwood Papers* in 1930. Mrs Bell was aunt to the present owner of that Journal, which the Ladies' friend, Miss Harriet Pigott, inaccurately believed to be written by Sarah Ponsonby. It was a Journal, Miss Pigott insisted (though she had never seen it), in which 'every person was mentioned, and though replete with genuine and humorous vein' was known to have not a single ill-natured word in it. On this particular point readers will of course decide for themselves.

Mrs Bell, by and large, made an excellent selection from Eleanor

Butler's closely written and often very difficult manuscript, lapsing only occasionally and then forgivably. In one entry the Ladies' gardener is recorded as nailing up fruit trees in a hurricane, Mrs Bell adding 'poor man', generously attributing feelings of sympathy to Eleanor which a study of the original manuscript proves she did not at the time experience. At other junctures Mrs Bell felt moved to improve on Eleanor's eccentric punctuation or her random order of events (in this selection I have refrained from correcting the smaller inconsistencies in the dates of the entries).

My own selection is in the main based on Mrs Bell's, though I have respected the current shift of interest from the formal to the informal, the national to the local, so that, like the Ladies themselves, I have considered the choice of a new pair of sugar-tongs of more moment than the restoration of the Bourbon monarchy. To Mrs Bell's selection I have added some hitherto unpublished extracts from the main body of the Journal as well as from an unpublished Journal for 1819. In all these extracts I have preserved Eleanor's own energetic punctuation. To these, by way of bridging some of the gaps in time, I have added excerpts from the unpublished letters of certain of their friends, as well as some published letters of their enemies, and I have garnished the whole with extracts published for the first time from their Receipt and Account Books. These *were* kept by Sarah Ponsonby, and here her own gently humorous spirit finds mild utterance, whether in describing the gymnastic exertions required to produce Mrs Worrall's enormous pound-cake, or the niceties of preserving cherries, not to mention those characters who make their shy bows from the pages of the Account Book: people like the 'flat faced carpenter', 'the little doctor' who attended their cows, the small boy who brought them a rare white foxglove, roots and all, from the wet tanks, to be rewarded with twopence, and the two Davies brothers mistakenly whipped for stealing the Ladies' strawberries and placated with shillings for the injustice. But of course the Account Book is only the gentle counterpart to the passion of the main work, which is Eleanor Butler's: her view is cosmic on occasion, sometimes spiced with Royal scandal, though mainly concerned with their own highs and lows, the business of their 'family' of servants, and the goings-on in the village of Llangollen.

The layout of the main body of the Journal which runs from 1785 to 1790 closely resembles the timetables employed by other ladies of the period, and like theirs it was very likely copied from that adhered to by Richardson the novelist's popular heroine, Clarissa. 'Rose at Eight' (and sometimes earlier) runs Eleanor's own timetable, continuing:

> 9 Breakfast
> 1–3
> 3–9
> 9–12

The blanks were to be filled in at will throughout the day. For it seems that Eleanor frequently went into the garden, to plant pinks, say, shortly returning to record the fact in the Journal. Or, gazing through the library window, she would record 'the Moon rising as I write this'.

The layout of the Ladies' Journal has to some extent influenced the scheme within which I have placed my selection. The truth is that the Ladies' lives were not so much a linear progression from point to point as a kind of dignified *eddying*. For though connected not a little slyly by gossip to the foibles of the fashionable world outside, their lives were in fact securely yoked, as were those of the Llangollen villagers themselves, to the seasons: to the promises of spring, the sultry charms of summer, the rewards of autumn, the wise putting-by for rigorous winter. Their life, accordingly, was repetitive, but it was a repetition which they loved and savoured year after year like connoisseurs, never taking it for granted, and always finding in its simplest manifestations a delight and beauty quite 'unknown', Eleanor would insist, 'to Vulgar minds'!

I have therefore discarded the linear method usually employed in selections of this kind, and instead I have grouped together all the thrawn Januaries of their lives, their ecstatic Mays, limpid Septembers and beloved candlelit Decembers, in the hope of giving a fuller and more sympathetic view of their quiet and enviable life together in the Vale of Llangollen.

Garsington, July 1983

Acknowledgements

I should like to thank Lady Martha Ponsonby and Major Charles Hamilton for so kindly allowing me to reproduce extracts from the letters and Journals of the Ladies in their possession; Mrs Lisa Baskin for kindly allowing me to quote from her collection of Sarah Ponsonby's letters; Mr Colin Franklin for most generously giving me his transcript of them; the National Library of Ireland for permission to use the 1819 Journal; the Bodleian Library and the John Rylands Library for allowing me to reproduce extracts from Harriet Pigott's and Mrs Piozzi's letters; and the National Library of Wales and the Llangollen Town Council for letting me use the Account Books that are in their possession. I also most warmly thank Mrs Rachel Davies of Wrexham for allowing me to quote extensively from the Ladies' beautiful Receipt Book which is in her keeping. Finally, I thank Faith Tolkien for so patiently reading and correcting this manuscript; Keith Taylor for seeing it through to publication; and Haro Hodson for help with the illustrations, which are by Thomas Bewick.

Some of the Principal Characters Mentioned in the Journal

SERVANTS

Mary Carryll had been housemaid at Sarah Ponsonby's old home in Ireland. She had aided and abetted the Ladies' flight, and afterwards accompanied them to North Wales. Her dignified social standing may be assumed because the Ladies (for whom she was very much more a friend than a servant) paid for her hair powder.

Molly Jones, kitchen maid. Discharged but reinstated. Much later discharged again for having the itch. Reinstated once cured. The cost: 3s.

Gwendolen, housemaid and, according to the Ladies, a pattern for all who followed.

Peggeen, indispensable 'daily' and maid of all work.

'The Irish Woman', usually referred to as 'IW' in the accounts. She was the Ladies' postwoman and trusted messenger.

Edward Parry, footman. He was eventually found to be too expensive and in other ways unsatisfactory, and so was discharged. Thereafter, the Ladies employed only female servants within doors.

Powell, Richard, William Jones, Moses Jones and *Simon* were all gardeners, and certainly the most tried of the Ladies' staff. All but the favoured Simon were in course of time found wanting and, like cannon balls, discharged. Poor Moses Jones in particular was reinstated and subsequently sacked a number of times.

PETS

Cows

Margaret, first and much loved; *Glory*, whom they used to accompany on walks with their friends; *Linda*, a present from Miss Harriet Bowdler – she walked all the way from Bristol to Plas Newydd; *Primrose*; and *Beauty*, perhaps the most loved of all.

Dogs

Flirt, their first dog in North Wales; *Rover*, her son; *Bess* and *Gypsey*, her daughters; *Sapho*; and *Phillis*, Lady Dungannon's 'little yellow dog', whom she was not permitted to take when she retired to Hampton Court.

Cats

Tatters, who lived to be eighteen; *Thomas*; *Babet*; *Muff*, lost in a snowdrift; *Brandy*; and *Gillian*.

SOME OF THE VILLAGERS

John Edwards of Pengwern, farmer, and their landlord. His son (also John) tried to evict the Ladies when he saw how attractive they had made Plas Newydd – fortunately he was unsuccessful.
Mr and Mrs Parkes of the Lyon, in and out of favour.
Mr and Mrs Edwards of the Hand, also in and out of favour.
Mrs Worrall, grocer and general supplier. She occasionally lent the Ladies money.
Mrs Parry of Ruabon, general grocer.

David the Miller.
Shanette, reputedly the witch of Llangollen.
Mr Baillis, builder and plasterer, known on occasion to present immoderate bills.
Mr Roberts of Dinbrenisaf, farmer. He supplied the Ladies with much of their butter and cheese, and also excellent geese.
'Poor Mary Green', whom the Ladies supported at the rate of one to two shillings a week.

COUNTY

The Dungannons of Brynkinalt.
The Lloydes of Aston.
The Lloydes of Trevor.
The Myddeltons of Chirk Castle.
The Myttons of Halston. Squire Mytton was a noted eccentric who once set his nightshirt on fire to cure himself of the hiccoughs.
Watkin Williams Wynn of Wynnstay.

PROFESSIONAL MEN

Mr Chambre, accountant.
Mr Crewe, surgeon.
Mr Turner, apothecary.
Mr Thomas Jones, apothecary.
Mr Wynne, solicitor.
Mr Hesketh, wine merchant.
Mr Appleyard, bookseller.
Mr Eddowes, bookseller.
Mr Sandford, bookseller.
Donnes, tailor.
Holiday, hairdresser.

FRIENDS

Mrs Tighe, girlhood friend and distant cousin of Sarah Ponsonby. They had been brought up together, and it was from Mrs Tighe's home in Ireland that the Ladies made their escape in 1778. Mrs Tighe gave Sarah a small yearly allowance.

Mrs Goddard, another friend from the old Irish past. To begin with, she was much against the Ladies' elopement. She later relented in face of their obvious devotion to one another, and when she died left Sarah a small annuity.

Lady Dungannon, yet another Irish friend. She was the Duke of Wellington's grandmother, spendthrift, eccentric and on occasion exceedingly tedious. (*See also* ENEMIES.)

*Mrs Elizabeth Barrett,** *Miss Laetitia Barrett* and *Miss Margaret Davies*. The Ladies' cow, Margaret, was very probably named after Miss Davies, which gives a curious tilt to some of the Journal entries. Their friendship with these three ladies was deep and intense until the Barretts made the mistake of parking their carriage at the Hand Inn during a period when our Ladies were conducting a vendetta with the proprietor. (So, regretfully, *see also* ENEMIES.)

Miss Harriet Bowdler, friend both of the Barretts and Margaret Davies. She was also the sister of Thomas Bowdler, who brought out a 'family' edition of Shakespeare from which all coarse passages had been extirpated. Harriet lived in Bath and was the Ladies' chief source of society news. For a time she became a kind of subterranean rival to Eleanor Butler for Sarah Ponsonby's affections.

Miss Harriet Pigott, rather younger than the Ladies, who first met her at some private theatricals where she played Busy, a maid. This was her nickname thereafter. She bravely left her tyrannical brother's rectory to make a life on her own, and was a favourite correspondent of Eleanor's.

Miss Anna Seward, known as 'the Swan of Lichfield'. In some quarters she was greatly admired as a poetess – in others, quite definitely not.

Mrs Piozzi, who, as Mrs Thrale, had been the close friend of Doctor Johnson. Now married to the opera singer Gabriel Piozzi, she had come to live over the hills from the Ladies in the Vale of Clwydd.

Mr and Mrs Whalley, a 'sensitive' little couple – Mr Whalley was an enthusiastic amateur painter – who came to live at Tower in Llangollen.

---

* Though unmarried, her age entitled her to the courtesy of 'Mrs'.

Some of the Principal Characters Mentioned

ENEMIES

Lord and Lady Ormonde, Eleanor's brother and sister-in-law. Throughout her life Eleanor maintained that they had cheated her out of a large sum of money due to her in the terms of her brother's marriage settlement. This particular vendetta did not extend to her nephews, who were regarded with pride and affection.

The Barrett sisters. (*See* FRIENDS.)

Margaret Davies. (*See* FRIENDS.)

Lady Dungannon. (*See* FRIENDS.)

Mr Edwards of the Hand Inn, frequently unreliable as to charges. On one occasion he was thought by the Ladies to be responsible for a scandalous piece about them in the newspapers. Dispensed with because of an exorbitant bill, but found too useful and reinstated.

Donnes the tailor, frequently unable to measure up to the exacting standards of the Ladies in the matter of their riding habits. He pleased sufficiently, however, to be retained.

Various joiners, plasterers, apothecaries, odd-job men, gardeners, sightseers and, in particular, chimney sweeps.

L.W.L.L.—2

21

JANUARY

1784

Sunday January 4th   Set out for Oswestry at the peril of our Lives – the road an entire Sheet of Ice – to visit the Barretts – supped and lay at the Barretts.

Sunday January 10th   Ill at night and all the morning . . .

(Eleanor Butler's Pocket Book)

1785

January 8th   . . . about a week before I received your last letter I was suddenly awaken'd in the middle of the night by a Person* requesting I would Agree to send for Our Vicar without delay to teach us Latin. He is a very good sort of modest Man – and was formerly a School Master – But as the Snow seems likely to go which will allow us to Work in Our Garden, we have agreed to defer it 'till next Winter When we hope if alive to put this Grand Scheme in

---

* Eleanor.

execution – to read the Sixth Book of the *Aeneid* – and then become Mistress of Italian – Our friend Miss Davies Who gave us the Receipt for the Bark Waistcoat sent us yesterday Barrettis introductions to that Language – We have a Grammar and Dictionary – We Cou'd have all sorts of Latin Books for Shillings from Shrewsbury – Our Pleasures though Very Sublime will not be very expensive for next Winter.

(Sarah Ponsonby to Mrs Tighe)

1787

January 4th   My Brother called here in his way to Bath – He is not improved – from being As I thought Six Years since, very pretty and genteel. He is grown monstrous tall and coarse and Clumsy and Irish – He talks of going to London But I shall not present him to you. I am not proud of Him . . .

(Sarah Ponsonby to Mrs Tighe)

January 31st   Are you ever tempted to go to Windsor and Visit Herschel.* We have heard wonders of his discoveries – and his new Telescope which I believe is by this time completed, must be admirable: I want to Know if it has really enabled him to discover whether there are any Works of Art in the Moon? as he expected it would.

(Sarah Ponsonby to Mrs Tighe)

1788

January 1st   Soaking rain. gloomy heavy day. Three. Dinner. Roast Beef. Plum pudding. half past 3 till 9. Still close night. Reading – making an accompt-Book. Then reading Sterne to My Beloved while she worked on her Purse. 9–12 in dressing room reading – writing to Mrs Goddard Bath. A day of Sensibility and Sweet Repose.

January 2nd   My beloved and I went the Home Circuit – fed Margaret who followed us from the Pales to the Melon ground door . . . Bought a whip from Davies the sadler . . . Reading Sterne to my Sally she netting a purse.

* Sir William Herschel (1738–1822), the Court astronomer.

24

Thursday January 3rd Rose at half-past seven. Soaking rain. Warm wind. Half past eight to nine writing. Drawing . . . Got the books cleaned and the shutters dusted. Went to the field before our cottage. Saw a man lying on the ground by the gate. Enquired. They said he was a stranger and supposed to be dead. Sent to see. Some signs of life. The Vicar's man came and proposed taking him to the workhouse. We sent him wine. He came to himself. Said he had been a gentleman's cook. Was going from London to Liverpool, had walked all night and probably fasted. Sent him something. Very little indeed.

Saturday January 5th My Beloved and I went the Home Circuit – fed Margaret – a very kind letter from Lady Dungannon – answered it with great Kindness also. 3 Dinner. Roast Beef. A day of uninterrupted and delightful Retirement.

Sunday January 6th Dined at One on giblet broth and boiled Mutton – this early as We invited our Landlord and his Wife, Son and Daughter in law to dine with Mary* – an annual custom.

Wednesday January 9th Harsh. Scowling. Black Wind. 3 Dinner. Roast Goose. Hogs puddings. *Mem* eat no more of the latter. too savoury – too rich for our abstemious Stomachs.

Thursday January 10th Three Dinner. Beef Hash. Hogs puddings. did not touch the latter. 9–10 Reading. finished *Melanges d'Histoire et de Litterature* which had been my Night lecture. A day of the most exquisite retirement.

Sunday January 13th Lead coloured clouds. Loud Storm. 9 till 1 in the Bedchamber over the Kitchen where We removed till our own, with the Dressing room, new papered and white Wash'd. A Hurricane. a day of delight and exquisite retirement.

Monday January 14th Showers of Sleet. Mountains covered with Snow . . . John Jones and Thomas Owen planting the Hedge in the new garden . . . Letter from Mrs Stanley (formerly Jenny Talbot) from the Hand on her way to Ireland from Bath, with a Rhubarb Cordial, two views of Bath from poor Mrs Goddard. Storm and gloom. John Jones planting raspberries. Lovely celestial night. Millions of stars, silver moon.

* Their maid, Mary Carryll.

Wednesday January 16th   Rose at half past 10. My head ached all night and my Sweet, tender Sally Would not leave me till the pain was entirely removed. gave me an Emetic which provided me Immediate Ease. Thank God.

(The Journal)

Expenses

Jan.   1   John Jones from Chirk Castle Gardens 1s.
     3   Post 1s.6d. Poor Man 1s.
     4   4 Strikes of Turnips at 1s.2d.
     5   Market 10s. Woman to Wrexham with Mrs Tighe's Beef 1s.6d.
   11   Mending Ventilator 3d. Bakehouse 3s. A New Whip 12s. Ed. Evans Carriage of Coals £1.8s. Ned the Butcher Due for Pork 16s.4d. Poor Mary Green 2s. Turkey 3s.6d.
   15   Pauper 6d. Oranges 6d.

Thursday January 17th   Dressing room papered. bed put up in the Bedchamber. Reading. Drawing. papering the Bedchamber. Cleaning Books. No letters.

Sunday January 20th   Richard Goosmere came to offer his services as a gardener – express image of the gardener of Andouillets as described by Sterne – little, hearty, broadset, chattering – I believe good natured and I'll swear hoping kind of a Fellow.

Tuesday January 22nd   Tempest. Gloom. Read *Betula Liberata* to my beloved. Explained all the difficult Passages – how delightful to teach her.

Wednesday January 23rd   3 Dinner. Boil'd fowl. hang Beef and Cabbage.

Friday January 25th   Sweet still day. Lady Anne Butler* came at three – dined – sat most comfortably over the fire talking of old times and laughing. Letter from Arthur Wesley.† Will breakfast with us to-morrow morning. Wrote to him and Lady Dungannon. Mr Owen of Porkington sent us a hare. Supped at ten. Retired at one.

---

* Eleanor Butler's sister-in-law, with whom they had a fluctuating friendship.
† Later the Duke of Wellington.

Sunday January 27th Rose at eight. Lovely misty morning...
Lady Dungannon and Arthur Wesley arrived. A charming young
man. Handsome, fashioned, tall and elegant. He stayed till two then
proceeded to Ireland. Lady Dungannon stopped here. Went away at
eleven. She was in the best Temper. Extremely pleasant and
agreeable. We sat till one.

Wednesday January 30th We rose at eight with the purpose of
going to Brynkinalt this day and to Oswestry tomorrow. Found this
morning so delightful, our cottage so silent and still, could not find
it in our hearts to stir from it.

Thursday January 31st My beloved and I went into the new
garden. Reading. Drawing. Read *Davila*. Then my beloved read *La
Morte d'Abel*. Nine till twelve in the bedchamber reading. Mr
Edwards of the Hand brought us a present of Hogs puddings. Old
Parkes of the Lyon came up to inform us that Mr Palmer, my
brother's chaplain had been at their House for a moment on his way
to Ireland. Had sent his compliments to us and Butler's love and
Duty... Very impertinent in them not to Deliver this message
yesterday morning. A day of sweet and delicious retirement.

(The Journal)

1789

Thursday January 1st The Dee is frozen all over. Shanette, the
reputed witch of the village, brought us for a new year's gift a large
parcel of apples Tied up in a neat white napkin. I met her as she was
coming in with her gift. She insisted on kissing my hand. A
compliment I could well have excused, but could not avoid for fear
of giving her pain. I think my hand feels chilled and numbed
since...

Expenses

Jan. 1   Shanette 1s.

Sunday January 4th Snow deep. A few sheep wandering about
the field in great distress. One of them apparently consumptive and
coughing up its poor lungs. Made my heart ache. I wish they cou'd
take money, or that I cou'd relieve them in their own simple way.

Monday January 5th   Letter from Miss H Bowdler Bath . . . 'I am told the King raves of the distresses of his People and only complains of restraint from an idea that he is prevented from doing the good he wishes.* When he first saw Willis† he said sternly "What do you come for? Go home and preach to your flock." Willis, with his usual gentleness and good sense replied, "Sir, our Great Master went about to heal as well as to Preach and my errand here is to heal your Majesty in which I hope and believe I shall succeed." "You are right" said the King. "Come hither and let me talk to you." '

Tuesday January 6th   Jonathan Hughes was last night appointed Cadereirfardd or the Bard who got the Badge of the Chair. The Chair was made by Edward Jones the village Carpenter and cost ten shillings. The subjects of their Poetry were Loyal expressions of sorrow for the King's illness, wishes and prayers for his speedy recovery. Praises of Mr Pitt. Encomiums on the Bridge of Llangollen, the River Dee, the Mill – which Mill can no longer work, the River having frozen and huge masses of Ice scattered about it forming a tremendous appearance.

Saturday January 10th   The moon steadfast over the center of our Field attended by a few Stars. What stillness in the air! Her Planet glittering in the deep blue expanse. The smoke from our Dressing-room Chimney spinning up in a thick Column. The whole Country covered with the purest most sparkling snow. The silence of the night interrupted by the village clock tolling nine, a dog barking at a great distance, the owl complaining. I could have staid in the field lost in admiration till morning.

Monday January 12th   The most bitter Cold I ever remember, cutting, shaving wind, lead-coloured sky, snow blown from the trees in drifts. Comfortable in the house if we could have any real enjoyment of our own Situation while so many not only of our fellow creatures but the Brute creation, who have a strong claim upon our feelings, are such Sufferers at this moment.

Thursday January 15th   The Vicar, Mr Jones, came to make a Collection for the Poor of the Parish who are in great want this

---

* At this period George III was suffering a temporary fit of insanity.
† Willis was his doctor.

piercing season. He staid for two hours. Wind, Rain, Snow, Sleet, Sunshine.

Expenses

Jan. 15   Post 1s. 2d. to relieve the poor 10s. 6d. poor Woman 6d.

Saturday January 15th   Confirmed thaw. Air soft. Sky gloomy. Letter from Miss H. Bowdler dated Bath the 13th. 'The King asked Willis if he thought he was mad? Willis said he had a Delirium on him at Times. "But what is the cause of it?" "Too much anxiety for the good of your People, too little sleep, too much exercise and an excess of Temperance." "True, that is all true, and now I will believe *all* you tell me." He complained that he had not what he liked to eat. "Why not?" said Willis. "If it is to be had in your Three Kingdoms your Majesty shall have it." "Shall I? then let me have Beef and Potatoes." His dinner was ordered accordingly, but they brought it minced for him to eat with a Spoon, having never Ventured to give him a Knife. The King turned to Willis with a look expressive of the most piercing Woe. "Look there, – is that the way for a *Man* to Dine?" Willis said certainly not, and ordered them immediately to bring him a Knife and Fork and to cut his dinner as he Chose it . . . The next day he said he wanted to write to the Queen, but nobody would take his Letter. Willis said he would take it, and accordingly the King wrote a few lines and Dr Willis took them to the Queen. She was in an agony of distress, but at his desire sent an answer that the King might know he had kept his word. When the poor Man saw that it was really her hand he caught Willis in his arms in such a Transport of joy and gratitude that he could hardly disengage himself. The first meeting was very trying to Both, but they have since been together several times. He shed tears, but seeing it affected her he said He would not Cry if *she* would not. He is gentle and kind to everybody and grateful for anything that is done by his attendants, except when he is particularly disordered and then he is dreadfully violent' . . . Soaking rain. Old Jonathan Hughes, the Bard of the Valley, with his poetical productions at the Eisteddfod one of which he has Translated. We sent for him into the Library – a tall Venerable figure. Can speak very little English . . .

Monday January 19th   Heard that Francis Evans, who was run over by his Waggon last Thursday returning from Oswestry with a Load of Malt, continued very ill, and that notwithstanding several doses of Physic and four Remedies he was still costive. We sent to desire he might immediately be swathed round with a Poultice of Bread and Milk and sweet oil as Hot as he could bear it, and that repeated till it had the desired effect. Reading. Drawing. Fine chill evening. The wife of Francis sent up thanks and Prayers for us. The first application of the Poultice had an immediate effect. Thank God.

Tuesday January 20th Freezing hard. Windy. Cold, but very Comfortable in the Dressing Room – an Excellent fire. Shutters Closed. Curtain let down. Candles lighted – our Pens and Ink. Spent the evening very pleasantly reading *Tristram Shandy* aloud – adjourned to the library. Worked – laughed. From Home Since the First of January 1789. Not once Thank Heaven.

Expenses

Jan. 20 A Glass in place of one I broke 6d. For Nitre 6d. Pig's head 2s.

Wednesday January 21st The Chimney Sweep came at last. A Child on Horseback, but tho' a Child in years an Ancient in understanding. A day of delicious retirement.

Thursday January 22nd Letter from Miss H. Bowdler. Dated Bath the 19th. 'At Windsor the P. of Wales took Lord L . . th . . n . . . to a Room so near the K that he could hear the Frenzy, at which both of them laughed etc. in a way too shocking to be related. He is now endeavouring to make his Mother detested. His Father irrecoverable. A Mother who adored him, and a Father whose Heart he had almost Broke before this disorder.' At one our Barretts arrived. Dined at 3. After dinner went to the Farmyard. In the evening the Irish woman we sent to Wrexham returned. No letters.

Friday January 23rd Prevailed with our dear Barretts to give us this day as they intended going at one. After breakfast we went to superintend our Work. Lovely, lovely day. Reading. Working. Became dark and gloomy. Poor Madam Bess grew ill. Wanted to go home. Sent for the Horses. The Servants luckily had gone to take their pleasure. When there was no remedy she grew better, thank

God. Eat her dinner heartily. Spent the evening very pleasantly.

(The Journal)

1790

January 1st   My beloved and I woke at seven. Found by our bed side Petticoats and Pockets, a new year's gift from our *truest Friends.* *

Saturday January 2nd   I prosecuted my notes on Dante – Scowling Wind, frost Yielding. Lowering Sky – My Beloved making a letter case for Mrs Tighe – White Satin and Gold – Cypher in the middle.

Sunday January 3rd   Mrs Blachford with her son and daughter came in. Staid an hour. Declined dining with us as her Daughter's extraordinary malady always seizes her at two and continues without interruption till nine. Pity, for she is a sweet girl.

Wednesday January 6th   The corn just springing up in the furrowed land. Cocks crowing in the different cottages.

Thursday January 7th   The field before our cottage quite green. Hum of bees and flies in the air. Birds preparing their future nurseries. Threw open the Library window. My beloved and I went over all our grounds, visited Margaret's stable, our pretty yards, admired our new Hedge. Then returned to the Library and our evening occupation of writing, reading, working.

Friday January 8th   Prices of stained glass – Blue, Green, Purple 5/6 per lb – Yellow 7/6 – Orange 11/7 – Deep Red 13/6 – made by Eginton at Soho (Square) Birmingham – One pound generally measures about a foot square – best mode of purchasing it would be to cut Patterns of Paste board to fit the Frames† and write on Each pattern the Colour wanted – a parcel from Halston by the Stage Coach. *Zelucco*‡ and *Beatrice*§ the first I may look over the other nonsense I am determined against.

Wednesday January 13th   Rose at eight. Birds singing sweetly, making all their little preparations for the lodging and maintenance

---

* Presumably Mary Carryll and the kitchen maid.
† No doubt intended to hold the coloured glass in the library.
‡ A novel by Thomas Moore.
§ A sentimental novel.

of their future brood. Hope he who 'Caters for the Sparrow' will protect them. Sky so placid, air so soft.

Thursday January 14th   A chorus of Throstles, Blackbirds and finches close beside our window. Mr Lloydde's Hounds in full cry on the opposite mountain. Mists rising from the river. Smoke from the village spinning through the trees.

Sunday January 17th   There is no describing the blazing beauty of this Morning. all the Mountains a glorious Purple and Gold. Woods Sparkling with Gems. Smoke Silently Spinning in Columns to Heaven – chorus of Birds Hymning their Thanksgiving in every Thicket – tender Transparent Mist Exhaling from the River and Brooks – the Hoar frost Melting before the Suns Brilliant rays and disclosing Such Verdure.

Saturday January 23rd   Met our good Landlord, good man. He said he never remembered so sweet a season, that the Birds' song is loud as in Summer – and this morning early he called his wife and daughter-in-law to listen to them. His daughter-in-law, after attending some time, said 'they would cry in May', but I trust she is mistaken.

Friday January 29th   Sent for Baillis – made him Examine the Chimney after that little Boy who Said he had, and whom we paid for Sweeping it. The odious Brat had gone no further than the Middle. Baillis with a long broom finished it.

1791

Saturday January 1st   Soaking rain and wind. Anne Jones, her grand daughter and old Parkes dined in the kitchen. *Mem* the latter old Brute never again to be invited. Owen, Mr Myddelton's Bailiff, came to demand a Christmas Box. Asked him for what? Sent him about his Business. A day of most sweetly enjoyed Retirement – a day according to our Hearts. Silent. Undisturbed.

Monday January 10th Parcel from Barrett. Powder. Essences. Bad Perfume. overgrown Cork Screw. Latter to be returned. European Magazine for December. Duller than ever. 3 Dinner. Our poor thin Turkey. Roast Mutton. Letter to that importunate Donnes.

Tuesday January 11th While we were at dinner Mr Crewe came, requested that his Two Daughters who had accompanied him to Llangollen might see this place. Gave the good man the keys of the garden. While they were in it hurried over our Dinner and when they were passing by invited them in. Modest, plump, well dressed young women. Asked them for that everlasting Hymen* at Crewe Hall. How she does transport that disagreeable person of Hers to all the great houses in the Kingdom! The Crewes departed – and we being Hungry ordered our boiled Salmon to be brought in which we finished with a very good Appetite. Then resumed our usual occupations.

Wednesday January 12th Man came with a Bill for so small a Sum that we were distressed at not being able to pay him. 'My Poverty but not my Will consents.'

Expenses

Jan. 15 Mr Davies for Salt, Baking etc. Dinbren for Geese etc. 7s. 6d. Butter 1s. Hand 1s. a Ham 3s. a Basket 5d. Poor Woman 2s. Sundries 1s. Market 10s. 4d. Moses Jones Weeks Wages 10s. Post 2s. Cooper's Bill 4s. 6d. Cream of Tartar etc 6d. Coalman's Bill for last Week £2. 2. 4.

Tuesday January 18th Letter and Pig from Mrs Mytton. Journey to Bath uncertain. Mr Mytton ill of a rheumatic fever which we are truly concerned for.

Wednesday January 26th My B and I went the Home Circuit – delicious Spring day blue Hepatica in flower. 9 Breakfast. half past 9 till 3 – grey. calm. Still. gloom increasing – Smoke attempting to

* Hymen was the Roman god of marriage. Mrs Crewe was obviously a matchmaker.

Aspire in Columns but crushed down by the Weight of the Atmosphere. That grateful Mary Greene brought a present of 11 eggs . . . Gloom – almost Darkness – Soft Calm Day. Very mizzling Rain . . . My B and I passed the greater part of the morning in the Garden superintending the Nailing our Fruit Trees. 3 Dinner. Roast Mutton. Pork Grinkins. Pork Paté. Mince Pye.

Monday January 31st   Hurricane Tremendous the entire night – fiercely sweeping thro' the Vale – Shaking our Cottage – ringing the Garden Bell in its August passage.

(The Journal)

1792

Expenses

Jan. 10   Baillis for Plaistering Whitewashing and Rough Casting 7s. Three Baskets for taking out Rubbish from intended new Shrubbery 1s.3d.
   14   Brandy for the Landlord's Cough 3s.
   15   Brandy for a Pudding 6d. Fowl 3s.
   17   Workman new Glazing 3 days 3s.6d.
   21   Workman in the Shrubbery 2 days 2s.4d.

1793

Expenses

Jan. 5   Clock Maker for cleaning Clocks 5s. Poor Woman 1s. Boiling thread for new piece of linen 1s.
   15   Robert the Mason for Wall around Dunghill 8s.
   23   Mr Evan's Man with Holly trees 2s.6d.

25   Edward Evans Carriage of Stone to Dunghill Wall 5s.
28   Little Workman to Stake the new planted Trees etc. 1s.4d.

1794

Expenses

Jan. 1   Stage Coachman's Christmas Box 2s.6d.
   14   Lame handed Woman 1s. poor man 1s.
   16   Expense of Mary's Evening Visit to Pengwern 2s.6d.
   27   To nasty Ungrateful Lloyd 6d.

January 25th Do not let anything shake your confidence in Mr
Pitt, I hope and believe it will be seen that he has done all that man
cd. do, but we have cowardly allies, and diabolical Enemies, and I am
afraid it is in the order of Providence that at present France sh'd
succeed. I hope no attempt will be made on England, but remember
what I said last year, and keep a few guineas *in the Drawer.* Whatever
distress such an attempt may occasion I hope it wd not be lasting,
and I dread its effect on Paper Credit much more than anything else.
I am persuaded our people wd fight like Lions, but we might feel the
want of a guinea to purchase Bread before all was settled.

(Harriet Bowdler to Sarah Ponsonby)

1795

Expenses

Jan. 1   Molly a New Years Gift 2s.
    2   Mathew Miller for Carriage 1s. Mary's Distress 5s.
    3   Market 13s.11d. Simon's Weeks Wages 9s. Dinbren in full
       for Butter – Geese – Mutton etc. £4.3s.
    6   Edwards the Oswestry Bookseller in full £2.8s. The Coal-
       man's Bill £4.
    8   4 Trusses of Straw – an excessive price 2s.
   18   Edward on the death of his Wife's Mother 1s.

1798

January 29th Your description of your valley, deluged by the late
long-continued wetness, and of the power of your gentle gravelly

elevation in its bosom, to digest all the rain the Heavens can afford it, delights me.

(Anna Seward to Sarah Ponsonby)

1799

Expenses

Jan. 6   Molly *finally* discharged for two Months wages came to 14s.
Knight the Butcher for 9 load of Muck £1.7s.

14   a Turkey – Dear Mrs Barrett 3s. 6d.

19   Simons Weeks Wages 9s. William Jones Do. He at length discharged 9s.
To Ned of the Mill going for Mr Turner* for Mary 1s.

1802

Friday 1st January   The Coal man came with his annual Bill, which notwithstanding the exorbitant rise of the coals was infinitely less than we had reason to expect from the Bills brought us in by Edward Evans, whom thank heaven we have dismissed at last.

Saturday January 2nd   Dr Darwin's† mode of Treating hysterics. To have the Back whipped well every morning with a bunch of green nettles. He ordered this to Mrs Preston, who submitted to the prescription and is the better for it.

Tuesday January 5th   Bought a hare from the old Poaching man.

Wednesday January 6th   Present from poor Roger Lever of Twelve Larks. How Barbarous to destroy these innocent little birds.

Monday January 18th   Dreadful account of the nastiness, misery, poverty and immorality which prevails at Paris. The Ladies so indecently naked that the sight is disgusting to the last degree. Mrs Fitzherbert in a very dangerous state, her disorder dropsical.

Tuesday January 19th   John Roberts brought up two Bacon Pigs. Their weight two hundred and ninety-nine pounds. The Robins and the Swifts began their first spring vespers.

* The apothecary.

† Father of Charles Darwin.

Tuesday January 26th   Friend from Berwick arrived with the loveliest of all lovely cows, called Beauty – sent by that dearest of Friends, Mrs Powys.

(The Journal)

1805

Monday January 7   We had a conversation at Brynkinalt with Mr Morhills Sen. who had been for Five years a resident in Prussia. He arrived at St Petersburgh the day after the assassination of the late Emperor Paul who had been dreadfully mangled – the Face cut – and one Eye beat out – nevertheless his Body was exposed to the populace the next day – extended on a Bier – Covered with a Black Velvet Pall – his Face painted and repaired.

(Eleanor's Day Book)

1815

Saturday January 14th   ... have you got Any Culinary receipts – we seek something *Very Good* out of *Nothing* ... the cheaper the more Convenient – the french understand these things better than any people upon earth – therefore I appeal to you to assist us in performing that Miracle – of making a great *Show* for *nothing*.

(Lady Eleanor Butler to Miss Pigott, then in Paris)

Receipts

FONDUE OF CHEESE

Rasp some Old rich Cheese and some common cheese equal quantities of each. boil half a Pint of good Cream and let it cool, beat up the whites of four eggs. Mix all together lightly, put them in little paper Cases and Bake them in a Gentle Oven.

LANGUES DE BOEUFS A LA REMOULLADE

Scald a fresh Neats tongue. Boil it in Broth with a little Salt and a Faggot of Parsley, Chives, Cloves and Bay leaves, When done, peel and Slit it, not quite in two. Make a Sauce with Parsley, Shallots,

Capers, and Anchovies, all very finely chop'd. A little Vinegar, rasp'd Bread, two Spoonfuls of Cullis, as much of Broth. A little Salt and coarse pepper, Boil all together a moment; then put the tongue in it to simmer for a quarter of an Hour. When you serve it up add a little Salt.

1819

Thursday January 5th   We this day Completed the Purchase of our House.

(The Journal)

FEBRUARY

1784

Sunday February 1st   I ill all night with an headache.

Receipts

White magnesia calcined 6 drachms.
Powder of rhubarb, sharp cinnamon, ginger, of each half a drachm.
Mix together in a fine powder. The dose: a teaspoonful to be taken
in mint tea every night.

Friday February 13th   Read *Cookes Voyage and Death* by Ellis to
my Love.

Saturday February 14th   Finished Spenser to my Love.
(Eleanor Butler's Pocket Book)

1785

February 7th   Mrs Herbert's conduct has shock'd Us ... My B thinks that if all Ladies who are guilty of that Crime, were Branded, with its Initial, a Great A in the Forehead – it would be the most likely means to deter others, from following the example. Don't you think it a good idea?

(Sarah Ponsonby to Mrs Tighe)

1786

February 17th   If you ever read Newspapers You will find that My B's scheme for Stigmatizing Adulterers and esses has been practiced at Connecticut – I hope and believe with Success – and flatter myself that in a little time the Old World will follow the example set them by the New on the Occasion – as a step to them being each better prepared for that which is to Come.

(Sarah Ponsonby to Mrs Tighe)

1787

February 26th   She was insensible to Six Blisters, the Seventh and two Cataplasms* rouzed her to a sense of Pain – and according to the present method of treating this dreadful distemper – she was obliged to swallow two Bottles of Port, besides a quantity of other strong Liquers every day.

(Sarah Ponsonby to Mrs Tighe, *re* the treatment of
Mrs Barrett, their friend, for a putrid fever and spots)

1788

Friday February 1st   Three o'clock dinner. Boiled Pork. Peas pudding. Half-past three my beloved and I went to the new garden. Freezing hard. I am much mistaken if there be not a quantity of snow in the sky. I read to my beloved No. 97 of the Rambler written by Richardson, author of those inimitable Books *Pamela*, *Clarissa*, and *Sir Charles Grandison*.

* Poultices.

Monday February 4th   Rose at eight. Celestial blue and silver morning . . . Compliments from Mr Owen of Porkington with a present of 4 sticks of black sealing wax. What a whimsical pleasant mortal he is! Compliments from Col. Mansergh St. George. Just arrived at the Hand, if we are unengaged will wait on us and receive our commands for Ireland. Our Compliments. Shall be glad to see him. He came at six. Stayed till nine. One of the most pleasing men I ever conversed with. Very pretty, slight figure, pale genteel Face. Animated interesting countenance. He was dressed in the deepest mourning, a black silk cap on his head which entirely concealed his hair. He had worn it these many years in consequence of a wound he received in America which has baffled the skill of the most eminent surgeons and Physicians in Europe . . . Related many curious anecdotes of Rousseau, and as he draws admirably we requested he would give us some idea of the face and Person of this unfortunate and inimitable genius. He very obligingly took out his pencil and drew two figures, I am persuaded striking likenesses of Poor Rousseau in a dress lined and trim'd with Fur, and a large Muff . . . We were quite sorry when this agreeable man made his Bow. Howling wind. Sharp keen night.

Tuesday February 5th   Millions of Birds singing sweetly; a Vast pillar of black thick smoke Issued from a chimney in the village then spinning up writhed with the Clouds forming a Singular appearance as it still retained its sooty appearance and from the stillness of the air remained suspended over the Vale.

Wednesday February 6th   Letter from Mrs Goddard. Written on the Cover Don't ope this till the Bearer is gone. Bearer went. Open'd Mrs G's letter – it contained nothing particular.

Sunday February 10th   Rose at eight. Ground thinly covered with snow – Blue sky. Flakes of snow gently descending and mixing with the foliage of the evergreens. Very cold . . . Ten my beloved and I drank a dish of tea. Our Mrs Bunbury is a charming woman in mind and person. Mr Bunbury* is a singular genius, but I think the pleasure of their company may be too dearly purchased by so many tedious hours of expectation – but it is his fault not hers. At half past one this really charming woman came, blooming and beautiful as an

* Henry Bunbury, caricaturist.

angel . . . Sweetly unreserved was this dear woman about her own affairs . . . Odd circumstance of two Ladies in Sussex personating us . . . Pretty idea of a Festoon of woodbine, convolvulus and hops taken from the Duc de Biron's garden. Receipt to preserve the Teeth recommended by Lady Fortescue – wash the mouth with Tobacco water.

Tuesday February 12th   9. My head aches. *Mem* not eat another boil'd Potatoe in haste.

Wednesday February 13th   I awoke at four o'clock with a desperate head, the darling of my heart arose, gave me some warm water which gave me a momentary relief, but it returned with greater violence and continued till three, during which time my beloved Sally never left me for a single moment. At three we arose, but I grew ill again yet determined to struggle against it. Read for three hours. Loud storm all day. Frequent showers.

Thursday February 14th   The Irishwoman whom we sent to Wrexham returned with a Turkey, six bottles of sherry – Letter from Miss Leslie Jan. 11th. *with a billet about nothing enclosed* . . . Threw her Letter in the Fire.

Sunday February 17th   Rose at seven. A sweet spring morning. Went to see our dear Barretts at Oswestry, the road entirely deserted. Met in the twelve miles only one horseman and the stage coach . . . Went to Church. *Mem* The Vicar, Edwards, reads prayers admirably well, the Curate dreadfully, the latter preached, singing charming.

Monday February 18th   Rose at eight. Soft Mizzling Morning. Nine. Breakfast. Half past Nine Till Three. Soft. Thick rain – Paid our rent £11. 7. 6 – half a year due Since the first of November 1787 – Writing. Wrote to Miss H. Bowdler little Stanhope Street May Fair London, with the green blank book. Sent it by a Mr Wales who was in the Stage Coach. Reading. Read Six *Sonatto di Petrarca* and *Davila*. heavy thick rain.
Three, Dinner. Roasted Goose.
Half past Three 'till Nine. Dinas Bran and the Surrounding Mountains Covered with Sleet. Reading. Writing. Read *Portrait de Henri 4 par Mercier* and what related to his reign in Hainault. Metastasio. Nine till Twelve in the dressing room Reading – a day of Such delightful and enjoyed retirement!

Tuesday February 19th Rose at seven. Misty soft morning. Went in the Hand chaise to Oswestry, on Chester Hill overtook General Pitt and his sister, passed them and flew on. Breakfasted with our Barretts, walked round their grounds with Mrs Barrett. Mrs Disbrone made what she calls coverlet but I know by the name of Lancashire Toughy.* Miss Maddock dressed our hair. We wore our new habits. At three went (Mrs Barrett in the Chaise with us) to Halston. Mrs Lloydd of Aston and her pretty children came soon after. Just before dinner *Miss* Webb made her appearance. I never beheld anything half so handsome. After dinner Miss Mytton played divinely on the Harpsichord, after tea Miss Webb spoke an epilogue in *Percy*, and another in *Douglas*, and another in *Jane Shore*† so finely, such a Voice, such gesticulation, a countenance so animated and lovely, every movement so graceful, that every person in the company burst into tears . . . At eleven we took leave, conducted Mrs Barrett home. Stepped in while the carriage was turning about and at half-past one arrived at our delicious abode. The library, parlour and kitchen chimneys swept in our absence, a disagreeable job well escaped.

Monday February 25th Rose at eight. Delicate morning. The stone cutter come to lay the stones in the Hall in the place of the odious Tiles which we have hated so long . . . Letter from Mrs Goddard, Bath, as usual no date. I wish she were not so tiresomely communicative of her odious dreams.

Tuesday February 26th Writing. Drawing. Sweet sunshine, blue sky. Soft smoke from the village ascending in spires . . . Mrs Jones, our late curate's widow, came to return us Thanks for having procured her a pension from the Bishop of St Asaph. Made her stay for dinner and coffee. Showed her the gardens, dairy and bleach yard. A sensible, agreeable, modest woman.

Thursday February 28th Rose at half-past seven. Hoar frost, dark cloudy sky. Ordered the Tiles to be removed from before the door, the dirt and rubbish which the stone cutters made cleared away. Spoke to our Landlord who was going up the Field. Told us the Birds in our garden sang as loud and as sweet as in the month of May. Nine breakfast . . . Fullerton came with compliments from Sir

---

* Toffee.
† Sentimental dramas of the day.

William and Lady Barker, Mr Ponsonby and Miss Staples – they will
be here immediately – how fortunate that the Hall is finished and all
the dirt and Rubbish cleared away.

1789

Wednesday February 4th   Rain and snow. Mr Daly and Mr Oliver
came on their way from London to Ireland whither they are posting
for the meeting of Parliament. Say the King was worse last Thursday
and Friday than he has been since his malady. He wanted to ascend
the Pagoda at Kew which being too publick they would not permit
him to. He then threw himself on the ground, wept and rolled about
in the most frantic manner, poor, poor man.

Thursday February 12th   The post brought us Cash for our Twenty
pound note. Paid corn man, coal man, the Butcher for our year's
provision of Pork. Some other small bills in the Village and cleared
ourselves thank God in this district.

(The Journal)

A Cottage 13th February   ... in the Mornings after Breakfast I try
to improve myself in drawing and am also proceeding in a tedious
MS which, if my eyes last – your Journal is to succeed. My B is also
improving herself though that is scarcely possible – in Italian – She
also Amuses herself with Compiling and transcribing Notes Illustra-
tive of Her Admired Madame de Sevigné. After dinner She reads
aloud to me till nine o'clock when we regularly retire to Our dressing
room (that Our Domesticks may go to rest) where We employ
ourselves generally till twelve – I work Cross stitch every evening
Below Stairs ... We continue to find all Our Hours too short.
Scarcely ever go from Home – and as seldom see any Strangers ...

(Sarah Ponsonby to Mrs Tighe)

Tuesday February 17th   Lever, the gardener of Chirk Castle, came
with Kendal the Carpet man, as we desired. We have not seen
Kendal these nine years, he was the first person from whom we had
carpets, a plain sensible man. *Vrai Anglais*. Lives in Cirencester in
Gloucestershire, deals most extensively in Carpets, Cyder etc., an
honest plain Yeoman, a character I revere. Ask'd him how the
County of Gloucester stood affected as to Politics. He, as freeman of

Gloucester, voted for Mr Howard. Said that at first the people wished for Pitt and approved of his measures, but now they begin to murmur and think he treats the Prince of Wales very ill. The King show'd symptoms of Insanity before he came to Gloucestershire. When Lord Berkeley heard that Cheltenham was proposed he waited on his Majesty to make an offer of Berkeley Castle for his residence. The King on hearing Lord Berkeley was in the antechamber ran out to him saying – 'What Berkeley, Berkeley, Berkeley.' When his Lordship informed him for what purpose he waited on him the King laughed like an Idiot and repeated 'Oh, Aye. Aye. Berkeley Castle, Berkeley Castle, Berkeley Castle,' and returned to his apartment without giving any other answer. Lord Berkeley told this to Mr Vernon. The profusion of Cyder this year is not to be described.

Friday February 20th   We removed to the Dressing room and got the Library Chimney swept, that Vile little boy from Oswestry not having proceeded beyond the turn of the Chimney.

(The Journal)

A Cottage February 22nd   We were alarmed at seeing a New Book intitled *The Cottage of Friendship* lately Advertised – but are informed that it bears no kind of resemblance to this . . .

(Sarah Ponsonby to Mrs Tighe)

Tuesday February 24th   Rose at eight. Storms, dark Clouds, faint sunshine. Writing. Snow on all the mountains. Nine Breakfast – half past Nine till three – Black sky – Bright Sun – High Wind. Artichokes planted – Writing – Drawing – Storms, fine light and shadow. The Duke of Leinster, Lord Charlemont, Mr Ponsonby, Mr Conolly, Mr Stewart, Mr O'Neil, all went thro' the village having first breakfasted at the Hand, on their way to London to offer the Regency of Ireland to the Prince of Wales.

Thursday February 26th   Letter from Miss H. Bowdler dated Bath the 24th . . . 'Last Friday the 20th the Chancellor had a Tête a Tête of two hours with the King, the subject was a sketch of everything that had passed since his illness (the bad behaviour of *some* excepted), the Lord Chancellor has declared that he never at any time has seen the King's understanding more clear, calm and collected, and what is still more he slept 8 hours after this conversation.'

(The Journal)

1790

Monday February 4th My head which has ached more or less these three weeks grew very bad. and My beloved ever Anxious – ever tender Made me take a Mustard Emetic, which Effectually removed my complaint. how could it fail when administered by her. I grew perfectly Well. and then My beloved and I sat by the Excellent Dressing room fire – got the Backgammon Table and played 'Till Twelve.

Friday February 5th The Woman of this Village who supplies Halston with Beesoms* returned from thence this evening, brought a letter from Mrs Mytton and a present of the first quarter of Lamb she killed this year.

Expenses

Feb. 11 Remitted for payment of newspapers £2.6s.
     13 Bill for Cheese £4.7.6.
         Do. Coals £2.8.0.
         Do. for Carriage of Do. 4s.
         Do. for Bacon £2.16.9.
         Do. Lion Inn for Wine, Muck, Carriage of parcels Oats etc. £9.9s.

Sunday February 14th Evening still and Misty. opened the casement, lighted Candles. this attracted Millions of birds who sang so Sweetly. Such a Variety of Notes. how delightful!

Saturday February 20th Sent the Irish woman to Halston with mushroom spawn, Periwinkle of sorts, American Saxifrage.

Tuesday February 23rd Spent the greater part of the morning in the field with our Cow. putting down Cuttings of Lombardy Poplar in the *Infini*.†

Wednesday February 24th My beloved and I went a delightful walk through our cow's field, up the lane, passed Edward Evans' field, the Lane to the Mill, the entire round of Edward Evans' field

* Brooms.
† The *Infini* was a planting of trees, dark grading to light to make it appear larger than it was.

returned by the lane. The richest glowing purple tint spread over the Mountain. Brilliant sun. Met in the course of our walk an old grey-headed man leading to the water a horse as ancient as himself. Edward Evans' son, with a dray full of thorns and Hollies from the Mountains to repair the Hedges. A good looking clean woman with three little children clinging about her, and a fourth in her arms. Told us she had eleven children. Edward Evans' clean and notable wife. A very old woman with pictures to sell. Told us she was from Carnarvonshire, had a blind Daughter whom she supported by the sale of these pictures which she purchased in Chester and Vended about the Country. The miller of Pengwern's son returning from school. Observed the Honeysuckle in the hedges in full leaf.

Expenses

Feb. 25   to Mrs Worrall due for Oranges 4s.7d.

    27   to our Kitchen Md. in part of Wages I forget what day 10s.6d.

Receipts

TO PRESERVE ORANGES TO KEEP ALL THE YEAR

Cut the Fruit into halves. and squeeze the Juice into a Bason. Pick all the Pulp into it free from the Skins – pull the peel from the Skins. Boil the peel in a good quantity of Water till tender, and when drained and Cold – Beat them to a Paste in a marble Mortar. that done to every 4 Oranges put One pound of Loaf Sugar. Beat them till the Sugar is well mixed, then put in the Juice and pulp stirring them well together, and Pot them for Use – They will Keep a Year – Lemons and China Oranges will Keep the same way –

Three Spoonfuls of the Above makes a pudding mixed with the Yolks of ten Eggs and the Whites of Two – half a pound of fresh Butter melted Very thick – and almost Cold – a fine Paste as usual.

OMELETTE

Four Eggs beat well, whites and all with two spoonfulls of fine flour – half a pint of Cream or good Milk – two Anchovies Chopt a little Parsley, a little grated Ham, pepper and Salt. Fry in Lard or dripping.

1791

Wednesday February 2nd Such a night of Tempests and Hail! Every pane of Glass in our Casements shook as if Agitated by an Earthquake. Rose at Eight. Bright sky. Keen piercing wind. Mountains and Valley covered with a thin surface of snow . . . Nine till twelve in the Bedchamber reading. A day of sweet Retirement.

Friday February 4th Removed the mushroom bed from the melon ground to the Farm yard. Letter from Bess Tucker with perfumed powders for sachets.

Sunday February 20th Message from the Dean of Ossory and Family. Arrived at the Hand late last night. Invited them to Breakfast . . . The Dean read Prayers. Mr Loftus and Mr Clarke came in while we were all kneeling. Prayers over we entered into conversation.

Expenses

Feb. 4 Nitre and Brimstone* 6d.
      5 Pork for Salting £1.1.8.
      6 Earnest to a new Kitchen Maid 1s.
    12 Poor Woman from whom we used to buy Trinkets 1s.
    17 Irish Woman to Wrexham for Medecine for Moses Jones 4s.
    19 Moses Jones in payment of Wages – more than he deserves 5s.
          Moses Jones for Spices etc. bought at Chester and Wrexham 19s.7d.
          A Pig's Head 1s.9d.
    21 Moses Jones discharged 5s.

1792

Expenses

Feb. 4 Moses Jones Weeks Wages 10s.†
      6 Miss Preston in payment of Her Bill for Tea £10.10s.

* For preserving beef.
† The unfortunate Moses Jones had obviously been reinstated yet again!

25 Mason in full for Cellar £1.2.1.
   Baillis in payment for Plaistering the new Cellar 10s.6d.
27 Pattern of Arch for new Room Chimney by Coach 6d.

1794

February 1st   I want to know that your teazing head-ach is perfectly removed, and that my ever dear Viellard* sings a French song as usual and is content to 'leave Dross to Countesses'. It is fair that in the distribution of this worlds goods everybody shd have something, and therefore the Money is commonly given to those who have nothing else to boast of − and so God bless them with it ... I am very glad to hear what you say of the Will tho' I wish I might add another 0 to the sum.

> (Harriet Bowdler at Bath to Lady Eleanor Butler,
> commiserating over her Mother's will in which Eleanor in
> spite of great expectations had been left only £100)

February 3rd   The following are the circumstances − Lady O† wrote to me on the dowager Lady O's death − promising that as soon as the Will should be Opened She would write to My B and send her a Copy − this Promise she *never* kept − we *know* from undoubted Authority that it bequeathed my Beloved £100 − and the Legacy would have been much greater − had she been suffered to have followed her own inclination − which in fact would have induced her not to make any Will. In that case My B would have been intitled to her Legal portion of an immense property. But Lady Ormonde longed for her Diamonds and Pearls etc etc − *all* of which She now has taken *entire* possession of − and to compleat the meanness − I might be justified in saying the *Treasury* of Her Conduct − a large Collection of Books known to be Lawfully belonging to Lady Eleanor are amongst these ill-acquired treasures − and she wishes to have it thought that My B's name was omitted in her Mother's Will − who but a little while since − sent her as I believe I told you − the strongest assurances of Maternal Affection by Dr Butler ...

> (Sarah Ponsonby to Mrs Tighe)

---

* Harriet Bowdler's current nickname for Eleanor Butler was the Viellard (old man),
with whom she carried on a sadly flirtatious correspondence.

† Ormonde.

17th February It is my B's intention, to pursue the same Plan of Moderation on which she has begun – to wait another month, and then address a second Gentle expostulation to Lady O. if that meets the same fate we will still rely on *Him* who has rescued us from much heavier evils – and who, we have an implicit Confidence will in his own good time reward the patience he has enabled my Beloved to exert . . .

(Sarah Ponsonby to Mrs Tighe)

Monday 24th February Dear Lady Ormonde, Your silence to the recent application I troubled you with the first of this month, (an instance of disregard to yourself and me, for which I was totally unprepared) will influence my abridging (much as is possible) the present intrusion on your attention. Last Thursday's post brought a Duplicate of the Will, Accompanied by your promise of letting me know 'when' I may be permitted to draw for the One Hundred Pounds my Mother had the Goodness to bequeath me. In Seven Weeks from the Event which added so considerably to your already Princely Resources could nothing be afforded except a promise of future information when I might apply for such a sum? . . . Let me also remind you that though for near Sixteen Years the constant Inhabitant of 'so remote a dwelling' yet when the Title of Ormonde is pronounced at St James this ensuing Birthday, the recollections of a Daughter and Sister of that House will consequently be awakened to the minds of some distinguished Characters in the circle, many of whom, as your Ladyship cannot be ignorant, I have the happiness to count in the list of acquaintance and not a few in that of my *real* friends. If the eyes of these persons should unanimously turn towards you on your first introduction to their majesties, let it be I entreat, with that degree of approbation which it shall prove my immediate business to convince them you are entitled to from all who feel an interest in my welfare – if by obtaining me the slender addition of One hundred a year you at once fulfil my utmost ambition and Secure to yourself my liveliest Gratitude. I have only one additional favour to solicit, it is the Obligation of not being kept in a state of painful suspense . . .

(Lady Eleanor Butler to Lady Ormonde)

[*4th March* Madam, I applyed to your Brother on your first application to me some years ago, for an addition of One Hundred a year to your allowance, and he refused my request, as he says that the addition he has already made to it, is in his opinion, more than you could expect from your former conduct towards him, and also he thinks it sufficient for you. I *then* and not till then, that I might not do you any injury showed him your last Letters to me. You can't be surprized that after such unmerited ill treatment as I have experienced from you in your last two letters, that I should decline all future correspondence. Your Brother desires I may inform you that your Legacy is lodged at Mr Le Touche's and that you may draw for it when you chuse . . .

(Lady Ormonde to Lady Eleanor Butler) |

1796

February 4th   So you have farming improvements on your hands at present. Thrice flattering to me is the observation interwoven with that intelligence. You, I am sure, will unite the *dulce* with the *utile*.* Beneath the wand of the enchantresses, Beauty starts up in her own form divine . . . I have already expressed to Miss Ponsonby my delight in the scenic fidelity, and elegant execution of the vignette for Llangollen Vale; but I cannot cease to feel pain, in the idea that my receiving it as yours and Miss Ponsonby's present, must render the publication so expensive to you. If you will have

* The 'beautiful' with the 'useful'.

51

the goodness to permit me to discharge the engraver's bill, you will extremely oblige me.

(Anna Seward to Lady Eleanor Butler, apropos Sarah Ponsonby's frontispiece to Miss Seward's extended poem 'Llangollen Vale')

1797

February 19th Mr Roberts of Dinbren is now here. I was, however concerned to hear him say you had lately been distressed by the illness, and alarmed for the life of your good Euryclea.* That she is recovering I rejoice. The loss of a domestic, faithful and affectionate as Orlando's Adam, must have cast more than a transient gloom over the Cambrian Arden. The Rosalind and Celia† of real life give Llangollen valley a right to that title.

(Anna Seward to Sarah Ponsonby)

1798

Expenses

Feb. 3   Fowl for Mary's intended Supper next Monday 2s.
   5   Postboy for oranges and lemons for Mary's guests this evening 4s.
   6   To Mrs Parks for Ale and Bacon for the Supper 8s.6d.
       Dolly Moses for Tea pot 2s.

1799

4th February ... our Vale is filled many feet deep with snow surfaced by an intense frost which renders it impenetrable to news by any sort of practible conveyance ... All this quiet and ignorance, however, would be the very reverse of disagreeable by such a fireside as that of our library if I didn't feel a wish of saying to you 'how do you do? I hope you are well' and if we had not too much reason to fear our beautiful, beloved and oldest cat Muff has been buried alive in this deep snow, for she has never been seen since its

---

* Mary Carryll! Euryclea was the nurse of Ulysses.
†'Rosalind' and 'Celia' (the close women friends in Shakespeare's *As You Like It*) were now fifty-eight and forty-two respectively!

commencement, nor never was known to be absent so many days together in the course of ten years life.

(Sarah Ponsonby to Mrs Tighe)

1802

Wednesday February 3rd   Mr Kavanagh left a cannister of Lundy Nicoles celebrated dry snuff for us at the inn. Thank God we never sully ourselves with the filthy dust, but it may prove an acceptable present for some of our snuffy friends.

Friday February 5th   The Rug man told us that in the tremendous storm forty two immensely large and very old Oak were thrown down in the Park. At Wrexham yesterday ten thousand pounds worth of the Trevor Hall, Abbey, and aqueduct timber were sold by auction. What an everlasting loss, what a disfigurement to this once so finely wooded, but now denuded country.

Wednesday February 10th   Visited our work. John Francis in the shed making the seats. Francis' man a fair-weather workman – found the morning too cold and chose to stay at home by the fire, but we sent for him.

Thursday February 14th   Universal snow. Birds singing sweetly this silver Valentines day.

Tuesday February 16th   Mr Roberts came at three. Brought him to the new seat. Beautiful in the snow. He admired it more than he would confess and suggested some unnecessary improvements.

Friday February 26th   ... the Welch call this premature summer weather a fox's day – to invite the birds to come out and then destroy them. Evening. Enchanting, emerald and gold. Wood pigeons, owls, thrushes, robins, blackbirds in full chorus.

(The Journal)

1806

February 11th We have once been at Oswestry . . . nor indeed out of our own house further than we could go as footpads – wishing to spend all we can and cannot afford in the manuring and hedging Our four beautiful Fields for our four beautiful cows . . .

(Sarah Ponsonby to Mrs Tighe)

1814

February 2nd Our poor driver, Patrick, and two horses out of four that were returning from having conveyed Mrs Piozzi to Ruthin escaped from absolute destruction by being lost in it [snow] last Saturday night. He was providentially discovered when quite exhausted after crawling on his hands and knees within twenty yards of the only habitation on that dreary road. One horse found its way home some hours after, the other, a blind one, had the extraordinary sagacity to remain stationary until she was sought and found in the morning.

(Sarah Ponsonby to Mrs Parker)

Thursday February 5th Your Most kind and Most interesting Letter Dearest Miss Harriet – with its beautiful enclosure. Should not have remained so long unacknowledged – had it been possible for me to find a place to write in – or even to write *on*! till this day. We have been Obliged to remove every article of furniture from the lower to the Upper regions – which we now inhabit. The difficulty was where to stow Books. Pictures. *Treasures* Tables. Chairs etc. etc. it is now Accomplished and the Spare bedchamber and Dressing room are converted into a State Apartment fit for the acception of that Gadding Dss. of Oldenburgh should her S. H. (which heaven Avert) ramble into this Principality.

(Lady Eleanor Butler to Miss Harriet Pigott)

1819

Sunday February 7th Letter from Mrs Mytton with the receipt for Potato Chips fried.

Tuesday February 16th ... a beautiful Lion Couchant* carved in oak – some centuries old – from the Warden of Ruthin.

Monday February 22nd Lady Georgina Wellesley's dreadful Account of the Caesarian Operation being performed on the Queen of Spain – while she was alive – She was *Murdered* by the inquisition.

Thursday February 25th Perfect Spring day – Soft – smiling – Verdant – employed in planting hollies ...

(The Journal – with an early violet
pressed between the pages)

* Still to be seen today in the Plas Newydd porch.

MARCH

1784

Monday March 2nd   Lovely Morning. Intense White Frost. Brewed.
(Eleanor Butler's Pocket Book)

1787

March 11th   Lady Dungannon Staid five days with us. and though
she was very civil and did her utmost to accommodate herself to our
Ungenteel hours . . . we are full as happy now the visit is over . . .
(Sarah Ponsonby to Mrs Tighe)

1788

Monday March 3rd   Rose at eight. Beautiful morning. Birds
innumerable. Air rather cold and harsh. Nine till three reading,
writing. The parish having sent a Warrant to Llandrdglee eight
people came last night as witnesses against that unfortunate wretch
who is suspected of having murdered her child.

Tuesday March 4th   High dry wind. Powder for the plate. Oil for the mahogany Table. Reading, writing. Loud storm. Three loads of muck from the Hand stables for the mushroom bed. Potatoes planted in the west border. Hay for Margaret from Pengwern Hall . . . finished *The Tatler*, began *The Spectator*.

Thursday March 6th   Letter from Miss Maddocks* which Pleaseth me not – from Mrs Goddard . . . Much ado about Nothing.

Saturday March 8th   Sweet day, purple transparent mists. Sun glistening thro' them . . .

Sunday March 9th   My beloved and I walked in the field before our cottage. Many decent orderly people hastening to Llansantffraid. A Methodist preacher there. The unfortunate wretch who was suspected of murdering her child taken up last night. The Body of the Infant being found by some persons who were in search of a Fox on the wildest part of the Merionethshire Mountain. The body was covered with sods under a great Rock. How shocking to Humanity!

Monday March 10th   Cold and gloomy. The Body of the poor Infant brought down the field in a basket. Three men and four women from the mountains with it as witnesses. The Inquest at this moment sitting over the Body in the Church . . . Letter from Miss Bridgeman. Coachman taken ill last night which prevents their coming. Her regret sweetly and tenderly expressed. Wrote to her. Inquest pronounced Wilful murder – poor wretched creature to go to Ruthin Jail to-night. Bell tolling for the infant who is to be interred in the Church yard, having been baptised.

Tuesday March 11th   White sky, pale sun. The poor unfortunate Wretch sent to Ruthin Jail last night, confessed the Infant was hers, but denied having mangled it in that shocking manner. May the Almighty in his infinite mercy give her grace to repent of this horrid deed. Writing, Drawing. Very cold and windy . . . our excellent Barretts fearing we should be unprovided sent a fine leg of Veal and a Calve's head with a letter written with their accustomed kindness . . . At half-past four a Rap at the Door. I was very agreeably surprised by seeing Monseigneur who is going to London to see his

* The hairdresser.

Brother, and our good Friend, poor Mr Butler of Ballyraggat, who is in a very dangerous state of health with water on his lungs.

Wednesday March 12th Nine till twelve in the Bedchamber reading – finished *Letters on Several Subjects* by the Rev. Martin Sherlock. I hope the Rev. Martin Sherlock will never insist upon knowing my opinion of Him and His Letters.

Thursday March 13th Letter from Miss H. Bowdler dated Portsmouth the 9th, from Mrs Tighe dated Harrow the 7th. Excellent thoughts on the Slave Trade in Mrs Tighe's Letter. Those who remain in their native country are treated worse than in the Islands, where, under most of their Masters, they meet with good treatment and are instructed by the Catholic and Moravian missionaries in the Christian religion. A reformation in the manner of bringing them over, and a general attention to their morals, manners and health afterwards, and having them well instructed in Religion and after some years set free, appears better than the abolition of the Trade.

Wednesday March 14th Cold insupportable. Excellent fire – Sopha and Table drawn quite close to it. 3 Dinner. Boiled Tough fowl – hang beef – greens.

Tuesday March 18th Soft chill day. A few flakes of snow. Letter from the unfortunate Creature in Ruthin Gaol. What can we do for her? Reading. Drawing . . . We then went the Home Circuit, told Richard we thought rolling four small Barrows full of gravel into the new kitchen garden was a very little mornings work. He gave us warning which (to his infinite surprise and evident regret) we immediately accepted, being determined never, while we retain our senses, to be imposed upon by a servant. Three dinner, boil'd Fowl, boiled mutton. Reading. Writing. Richard sent in his keys. We sent out his wages. He went away with great reluctance. But not chusing to let our servants change places with us We resolved when He gave Warning in the morning that he should take the consequence of it in the afternoon. Soft moist mild night . . . Nine till twelve in the Bedchamber reading. A day of sweetly enjoyed retirement, the little Fracas of Richard's sauciness not having disturbed us, as we think we acted with becoming calmness and presence of Mind.

Friday March 21st Three Dinner. Fresh Flounders, a bad Lobster and Indifferent Oysters.

Saturday March 22nd   Celestial glorious spring day. Through the Lenity of Pepper Arden* the girl acquitted of the murder of her Infant, which we are truly glad of, as had the Judge enquired minutely into the particulars she must have been hanged this day on the green in this village.

Saturday March 29th   Celestial lovely day. Reading, drawing. Saw a White lamb in the Clerk's hanging Field. The Parlour getting a general scouring, sweeping and cleaning. My Beloved and I went the Home Circuit. Walked round our empty garden many times, like it infinitely better empty than occupied by that Drunken idle Richard. Sweetest lovely day, close, nay even sultry. Lambs bleating, Birds singing, everything that constitutes the Beauty of solitude and retirement . . . The Irishwoman whom we sent to Wrexham returned. Soft fine rain. Began *Les Memoires de Madame de Maintenon*. I doubt whether the Vulgarity of stile, absurd anecdotes, and impertinent reflections will permit me to read it.

Monday March 31st   Heavenly evening. Reading. Drawing. Went to the white gate – still – owls hooting. Nine till twelve in the Dressing room reading – finished *Les Memoires de Maintenon* – Began her letters. Company Here since the 1st of January.
Lady Bellamont drank coffee and breakfasted.
Lady Anne Butler came – went away the 29th.
Mr Lee came for a moment. Lady Mary Fitzmaurice.
Mr Myddelton breakfasted here.
Mr Wesley breakfasted. Lady Dungannon breakfasted here.

1789

Tuesday March 10th   Gypsey came to the Door, wanted to tell fortunes. Dismissed her. Hate such people.

Saturday March 14th   Letter from Miss Shipley dated Bolton St. Thurs. 12th. 'Dowager Lady Spencer says she is wild to be acquainted with *Les Amies* and their lovely Cottage, and had Lord Spencer gone to Ireland she had determined when she visited him to spend the day in the sweet Vale of Llangollen.'

* The judge.

Tuesday March 17th   Still – muggy evening. The Coal man came with his bill according to annual Custom at the March Fair in Llangollen. Thank heaven we had the money to pay him.

Thursday March 19th   Mr Chambre's Clerk brought a Letter from Mr Chambre and £20.13s.4d. The first quarter of our Pension and receipts for each of us to sign. A Letter from Mr Child* to Mr Chambre. The Certificates would not do. They must be signed by the Minister and Church Wardens. If there is only one Church Warden He must sign his name as the Church Warden. This is a sad inconvenience as our Church Warden lives beyond Trevor. Dismissed the young man with a perquisite and many many thanks to Mr Chambre.

Friday March 20th   Sent for Mr Edwards of the Hand about *very Particular business*. He came immediately and acted as we expected and indeed always experienced. Sent to invite the Vicar to coffee. I am so puzzled I scarce know what I write. The Vicar came to tea. Our Landlord came. Paid him his half years Rent, which was due last November but we had not money. Now for the Cause of my Puzzle. Peggy, our undermaid who had lived with us three years was this day discharged our service. Unfortunate girl. Her Pregnancy she could no longer conceal, nor could she plead in her excuse that she had been seduced by promises of marriage. Nine till twelve in the Dressing room concerning that Poor Peggy Jones. Her father would not admit her to return to his House. We prevailed on the Weaver and his wife to receive her. What is to become of her?

Saturday March 21st   Lovely delicious day. The Vicar came. Mr Chambre's Clerk James Price, the Churchwardens John Ellis and John Jones. The Certificate† signed at last . . . Peggy Jones went to Trevor Hall this morning and I fear perjured herself. The Person to whom she swore her pregnancy was due was not the man to whom she was attached. Ordered her to be dismissed from the Weaver's which was instantly done.

Thursday March 26th   The turner came with the Fitchet‡ alive in a Trap. He caught it last night by the Brook side. This the felon who

* The banker.
† For their pensions.
‡ A polecat.

has committed such depredations in our Poultry yard. He killed our Turkey cock and Hen, two beautiful cocks, one the gift of our Landlady, the others of our Barretts, and above all he slew our ever to be lamented Hen . . . Most delicious lovely day, gentle fleeces of snow falling down, sun shining, the whole country smiling. Birds melodiously chanting. Village Bells ringing. Populace shouting for whom we ordered a Sheep to be roasted. A Bonfire illuminated to Celebrate the happy Restoration of His Majesty's health, our Benefactor.

Saturday March 28th The little Brynkinalt woman from whom we have the cheese came to be paid. Thank God we had it for her. She brought two fowl and six pounds of Butter. Poor Brynkinalt, the Hospitable Doors of that venerable mansion are I fear closed for ever by the rapine and plunder of Servants, who imposed on the extravagance and weakness of their old Mistress.* Soft gloomy evening. Field perfectly covered with sheep and lambs. A Plough at the end moving slowly under the trees. Ploughman whistling, the wildest and most plaintive tune I ever heard.

Sunday March 29th Letter from Lady Dungannon dated Lille March 22nd. Thank God the poor Woman has recovered her health and spirits amidst all her sufferings, and Lord Dungannon, her most excellent grandson, with a generosity and goodness of which there are but too few examples, has by paying her Debts (to which no law could oblige him) extricated her from all her difficulties, and she hopes to return to England the latter end of the ensuing month.

* Lady Dungannon.

1790

Monday March 1st   Receipt to destroy insects on trees – a handful of Coarse Salt in 6 galls of water – wash tree with it.

Tuesday March 16th   Splendid evening. Reading. Writing. My beloved and I walked by the Mill, the Pengwern lane and the beautiful fields near Pengwern wood. Bull bellowing fearfully at some distance. Met three innocent boys, one with a Spinning Wheel on his head.

Friday March 19th   Discovered an artichoke, two months earlier than I ever remember, and there are more appearing.

Monday March 22nd   ... thanks to God for the Seasonable remittance which enables us to discharge some, in particular one heavy debt which pressed like a dagger to our heart.* My Beloved and I talked the Matter over.

Tuesday March 23rd   My beloved and I walked to Blaen Bache. The vale has lost none of its beauty as cultivation has succeeded to woods and waste. Cornfields and Meadows smiling on the summit of the mountains. Entered a cottage situated in the declivity of the mountain in the only wood remaining, over the babbling Brook. Found a very pretty young woman spinning, a weaver at his loom, a little child with a Doll, two fine dogs, which the young woman with native politeness took up in her arms and locked in the outhouse. A black and white cat. My beloved and I gathered holly berries, primrose and strawberry plants for our Bank. Such an evening.

Accounts

Receipts. March 27th. My B by a Bill of Exchange from Her Brother £92.19.1.

1791

Tuesday March 1st   Rose at eight. Intense frost. Brilliant Day. My Beloved and I walked in the field before our Cottage. 9 Breakfast.

* A loan from the Barretts, who were embarrassingly now enemies!

Half past 9 till 3. Splendid Superb Day. My Beloved and I went the Home Circuit. Writing. Drawing. Walked in the *Infini*. 3 Dinner. Mutton Roasted. Mutton Chops. Cockles and Mussels. Half past 3 till 9. Sweet Evening. Calm – Still – Delicious. Home Circuit and *Infini*. Reading. Working. 9–12 in the Bedchamber. Reading. a day of the most delicious retirement most delicately employed.

Friday March 4th Storm all night. Whistling wind. Summits of the mountains enveloped in purple mist – sweet sheen of tender light. 3 Dinner. Boiled Fowl. Bacon. Sprouts. Boiled Fruits.

Wednesday March 9th A chimney sweep sent by Mrs Worrall arrived. Instantly adjourned to the Bedchamber and got the Library chimney swept which was in great want of it. A day of silent and sweet retirement.

Friday March 11th Birds so melodious. Lovely day. One gentleman two ladies walked up the field then Rapt at the Door and desired to see the House. Refused them with proper contempt. Creatures without names. Certainly without manners. With a consummate stock of courage.

Friday March 25th Made the Ginger Wine.

Wednesday March 30th Sweet Evening. My beloved and I walked in the Field. Met a native of North America. His name Benjamin Pitt. A perfect Copper Colour with a hideous mouth and such eyes!

1792

Expenses

March 1 Mason in part for new room 6s.* Peter the Smith 1s.
Coach for new Windows 1s.2d.

10 Shanette deceased.
Mason and Labourers 8 days at Little Room 19s.6d.

17 Edward Evans bringing the Marble from Oswestry 5s.

22 Smoking our Bacon 2s.6d.
Our Landlady for Bricks and Lime for new Cellar and Little Room £1.7.6.

* This signifies an unwise burst of spending on a new room, new cellar, new marble chimney piece, carpets, curtains, etc. They were soon in financial difficulties.

27   Peggeen preparing Yarn 3s.6d.
31   Marble Masons 4s.6d. – Mr Evans Man with Portugal
      Laurels 2s.

1793

March 26th   The Times are so alarmingly frightful . . . Mary nearly
fractured her skull falling upstairs. Her favourite Cat having followed
her for Victuals unperceived occasioned her making a false step . . .
We believe the end of the World is at no great distance – what is
your opinion?

> (Sarah Ponsonby to Mrs Tighe, on the alarming
> course of the French revolutionary wars)

1794

March 4th   I have of late received so few letters from you, and
none at all from your charming friend, that I cd not help fearing I
had offended you . . . I still anxiously wish to hear from my Viellard
who I hope will set my heart at rest, wch it *never* can be, except I
receive frequent and kind letters from both my beloved Friends.

> (Harriet Bowdler to Sarah Ponsonby)

March 13th   Do not let my Viellard grow Idle again!

> (Harriet Bowdler to Sarah Ponsonby)

Receipts

MUTTON HASH

Make a proper quantity of Flour and Butter in a Stewpan – Stirring
it continually till it takes a good brown colour, add a very thin Slice
of Ham, pepper and Salt, some Capers cut very fine. Simmer it
slowly 'till the Ham is thoroughly done, then put in the Mutton cut
in thin slices, warm it without boiling, garnish the Dish with Pickles
Horse radish and fry'd bread. Serve the Blade Bone boil'd upon the
Hash.

March

BREAST OF VEAL — MARINATED

Cut the Breast of Veal in pieces Boil it in Broth till three parts done then Soak it about an Hour with two Spoonfuls of Vinegar, a little of its own Broth, Pepper and Salt, four Cloves, a little Onion, Thyme and Bay Leaf. Drain and fry it a Good Colour with Parsley.

AU CONT BOUILLON

Put a Whole Breast of Veal into a Stewpan its own length with a good Glass of White wine. a little Broth. a faggott of Parsley Winter Savoury Thyme, Sorrell, Basil, Chervil and Slice Carrotts, Celery, Turnips, Parsnips, Parsley roots and Onions. Pepper and Salt. Pass the Sauce through a Sieve. Skim and Serve it upon the Meat.

ALMOND CAKES

Eight Eggs and two Whites, three quarter of a pound of Sugar a quarter of a pound of sweet Almonds half an Ounce of Butter. half a pound of Flour. Bake them in little Earthen pans.

1796

Lichfield March 23rd   Ah! I am afraid you are too partial to my attempted poetic consecration of your own Langollen Vale, and its bright mistresses.
(Anna Seward to Sarah Ponsonby, about Miss Seward's collected poems. The final verse of the title poem runs thus:

> Through Eleanora and her Zara's mind
> Early through genius, taste and fancy flowed,
> Through all the graceful arts their powers combined,
> And her last polish brilliant life bestowed;
> The lavish promises in life's soft morn,
> Pride, pomp, and love, their friends the sweet enthusiasts
>   scorn.)

1797

March 3rd ... these desperate times – The Banks shut up – Only Paper Money Current and not a fragment of that in Our possession ...

> (Sarah Ponsonby to Mrs Tighe, with Britain
> standing alone against the French, Ireland on the
> verge of rebellion and a financial crisis at home)

1798

Expenses

March 1 Amongst our 3 men for Drink 1s. 6d.
2 Amongst Our five men for drink 3s.
3 Amongst Our Ten Labourers for drinks 5s.
Lodwick's Widow for sending Her Son to the great Work* 2s.
5 5 hundred Quicksets at £2.15.6.
6 Amongst Our 10 Labourers for drink 5s.

8	20	10s. 6d.
9	9	4s. 6d.
10	11	6s.

Lodwick's Son for good work 1s.
17 Baker for bringing Quicksets 1s.
Irish Woman to Wrexham for Mary's Rheumatic side 1s. 6d.
19 Simon for placing our beautiful Tommy by his poor Mother 6d.
20 Cutting hair 5s.
27 Mr Robert's Simon and his Boys ploughing and harrowing the Abbert 4s.

1802

Sunday March 14th Went to our village church. An English sermon that might have been Hebrew for anything we understood of the matter, so dreadfully was it preached by the poor curate.

---

* The strangely named 'Potatoe garden'.
† One of their fields.

Monday March 15th   At half-past ten in the Hand's new Chaise,
Dick Morris driver – My beloved and I went to Chirk Castle. Roads
capital. A Porter at the gate. Drove up to the old entrance gate,
alighted and walked through the great gates, found the Lawn
covered with sheep and lambs, all milk white ... Staid there a
quarter of an hour and proceeded to Oswestry through the Park.
Saw with regret the 64 old oak lying about which had been thrown
down by the late tremendous storms. Met cattle innumerable driving
from the fair. Stopped at little Edward the Bookseller's, paid him his
bill. Left some newspapers to be bound. Next, to little Edward the
Silversmith, bought a Pen knife, a silver pencil and gold locket, and
some Honeysuckle Soap. We then went to Mrs Barrett's. Found her
battling with a rebellious Tenant to whom she forgave thirty pounds
arrears of rent. When the contest was over she and Margaret went
with us round her ground.

Wednesday March 17th   Fair in the village by much the poorest
since we came to this Country, the season considered. Neither Beef
nor Veal, the price of meat being so exorbitant that few can afford to
purchase it. Many market days formerly were better attended,
greater number of buyers and sellers than there are at this Fair.

Monday March 22nd   Our lovely little Primrose calved in the night.
A son.

(The Journal)

Llangollen Vale March 24th   The hog's head arrived in the precise
season of perhaps all others in our lives when it best suited our
farming arrangements to make an immense plantation of this first
of fruits to which the contents of that well-filled vessel were indeed
amply competent, and as the apple potatoes which composed a part
of them were a kind absolutely unknown in this country, you have
enabled us both to benefit and oblige numbers of our neighbours by
distributing a few to each, which we have every reason to believe
will provide an important and lasting advantage to many poor
families.

(Sarah Ponsonby to Mrs Tighe)

1810

Friday March 16th   I dare say We could have discovered Aches and pains in Abundance had we professed leisure sufficient to attend to them. but Tuesday we had an MP – and a Young Divine to entertain – Wednesday we had that most interesting of Beings Lady Erne to admire – Thursday We had Lady Erne Again – and this day our beloved Ancient Cow Beauty for So Many – Many years the Grace and Pride and Ornament of Our Pastures – Well – this day – No Matter – I am convinced She is now grazing in the Elysian Fields – dear Busy* I wish you had Assented to Accompany Mrs Kenyon – We should have found it Comfortable to expect you. and we want Comfort for dearly did we Love Beauty and Sorely do we regret her –

(Lady Eleanor Butler to Miss Pigott)

1815

March [undated]   The News is Glorious indeed. but the Demon† has effected his escape and we fear will direct his steps towards France. how will he be received there?

(Lady Eleanor Butler to Miss Watkins Wynn)

* Harriet Pigott, who played the part of Busy, a maid, at a theatrical party, and thereafter was called Busy by Eleanor Butler.

† Napoleon.

Thursday March 8th Sunday. Monday. Tuesday. Wednesday. Thursday – and not a line – We Therefore conclude that as each was primed and ready for Battle the Combat ended fatally – Similar to that of the two Kilkenny Cats – Who Fought 'Till only the Tail of One was left – I am Convinced if Dear Busy had a Single Claw remaining it would have been employed in transcribing the So Solemnly promised Egg-receipt . . .

(Lady Eleanor Butler to Miss Pigott)

1819

Monday March 1st The skill of Dr Darwin who has saved Mrs Talbot by prescribing Cinnamon instead of Ordinary tea. Protect young peas with furze. Recipe for poor old Evans who was suffocating with Phlegm.

Thursday March 4th The old Duke Hamilton who died lately left estate Eighty thousand pounds to an *improper* who lived with him – he has not bequeathed a farthing to his Son Lord Archibald Hamilton or his daughters . . . a poultice of Bruised and pounded Water Cresses fresh from the Spring – laid over every other application – changed twice in the day each time quite fresh – prevents the offensive smell so dreadful in that unfortunate complaint.*

(The Journal)

March 4th Llangollen is at this moment in a State of Terror, Confusion and approaching Distress from the termination of the Cotton Manufactory and the shutting of its Bank . . . Some of our neighbours and some of yours in Oswestry have been weak enough to have deposited considerable sums in the latter . . . the Bankrupts can only offer 2d in the pound. We have been too wise or too poor . . . Next Saturday night Scores of poor little creatures are to be dismissed from that odious employ, and unfit for any other whatsoever, and whose parents are as incompetent of finding them a maintenance as we are in finding the Longitude.

(Sarah Ponsonby to Mrs Parker)

* Cancer.

1826

Requirements for a Plas Newydd housemaid.

Wages Six guineas a year – Scouring of Rooms – Only required for
the Maids and Mangle rooms – and the Hall and porch – which last
are of free stone – all the other rooms being covered with carpets –
and only scoured thrice a year – perfect neatness in Appearance and
Work – and Simplicity of attire in which qualities She will have a
very excellent pattern in Gwendolen – A good washer – and a Strong
assistant in the Laborious part of Brewing – a Good Sharpener of
Knives is most particularly requisite to Our peace of Mind –
Assisting the Dairy Maid in Keeping the Kitchen and all its utensils
and furniture in perfect Neatness – and making Winter Fires in Our
Library – and eating Parlour and at night in Our Bed Chamber –
seems the heaviest part of her requisite Duty – a good humoured
Willingness – Occasionally to assist in Other miscellaneous Services
will We can pledge Our Words – neither be imposed upon – nor
unrewarded – No fine Plain Work nor much Coarse – nor any Ironing
of fine or small Linen expected – Lady Eleanor personally asks that
she May be a Merry Creature Given to talking and Singing –
provided they are neither *Raw* Songs nor Methodist Hymns.

(Sarah Ponsonby to Mrs Parker)

APRIL

1784

Monday 5th April   Pain in my eye!

Friday 16th April   Finished Swinburne's *Travels Through Spain* to My Love.

Monday 19th April   Copied the extract of my Father's Will for Lodge. Lady Morris.

Wednesday 28th April   . . . to the Hand in the Evening – fainted there.

(Eleanor Butler's Pocket Book)

1785

April 11th   I have also a foolish Vexation of my own – which I am ashamed of being teazed by but cannot help. Somebody I know not who at Kilkenny wrote Mrs Goddard word that I was going to be married to I know not whom neither. But I am more tormented by Mrs G's having a momentary doubt of its truth than at the report. I have reproached her for her folly and told her in the words of Mrs Ford in the Merry Wives of Windsor – 'What – have I 'scaped such reports in the holy day time of my beauty and am *now* fit subject for them!' – If you hear it – I need not bid You do me justice ... My B has a Book of (I think) Very well chosen Extracts from all the Books She has read since We had a home. She intends writing a fair copy of it in her own hand for You – I have ventured to assure her it will be acceptable, which her diffidence led her to doubt. She will also write Her historical opinions – and we expect Flechier Very soon ... We have Summer Weather but want rain. We have now every Shrub and Perennial that was admired at Woodstock* – in which My B's excellent heart makes her feel as tender an interest as I do – Amongst the rest the Hypericum Balearicum which is one of our first favourites – though it had all perish'd at W: before I left it –

(Sarah Ponsonby to Mrs Tighe)

April 15th

GINGER TEA

It is made by shredding twelve or fourteen large lumps of the best ginger – pretty small – which are made into Tea – in the common way – the Dose a Tea Cup Full when perfectly cold, taken at any time when the Head is affected or the Stomach indicates a likelihood of its being one – for our practice convinces us, that though Head aches may proceed from nerves as well as a disorder'd *Stomach* – *That* being strengthened† seldom fails to relieve if not remove the complaint, which the Ginger tea seldom fails to effect ... I cured my B of one of her Bad head-aches (which fully deserve that Epithet) by a vomit of Weak Ginger tea which I wish you wou'd try for *Our* sake when next you have one.

(Sarah Ponsonby to Mrs Tighe)

1786

April 12th Italian is my B's present Hobby Horse. I think she

* Sarah's old home in Ireland.
† It was commonly believed in the eighteenth century that strong-tasting substances strengthened.

makes great way – but she is modest. We have sent for Duché's
Sermons and expect them soon, along with Chamber's *Dictionary*
which has gone to be bound. My heart beats at the idea of the
Scientific knowledge which I shall find in those volumes.

(Sarah Ponsonby to Mrs Tighe)

1787

April 13th My B and I have made our resolution known in the
Village, that We would never visit, or be visited by any persons who
became residents in it, as it would subject us to perpetual and
sometimes very disagreeable intrusions . . . We have been obliged
to adopt the resolution of making no acquaintance with occasional
neighbours – as our Village is now almost always crouded with
Strangers . . .

(Sarah Ponsonby to Mrs Tighe)

1788

Thursday April 3rd Letter from Lady Dungannon. It is at length
determined that she leaves this country. She is to have an apartment
at Hampton Court. Poor woman, we shall miss our old very good
friend and neighbour, but 'thus the wheel goes round'. Wrote to
express our great regret. It's late in life to move, but she will perhaps
find it pleasanter than the uninterrupted solitude of that old and
lonely mansion.

Friday April 4th . . . boiled skate – what a Vile dish!

Receipt

SAUCE FOR SKATE

Make a Sauce with a Bit of the Liver bruised and Boiled a Moment with two Glasses of White wine – two spoonfuls of Chopt Parsley, pepper and Salt – a good Bit of Butter. Thicken with the Yolk of One Egg and some Cream – Serve it Over the Fish.

Thursday April 10th   Fine evening. Gentle wandering light on the mountains . . . My beloved and I took a delightful walk, ascended the Hill then descended into the narrow deep valley which leads to Llansantffraid. Steep hills on either side clothed to the summit with wood. The Cyflymen gushing rapidly over the Rocks and hastening to the little Mill of Pengwern. That mill, a wooden bridge, our Landlord's cottage closing the scene at one end, the other terminated by the small hamlet of Blaen Bache, the Berwyn Mountains rising behind. Walked by the brook side to Pengwern. Our Landlady came out with great expectation of joy in her countenance, said she was rejoiced to see us, that she thought it a long while since she had that satisfaction. When we had returned her greeting crossed the large wheatfield, then the Miller's field of Peas, the meadow, crossed the lane, returned hence by our own field. Met besides our Landlady the Hand Husbandman with his Team, the old man of Pengwern our Landlord's eldest brother, and a civil modest young woman who removed a great stone which closed a gate we were going to climb over.

Sunday April 13th   Superb evening. A riot with the Weaver's Mastiff, ordered him to be shot or sent away. Relented. Gave the man half a crown for sending him away immediately. Thought the woman looked sorry for the Dog. Bid them send for it again on condition that it is to be chained up all day.

Expenses

April 13   Weaver for his civility about the Dog 2s. 6d.
   19   John Jones for 2 Mole traps 4s.   for himself 1s.

Sunday April 20th   The Library windows thrown open. Gentle wind rustling through the leaves. Cooing of wood pigeons. Sweet pipe of the Thrushes and Blackbirds. Finished 'Thoughts on The Importance of the Manners of the Great in General Society'.

Wednesday April 23rd   My beloved and I went the Home Circuit – delicious Soaking rain – how we enjoyed it! A day of the most delicious retirement and Sweetly peaceful Occupations.

Thursday April 24th   Soft grave still day . . . My beloved and I went to the shrubbery. While we were thus employed heard loud and repeated lamentations from the Sheep and lambs who were grazing in the little verdant meadow by the Cyflymen. Ran to the pales to see what was the occasion of the plaintive bleating. Saw the entire flock ranged by the brookside, apparently in the greatest distress. At length observed one sheep hanging from the hedge on the other side of the stream just strangling, as the Briar with which it was entangled was got about its neck. Sent instantly and had it released just in time. The moment it was freed all the cries of its companions were appeased. They gazed kindly at it and returned cheerfully to their simple repast. A single lamb attempted to wade over to it, but the tender parent prevented its fond impatience by her own, and rushing thro' the water meekly stood while he plentifully sucked her.

Friday April 25th   Reading. Writing. My beloved and I went the home circuit. A mole caught in the new trap. A boy in the field with three fine young Thrushes which he took from the nest on Pentrefelin – a piteous sight.

Monday April 28th   Rose at six – delicious dewy morning. bright sun. blue sky. From Wrexham new spade. Parcel from Appleyard containing one quire super royal paper for mounting drawings –

hundred quill Pens . . . My Beloved and I went to the garden, sowed the tender annuals in their hot bed. The Irishwoman whom we sent to Chirk gardens at 7 this morning with a letter to Lever returned with three pots of cucumber plants. Planted them. Sowed three sorts of cucumber seeds. Reading. Drawing. Oiled the Parlour eating table with the Spinhamland receipt. Dined in the kitchen to let the oil soak in it. Shut the shutters of the kitchen window and dined very comfortably on lamb and cold mutton . . . Delicious heavenly evening . . . My Beloved and I walked round Edward Evans' meadow, then up the Mill lane, turned into the meadow which slopes from the Blaen Bache hill and hangs over the Mill stream. John Edwards, and his little son with him, repairing the hawthorn hedge. He moved the stone from the gate. Walked round the field, returned home by the lane. Found Margaret at the gate waiting for admittance. Opened it for her. Walked round our little demesne . . . In our walk met a little boy, asked him where he was running. To rob a nest which he had observed in the morning. Scolded him and forbad him to molest the birds.

Tuesday April 29th Rose at half-past six. The loveliest blue and silver morning I ever beheld. My Beloved and I went the home circuit. The air perfumed with sweetbriar, violets, and the Blossoms of the various kinds of Cherries. A Choir of Birds. The Cuckold for the first time this year. We visited our cucumber plants and tender annuals. Then walked in the field before the cottage. The country in a blaze of beauty.

Wednesday April 30th Rose at six. Enchanting Morning – My Beloved and I Went the Home Circuit. The Morning So heavenly Could not leave the Shrubbery 'till, Nine, Breakfast. Half past Nine Till Three – again went the home Circuit, how Splendid. how heavenly. came in for a few Minutes to Write, went out again. Staid Till one. Reading, drawing. then Went again to the Shrubbery. brought our Books namely *Gil Blas* and Madame de Sevigné with us. Such a day! Three. Dinner. roast breast of Mutton. boil'd Veal. Bacon and Greens. Toasted Cheese. Half past Three Till Nine. Such a heavenly evening. blue Sky with patches of Cloud Scattered over it. My beloved and I went to the Shrubbery. Spent the Evening there. brought our Books, planted out our hundred Carnations in different parts of the Borders. heavenly evening. Reading. Writing. Nine till

One in the dressing room Reading. A day of such Exquisite Such enjoyed retirement. So still. So silent –

(The Journal)

1789

Friday April 3rd   Mr Edwards of the Hand's Cow calved Twins. The farmer of Pengwern Hall's two cows calved Twins. This is looked upon as a Sign of a prosperous year, and particularly as the King's recovery is looked upon by the Loyal Inhabitants of this lonely Vale as the most signal instance of the particular care of Providence for these Islands.

Saturday April 4th   Mutton from Oswestry of a great Size and Vast price . . . My beloved and I walked many times on the Esplanade. Clear evening, but sharp and cold beyond expression. A comfortable well clad old woman rode up the field with a pipe of Tobacco in her Mouth, the Puffs from which softened the keenness of the air and must make her journey over the mountains delectable.

Sunday April 5th   Bright sun gilding the Rocks and Mountains. Evan Williams and his Wife walking slowly and pensively round their hanging Field, examining the Thread which lies there for bleaching, and counting the Lambs which, with their Dams, are on this sweet spot.

Monday April 6th   Fine evening. Reading. Drawing. My Beloved and I walked for an hour admiring the beauty of the Evening, the heavenly light and Shadow Wandering about the Mountains, the Plough close beside us, Sheep and Lambs in the field. A Woman riding up the road which undulates through it, the Miller driving his horse laden with Sacks of Corn, Children returning from School, an old man bent double with years and leaning on short crutches.

Saturday April 11th   A crowd of people, the attendants of a wedding from Wrexham, with the Bride and Bridegroom, entreated permission to see the shrubbery. Could not refuse them on this, most probably, happiest day of their lives. Looked at them as they walked. Very well dressed in a plain clean way befitting their station in life.

Tuesday April 14th   Glorious day. A Plough at one end of the field, plough man whistling melodiously. A Harrow in another part. Sheep and lambs dispersed about, some grazing, some at play, others lying down. Smoke ascending from the cottages with which the sides of the mountains are dotted. Writing beside the window. I must write down the Scenery which adorns this field at this moment. Richard Griffith's Plough is under the window. Edward Evans with a Harrow. Evan Williams sowing oats. The Pinahin man's cart with Dung in a remote corner of the field for Potatoes. The Miller and his horse laden with sacks of corn coming from the Mill to the village. Sun shining, birds singing, lambs bleating. Ploughmen and sowers whistling and singing. Village bells ringing for Church.

Thursday April 16th   Warm and comfortable beyond description. Our fire most excellent. Table strewed with Books, pens, Ink, paper, every implement for Drawing. From the window we see our Landlord sowing.

Sunday April 19th   Our good landlord came with a letter to us from that Price who was condemned for sheep stealing. His sentence was reserved and the judge promised to recommend him as an object of mercy and that he should be Transported. He writes to us, to entreat we will get him off from Transportation. Threw his letter in the fire as we cannot consider a noted Sheep Stealer entitled to much lenity even had we interest to get him off.

Monday April 20th   Planted a great quantity of Primroses on the bank by the Shed. A Storm parching and withering everything . . . I went to the Shrubbery to see the funeral of old Parry of Llangollen Vale who died last Thursday. He was the most opulent farmer in this Parish. His Burial was extremely decent and respectable, a hearse and six, one postchaise, and all his kindred, who are the most respectable Farmers in the Country, attended on horse back with hatbands. He left twopence apiece to all the poor Wives and a penny apiece to all the Children in this Township. He was very old, lived in a beautiful place under the Mountain about a mile from this Village. The moment the procession entered Llangollen the Clerk and a number of well drest people with their hats off began to sing a Psalm, which they continued till the Body reached the Churchyard.

The first person who preceded the procession was old Roberts of Dinbrenisaf who is past ninety years of age. After him came the old farmer all in black who had lived with Parry twenty years.

Expenses

April 1 Jacob for Primroses 6d.
      3 Bonfire Sheep and Bell ringing for the King's recovery £1.16s.
    10 Baillis for Repairing the Roof of our House. Chimneys etc. 3s.8d.
    23 Carriage of Cyder from Worcestershire 11s.6d.
    25 Mr Bishop the Painter in part of payment £1.1s.

Tuesday April 21st Little Bishop the painter came at last and his man. We intended to diet him and his Journeyman at the Hand but as they arrived late last night and Mr Edwards was from home they would not admit him. So he went to the Lyon and there he must remain which is a great Mortification to us who had agreed with Mr Edwards for their board.

Wednesday April 22nd Visited our painter and whitewasher. Staid with them some time, Then came to our Apartment which I admire more every time I see it. I am so sure it is like Madame Sevigné's Cabinet . . . A little dwarvish smiling man all in Tatters came to offer his service as a Portrait Painter.

Saturday April 25th The Parlour and Library windows painted a beautiful rich white – the Doors varnished. Skirting board chocolate colour. Kitchen Window white. Seat and settle chocolate colour and linen press Door Varnished. Hall and Door going to the cellar and Larder varnished – Stairs and Skirting board Bannisters painted – the ceilings of the Library – Parlour – Hall – Kitchen whitened . . . This vile Mrs Vent* counteracts all the Salutary effects which Madame Pluie's† presence would have done our Trees . . . My beloved and I walked in *l'infini*.

Monday April 27th Mr Edwards of the Hand came up to tell the melancholy Tale of his youngest child, an Infant of Four Months old,

* The wind.
† The rain.

who has been pining and wasting away these six weeks and has now become quite a skeleton, tho' it eats heartily. It has got the oldest keenest Look, and the eyes penetrate through everyone that comes near it. They attribute this singular case to its being bewitched and Shanette the oldest woman in the Parish is suspected of having committed the Deed through Malice, because she was refused charity at the Hand, six weeks since. She was then observed to look eagerly at the child there several times, who was in perfect health and spirits, and from that moment Drooped and pined. The Father and Mother are firmly persuaded of this and have applied to Edward Jones the hump-back Carpenter for a remedy of which he is possessed, and has inherited from his Father to whom it had descended through many generations. This remedy or charm to counteract witchcraft consists of a Prayer. He first visits the Person or Creature affected, takes something from it, a pin if a human being, a Lock of hair or Feather if Beast or Fowl. He then returns to his house and says a Prayer, after which the Patient never fails to recover. Please God I shall attend to this case and know the whole process of it. Powerful as Fancy is on the human Mind, it cannot operate on that of an Infant.

Tuesday April 28th   Sir John Heatly sent to desire permission to see this Cottage and Shrubbery. Our compliments to him, he was welcome to see the Shrubbery but the Library and Parlour being just painted the furniture was removed. He came. Saw him through the window. A great Vulgar looking man with a riding coat. Hair well dressed.

Wednesday April 29th   Rain. The cuckold for the first time this year.

Thursday April 30th   Storm. Writing. Mr Edwards of the Hand came with Walpole's note. Asked him about the bewitched child. Edward Jones the Carpenter came on Monday night, took a pin from the child and for nine times he is to read the Prayer, every morning before sunrise and every night after sunset. The child now sleeps and is easier, not screaming so often or so loud as it did before, and they hope it will recover.

(The Journal)

Thursday April 1st   Letter from Mrs Barrett with £41.9.10. being the cash due to us out of the £91.19.10. which we sent her to pay herself fifty pounds which We were in her Debt.

Expenses

April   1   to Mrs Parks 4 and a half Load of Muck 19s.2d. to Do for
             Half a Ton of Hay £1.10s.
             To Mrs Parks for the Debt of Bishop the Painter in 1789.
             £1.1s. *Mem* Mrs Parks's extreme Gentility.
             Our Half Years Rent due 1st. November 1789 £11.7.6.
             For Shandy to Our Landlord 5s. a piping Boy 6d.
        3   Liam for Salmon and Oysters from Salop. Our Kitchen
             Maid earnest for another Year 1s.
        8   A poor Turk 1s.
       14   to Mr Speakman with a *Pine Apple* £1.1.0.

April 18th   Planted Scotch fir. Sent for Evan the Clog maker to water them, then my beloved and I went to the quarry and planted seven Scotch fir there. Then we took a most delicious walk behind Pen-y-Coed. Returned over the Pengwern road. The Country superb. Observed a little cottage roofed with stone and covered with sod erected on the side of the Mountain. From above the little abode all the rubbishy stone has been swept away, the ground cleared, an orchard planted behind the house, a little garden secured by a Box hedge from the encroachments of Sheep. This garden contained flowers such as primroses, dianthus, snowdrops and sweet briar, jessamy, roses, all for the use of a Hive of Bees. A little well beside – but I could expatiate for ever on the delights of this delightful little habitation.

Wednesday April 21st   My beloved and I ran the Home Circuit enjoying the Rain.

Friday April 23rd   Spoke to the joiner about the quarry which Edwards of the Hand was going to open on the hill opposite our window and which we sent to the workmen not to proceed with. They civilly desisted immediately.

Saturday April 24th   My beloved and I went the Home Circle.

Discovered Edward Evans' son going to climb over the Hedge by the Shed. We stop'd him, and walked instantly to his Mother's house, dark as it was, to complain of him. She threatened to 'wand him' but we got him off.

Monday April 26th　Tuesday was the most superb and brilliant day I ever beheld. Went to the joiners. Sent him to Mr Edwards of the Hand about the Masons opening a quarry in our View. Received a Saucy answer in return. *Mem* to recollect it in proper time and season.

(The Journal)

1791

Friday April 1st　Bedchamber and dressing room whitewashed.

Wednesday April 6th　Letter from Sidebottom recommending John Francis as a gardener qualified to please us. Went down to him. A little old crafty looking being. Spoke to him. *Deaf*. Went the home circuit with him. *Lame*. Never managed wall trees. Sent Sidebottom back as good a Thing.

(The Journal)

Expenses

April 12　Bell ringers for my dear Lady Eleanor 10s. 6d.*

April 30th　... though the World seems unanimously of the opinion that it affords her a new claim to that One hundred per Annum in addition to her present *two* which wd. gratify Our utmost ambition – We have no reason to think Ld Ormond will be Prevailed with to adopt it ... Though we have known her right to the Appellation of Ladyship, a considerable time past – It was only the day before I last wrote to you that she was induced to accept it from a report having been propagated in Kilkenny ... that she disapproved the restoration of her truly illustrious family to their Hereditary Honours. She would otherwise have been much better pleased to have resigned that share in them which seems attended with much more pain than Satisfaction, to her truly amiable feelings.

(Sarah Ponsonby to Mrs Tighe)

* The forfeited Ormonde titles had been restored, which meant that Eleanor Butler, as an earl's daughter, had the courtesy title 'Lady'.

April

1793

April 4th   I must thank you again for the excellent introduction to the Spanish language which has enabled my B to read whole cantos of the *Araucana* without looking above once or twice into a dictionary. I also can read three or four successive lines after she has explained them to me with perfect facility, so that, between us, a wonderful progress has really been made . . . We begin to hope from the success of the Austrian arms that peace will soon be restored to the world and a counter-revolution take place very soon in France . . .

(Sarah Ponsonby to Mrs Tighe)

April 6th   I look at the little Drawing in my Day book, I read your precious letter and think of all the happiness I enjoyed with you and my own Viellard during the most delicious days of my life, but at present I can only enjoy the pleasures of Memory –

> For Joy's bright sun has shed his waning ray,
> And Hope's delusive metre cease to play:
> While Clouds on Clouds the smiling prospect close.

(Harriet Bowdler to Sarah Ponsonby)

April 23rd   I wish the newspapers wd. not torment us with so many falsehoods . . . I feel more dread of famine than of war . . .

(Harriet Bowdler to Sarah Ponsonby)

1794

April 29th   I have a letter from my Viellard wch. I shall answer on the first of April 1795 if I can think of anything in the meantime to teaze and provoke him heartily. Till then I have nothing to say, except I receive a letter which is worth answering – I wish I knew where to get another Husband* . . . My Mother (with all her knowledge) cannot imagine why Sea Kale shd. make your head ache. We dress it like aspargus and find it very wholsome as well as pleasant: but my mother thinks it wd. be good stew'd like cellery, and I am sure my friend Mary wd dress it nicely.

(Harriet Bowdler to Sarah Ponsonby)

* In this rather bizarre game of coquetry Harriet Bowdler seems to be pretending to be Eleanor Butler's fiancée!

Receipts

A FORCED CABBAGE

Take a fine White heart Cabbage, lay it in water two or three hours, then half boil it, Set it in a Cullender to drain – then very carefully Cut out the heart, but take great care not to break off any of the outside leaves. Fill it with Forced meat made thus: Take a pound of Veal, half a pound of Bacon fat and Lean, together. Cut them small, and beat them fine in a Morter with four Eggs boiled hard. Season it with Pepper and Salt a little Mace a very little Lemon peel cut fine, some Thyme and two Anchovies. When they are beat fine. Take the Crumb of a Stale Roll, and the heart of the Cabbage You cut out Chopped fine – Mix all together with the Yolk of an Egg. Then fill the hollow part of the Cabbage and tie it with a Pack thread, then lay some slices of Bacon to the Bottom of the Stew pan and on that a pound of Coarse lean Beef Cut thin – put in the Cabbage – Cover it Close, and let it Stew over a Slow fire 'till the Bacon begins to stick to the Pan. Shake in a little Flour, then pour in some Broth – one Whole Pepper – a Handful of sweet herbs. Cover it close and let it Stew Very softly an hour and half. put in a Glass of Red Wine, give it a Boil, then take it up, lay it on the dish, Untie it – strain the Gravy and Pour it over. This is a fine 'fill' dish and the next day makes a fine Hash with Veal Steaks Boiled and laid on it.

1796

April 7th Amidst the number of polite letters, with which my various literary acquaintance have honoured my Llangollen Vale publication, yours is super-eminent in the ingenuity of discriminating praise, which, above all general encomiums, gratifies a writer. I have sent it, with its fascinating predecessor, to the accomplished Recluses* whose whole warm hearts are in the reception which my lately emerged poems shall meet with from the distinguished few that make encomium fame, and whose praise is potent to recompense the stupid strictures of my anonymous foes amongst the public critics.

(Anna Seward to Christopher Smythe, Esq.)

* Eleanor and Sarah.

April

1798

April 24th   You must each have been deeply disquieted by the miserable scenes which have been acted in your native Ireland since I last had the honour to address you. None of your particular friends are, I trust, on the dire list of those who have fallen the victims of its assassinations. Had my gallant friend, the murdered Colonel St George, the happiness of your acquaintance? . . . What lovely weather! Our valley is bursting into bloom, and the fruit trees of a large public garden in one part of it, now in full blossom, presents a grove of silver amidst the lively and tender green of the fields and hedgerows. Alas! the melancholy of the apprehensive heart is rather increased than abated by this vernal luxury. It seems but as gay garlands on the neck of a victim. In every frame of mind, I remain, dearest ladies and etc.

(Anna Seward to the Ladies of Llangollen)

1799

April 3rd   That your and Lady Eleanor's kind attentive cares have restored the health of your humble friend and follower* of your fortunes, I congratulate you, my dearest Madam. Concerning your own and mutual health, the kind letter, which I have now the honour to acknowledge, makes no mention. I therefore flatter myself it is unimpaired. Would to Heaven I could entertain for your peace as dear a certainty! – but let me forbear to touch the jarring string, which you shun to vibrate; – nor will I descant on my own increasing weakness from the augmenting tyranny of rheumatic disease.

(Anna Seward to Sarah Ponsonby)

April 22nd   The rivers of blood now deluging on the Continent† May not establish peace in these Islands . . . The terrible Income Bill must be answered this very day without any mitigation of the other Taxes . . .

(Sarah Ponsonby to Mrs Tighe)

* Mary Carryll.
† The Napoleonic Wars.

1800

April 16th   Possibly I was the only person who perceived the Earth quake – it was early in the morning you mention – I awoke Miss Ponsonby to say – that if there ever was an Eruption of the Earth in Wales I experienced it at that moment.

(Lady Eleanor Butler to Mrs Piozzi)

1801

Brynbella 5th April   The Ladies at Llangollen enquired much for you. They have more news and more stories than one could dream of. Their *best* however is concerning their own old Maid Mary from whose character one would think Sophia Lee had portray'd that of Cawnor in her tale of *The Two Emilys*. Mary seeing her Ladies eyes fix'd one fine night lately upon the stars, said to Miss Ponsonby, 'Ah! Madam, you once showed me a fine sight in the heavens, the Belt of *O'Bryan**: but I suppose we shall see it no more now since the *Union*'. To this nothing, sure, can be added.

(Mrs Piozzi to Mrs Penelope Pennington)

1804

April [undated]   . . . as the Chief Consul of France seems likely to have sufficient trouble at home to prevent his taking that of coming to invade us, and we hope that we have at length become Conquerors in the Cotton manufactory War, which was if possible still more formidable to us . . .†

(Sarah Ponsonby to Mrs Tighe)

1814

April 5th   The choosing of a new pair of Wafer tongs as important to us as the restoration of the Bourbons . . .

(Sarah Ponsonby to Mrs Parker)

* An Irish patriot of the time whom Mary had confused with Orion.

† The Ladies were great conservationists – witness their opposition to Mr Edwards of the Hand opening a quarry in sight of their windows. In this case they were fighting against a cotton mill being built on the banks of the River Dee. In the event they were unsuccessful.

Lady Eleanor's Prayer to Diana

Since thou and the stars my dear Goddess decree
That old maid as I am, an old maid I must be,
Oh hear the petition I offer to thee,
For to bear it must be my endeavour!

From the griefs of my friendships all drooping around
Till not one that I loved in my youth can be found,
From the legacy-hunters that near us abound,
Diana! thy servant deliver!

From the scorn of the young, and the flouts of the gay,
From all the trite ridicule rattled away
By the pert ones who know nothing better to say,
Oh a spirit to laugh at them give her!

From repining at fancied neglected desert,
Or vain of a civil speech bridling alert,
From finical rudeness or slatternly dirt,
Diana! thy servant deliver!

From over-solicitous guarding of pelf
From humour unchecked, that most obstinate self
Or ridiculous whim whatsoever

From vapourish freaks or methodical airs
Apt to sprout in a mind thats exempted from cares,
From impertinent meddling in others affairs,
Diana! thy servant deliver!

Nor let satisfaction depart from her lot
Let her sing if at ease, or be patient if not,
Be pleased if remembered, content if forgot,
Till the Fates her slight thread shall dissever.

1819

Sunday April 4th   The vicar was three hours at Church – to the great weariness of the Congregation whose dinners were spoiled.

Thursday April 22   Cuckold heard. 63 Asparagus cut. The way of telling a true from a composition stone – applying to the tip of the tongue – Stone is invariably Cold – composition warm. Not knowing there was to be an English Sermon did not go to Church.

(The Journal)

MAY

1778

Monday May 25th Lay at *Llangollen* a pretty Village on the river *Dee* over which there is a *Bridge* esteemed one of the wonders of *Wales*. Built upon a solid rock in 1395 – went to see the *Church* which contains nothing remarkable except for the tomb of a Knight of the Owens Family with a Banner over it.

Tuesday May 26th Walked in the Morning to see Crowe Castle – Trevor Rocks commands an extensive Prospect over the Beautifullest Country in the World. Went in the afternoon to see the remains of an *Abbey* called *Valede Crucis* two miles from Llangollen. There can scarcely be imagined a more beautiful Situation than this *Abbey* . . .

(Account of a Journey in Wales Perform'd in May 1778 by Two Fugitive Ladies*)

---

* The only extant Journal kept by Sarah Ponsonby. This was shortly after their elopement.

1783

May [undated]   Your Pork lies heavy on My Stomach, it was too fat and High fed. I am Sure you were Sick after it. I had rather Sup than dine with you. But pray Poll Davy when will you come and eat with Us. I'll give you a bill of Fare. for breakfast you shall have a Couple of new laid Eggs from our Jersey Hens who are in the Most beautiful Second Mourning you ever beheld with plumes of Feathers on their Head which the D. of D.* would not disdain to Wear. Your dinner Shall be boil'd chickens from our own Coop – Asparagus out of our own garden Ham of our own Saving and Mutton from our own Village. Your Supper Shall consist of Gooseberry Fool – Cranberry Tarts roast Fowl and Sallad – don't this Tempt you – You Shall have a green goose and gooseberry Sauce. No Savage admitted to distract our inspection of it . . .

(Eleanor Butler to Mrs Goddard)

1784

Friday May 14th   I ill of an head ache.

(Eleanor Butler's Pocket Book)

1786

May 28th   My B and I received by Yesterdays post – an acknowledgement from our Friends at St Denys for the Pacquet You were so kind to forward for us – I have the pleasure to tell you that the Sentences were so much approved of that more have been desir'd – And the Princess† has done me the high honour to say – that if I went thither the Grate should be open'd – and I should be permitted to see and converse with the Nuns. The first is a favour seldom granted to any Protestant (My Beloved would be admitted of Course) as strangers are never allowed to see them but through the Grate – when they appear in long Black Veils – and white Kirtles and must

---

* Duchess of Devonshire.

† The Mother Superior of the Carmelite Nuns of St Denys, where Eleanor had a cousin. She was sister to Louis XV. Sarah appears to have sent her some embellished mottoes.

observe a strict silence . . . They Complain'd of the Musk with which
Our Letter was scent'd – Did you perceive it?

(Sarah Ponsonby to Mrs Tighe)

1788

Thursday May 1st Went into the Weaver's garden. Never saw
anything more neat and comfortable. A great quantity of Thread
whitening on the grass. A neat sodded hovel with a good bed of
straw for the Dog who guards this little property. The honest man
just returned from Oswestry Fair where he had been to sell a piece
of Cloth, three little children cleanly drest playing before the door.
The Wife scouring her chairs and Tables.

Expenses

Weaver *Our* neighbour 1s.

Saturday May 3rd Mr Woolham from Wrexham came with his
bill. A very good sort of man, sensible and intelligent. Asked him
many questions concerning the Charlestown, South Carolina, where
he resided some years. He gave us an account of the Rattle snake
and the discovery which a Negro accidentally made of a Cure for the
Bite, which before was thought Mortal. This man was bit in the
woods and in the Anguish of mind and Body pulled up some leaves
of American Plantain which grew near him – he chewed their leaves
and applied them to the Wound. He returned to his master and
informed him of what had happened and prepared to die, which
was always the consequence a few hours after the bite, but to the
Surprise of every person the negro felt no inconvenience from the
wound. Which attributing to the Virtue of the Plantain, he suffered
himself to be twice bit by a Rattle Snake, and each time applying the
leaves, as at first, felt no Pain from the Wound. This discovery was
of so much importance, so many dying every year by the Rattle
Snakes, that there was an assembly held, the negro was freed, fifty
pound per annm. settled on him, and the cure has been every year
published in the Almanacks of that Country.

May 5th Edward Evans of whom we enquired for his eldest son,
a lad about fifteen, told us he has gone to London with a youth of his

own age, son to old Jonathan Hughes the famous Welsh Poet. They walked to Birmingham, then got on the Stage Coach, arrived in London on Monday, and the Wednesday after both got places. Edward Evans' son hired to a person who keeps a lace shop.

Wednesday May 7th   The Irishwoman brought us a letter which Francis the Carrier got at Oswestry. It was from the Barretts and written on Sunday, but forgot by Mr Francis Berkeley, the postman, in his Bag. How very provoking. Writing in a rage to complain of the postman to the Barretts, who probably are raging at us. Went again to the Shrubbery and Potager. As we were going to our new Potager met a large Bundling fat elderly woman toiling up the lane, who apologised for the liberty she took in looking about her. Told her she was very welcome to see the shrubbery. Rang the Bell to have it shewn her. We came in. Glorious light and shadow. A thin spare upright figure from the Village who conducted her up told us her name was Payne, that she was a relation of Lord Bulkeley's and was going in a *Chaise* to the Island of Anglesea.

Saturday May 10th   My Beloved and I went to walk in the fields by Pengwern. Met Davy the Miller – Asked him for his Father (old Silenus). Very ill was the reply, which I am sorry for. Walked sometime in the delicious meadows under Pengwern wood. At our return met our Landlord in the Mill lane. Made him come back with us. Ordered him ale, and sent him round our Shrubbery and Gardens ... The Venerable worthy man prayed fervently for our health and happiness. Heavenly evening.

Expenses

May 10   for a Scythe and Shovel 8s. for Mushroom Spawn to Wrexham 4s.

Sunday May 11th   As we were returning from the Shrubbery met old Parker, who came with compliments from Mr and Mrs Cooper desiring permission to see the cottage and shrubbery. Our compliments. They shall be welcome. We retired to the State Bedchamber till they were come and gone. Observed them from the window. He a tall man (a Clergyman) she a little woman in deep mourning. They left their Compliments and thanks ... My Beloved and I walked in Edward Evans' cornfield and meadow. Then before our Cottage. All the pretty neat Peasants in their best apparel returning to their mountains from the Village. The elders soberly conversing returning from the Methodist Chapel.

Tuesday May 13th   Went to those enchanting meadows under Pengwern wood. In the Lane the Tanner's son, a creature whom when we first came to this country we frequently took with us as a guide on the mountains. Asked him where he had been these three years that we had not seen him. Told us that he had married a young Woman in Llansantffraid, that his wife and he were parted, the cause of their discord his 'Ebriety', of which he acknowledged himself too frequently guilty. Met Davy the Miller. Enquired for his Father (old Silenus). Something better. Proceeded to our walk through the sweetest meadow, shady, a small narrow rivulet gurgling on one side. The meadows in more splendid Beauty than I ever remember them. Pengwern Wood hanging over them dark and gloomy. The Boughs rustling with the wind. Rooks cawing, Kites screaming . . . Moel Morfydd with its rich purple heather and golden yellow gorse. The Village smoke. Church Steeple. Dinas Bran. The rocks, cottages, gardens, pastures interspersed, clumps of wood, single trees, quarries – with sheep goats cattle scattered about. When we had walked many times round these enchanting fields returned slowly towards our cottage. At the Termination of the little Lane met Peggy running to inform us that some Company were coming to our House (her expression) a few yards further met L. in the same breathless state to acquaint us that a Chaise and Four with many attendants were just arrived, an old gentleman and a very genteel young one alighted and waiting for us in the Library. We hastened home with some degree of anxiety, endeavouring to guess who our guests could be. At the little gate met Lord Nugent who, with great politeness, said he came this Road on purpose to pay his compliments to us. Then introduced his kinsman, Mr Nugent, who I think without exception one of the prettiest young men I ever saw. They staid an hour and then made their Bow.

Friday May 16th   High blustering wind. Splendid sunshine. Reading. Drawing. Compliments from Mr Pierce (of Ruthin) desiring to see the cottage and Shrubbery. Our Compliments. He may see the Shrubbery but not the Cottage. We have no notion of being disturbed by Welsh parsons.

Saturday May 17th   Cut the hedge of the Bleach and Fowl yards. Lovely, delicious day. A very genteel looking young man attended by the Hand driver walked about the field, advanced to the new garden, but seeing us in it politely retired. Reading. Drawing. Compliments from Mrs Mytton. If we are at Home will wait on us. Our Compliments, are at Home and shall be pleased to see her. She came with her two nieces, twins, Pigotts. Very pleasant unaffected good girls. Went the home circuit. They were lost in astonishment and admiration of the profusion of lilacs in full Bloom. Prevailed with Mrs Mytton to stay for dinner. My sweet love went with the Pigotts to the Bridge where the Phaeton waited for them . . . When this agreeable and friendly party drove off we went into poor Mrs Jones, asked her and Miss Pryce how they did. Returned to our Shrubbery and kitchen garden. Saw a lady walking before the door. Mrs Otway's compliments. Beg'd leave to see the garden. Permitted. Staid in the potager till she, her little girl, and Dog were gone. Lovely evening. My Beloved and I went our accustomed walk and returned by moonlight – but such a night! The Moon hanging from the richest clouds and casting her silver light over the mountains, the summits of which were flaming, the farmers having kindled fires to destroy the Heath and procure grass and herbage for their sheep and goats.

Monday May 19th   Splendid beauteous morning. Bells ringing for young Myddelton, who is expected in the village from Chester on his way to Denbigh, for which town he is to be elected tomorrow, his Father having vacated his Seat . . . Three dinner. Roast lamb – asparagus – peas porridge. Celestial evening. My beloved and I went to the Shrubbery. Heard loud shouting. Went to the pales. Saw young Myddelton make his entry preceded by the village Bailiff with twenty men under arms. Blue and yellow Cockades in their hats a great number of the Tenantry on horse back. Young Myddelton in his own Carriage. A great mob shouting, bells ringing etc. etc. Reading. Drawing. The Bailiff and his twenty armed men came up to our Cottage and saluted us with two round, according to *his* custom when there is any rejoicing in the Myddelton family.

Expenses

May 19   Owen the Bailiff and his Men rejoicing for Mr Myddelton
3s. 6d.

Friday May 23rd   Little Gillian kittened in the Cow's stable this morning.

Monday May 26th   My beloved and I went to the sweet hanging meadows over the Mill – what a pretty simple scene did we behold. Between the branching oaks just over the Wheel the Bridge of one arch – the young Miller his wife and children sitting on the battlement. An ancient man resting on his crutch – his wallet and faithful dog lying at his feet. Beyond, Edward Evans' farm yard – his cows all standing to be milked. The Team led home by his youngest son. Himself bringing out sheaves of straw from the barn. Lovely still night – the Thunder clouds gone.

Saturday May 31st   Letter from Mrs Keatinge desiring permission to introduce herself to our acquaintance. She is my relation, but I never saw her ... We thought it but proper to go down to the Hand to invite her here. We went and found Mrs Keatinge in the Great Parlour of the Hand, writing. A beautiful Tame Fox in one corner of the room ... She ordered her servant to bring in her Dogs – three beautiful harlequins and a noble Newfoundland dog. Then the cat was led in on a Collar. They all came from the Stables where we went also to see her charming Merlins* and a magnificent horse which Mrs Keatinge always rides.

(The Journal)

1789

Friday May 1st   Rose at seven. Mr Edwards of the Hand came to know our commands for Oswestry whither he is going. Asked him about the child. Much better. There was a Vestry held at the Hand last night, about the Poor of the Parish, at which Shanette, the reputed Witch, attended. She beg'd two shillings of the Parish Money, which Mr Edwards of the Hand obtained for her of Mr Pleydell. She seized Mr Edwards hand, pray'd to God to bless him and all his family. He thought that a proper moment to have his child cured if she was really bewitched, and had it brought to Shanette, who took it in her arms, kissed it, bid God bless it, and muttered to herself Some Words, which they say are peculiar to

* Welsh ponies.

Witches, and never repeated by them, but when they are desirous to revoke their witchcraft. Mr Edwards of the Hand has promised to send me the Words. The child smiled, ate heartily, slept all night soundly, and this morning has no appearance of that Eager Sharp look which she has had these six weeks. Tho' this is May day neither ash, oak, elm, nor Beech nor Lime have expanded a single leaf, nor are the buds much swelled. Not a single bloom on the black thorn.

Saturday May 2nd   Mr Edwards of the Hand sent up the three words pronounced by Shanette over the Child – *Maeth A Chynnydd.**

Monday May 4th   Met our Landlord. Asked the good old man to come in and ordered him some ale. Enquired where he had been this long time, told us he was lately at Oswestry with his Daughter-in-law and his grand-daughter, little Maudy, on whom he dotes. We asked him how he travelled to this fair. His daughter-in-law rode behind him. Maudy rode behind a Mantua Maker, a friend and neighbour of theirs. John (his son) carried the little boy behind him.

Thursday May 7th   Sweet evening . . . Spent some hours in the Garden. Sowed our Pink seeds, Planted new Potatoes. Melon ground cleaning . . . Reading. Drawing. Saw the Swallows, the first this Season, Swim over the Field. Went out again. Walked up the sweet winding lane then towards the Mill. Met a Drunken Man – grew afraid of him which we needed not for the poor man the moment he saw us left off singing, took off his hat with the utmost respect, bid God bless us, and stood still as we passed him. Walked in the Shrubbery. The loveliest moon I ever beheld in the softest richest clouds then emerging in full splendour, the owls and reed sparrows hailing her approach. A day of sweet occupation and enjoyed retirement.

Saturday May 9th   Letter from Miss Louisa Shipley . . . a paragraph enclosed from *The World* – 'Miss Ponsonby and Miss Butler, the Irish Ladies who have settled in so romantic a manner in Denbighshire have been very Conspicuous in their Rejoicings for the King and Queen' . . . Delicious evening. A short thick ill looking fellow in black with a long whiteish riding coat, black hair, slouched hat, pretending to have the toothache, came to the House and

* Increase of nourishment.

desired to speak to one of us, saying he was a Portrait painter, that his mother was Housekeeper to the Prince of Wales etc. We sent him word we had no occasion for anything in his way. He walked into the Kitchen, called for Beer, and seemed inclined to establish himself. My beloved and I grew alarmed. She walked down and ordered him to leave the House directly, which he did. I am sure he belongs to some gang or has made his escape from some jail . . . Saw that ill-looking man in the field. If he continues to lurk about this house he shall be made to give an account of himself.

Sunday May 10th   Very polite sentimental note from Mrs Scanlan with a present of the most beautiful Tree in Seaweed elegantly arranged. Storm very unpleasant. We set up the eolian harp* in the Pantry window. Had a sublime and delightful effect.

Monday May 11th   My beloved and I then walked on the Velvet Carpet of the Mountain . . .

Sunday May 17th   . . . dined at Oswestry – drank coffee at Halston – sup'd at Oswestry – one of the horses got the cholic – had many times a great mind to lye down on the precipice . . .

Tuesday May 19th   Opened the window – David the Miller coming down the field, driving his horse laden with corn before him – his daughter in his arms. Asked him why he would take her out so late. He said 'Why I should have no peace in the house without she came' as she was so fond of him. Next figure an old woman leaning on a stick with a large bundle of wood on her head tied up in her apron for firing. Third figure a young man with a plough share going to be mended. Fourth figure our Margaret followed by her maid going to her Stable for the night. Fifth figure Mr Edwards of the Hand with a large dish of trouts just caught – a present.

* The wind played on its strings.

Friday May 22nd   Sweet morning. At nine my beloved and I set out in the Hand Chaise. One of the horses fell down just by the gardens of Chirk Castle. Many workmen, among them our friend John Jones ran to our assistance. The Horse was set on his feet and again we drove on . . . At the bottom of Chirk hill met the Stage – empty of all its passengers except one woman. Six or seven great men of all sizes and descriptions puffing up the steep in order to ease the horses. Met Venables and several well dress'd people, Men and women, at different times riding to and from Oswestry. Coal and lime carts without end.

Saturday May 23rd   Visited Margaret in her field opposite the workhouse. Found her in excellent grass accompanied by three calves and one lamb.

Tuesday May 26th   Our dear cow having showed symptoms of calving she was brought home to her stable. She grew very bad. Sent for the old man of Bala. He came though he said to no other cow but ours would he have come, as he is become so old and infirm. He found her very ill. The Irishwoman came. Sent her for Edward Evans. He was not to be found, but Davy the Miller came, and John Edwards' wife with the greatest kindness. Among them they delivered her of the largest heifer calf quite dead, but she is safe and we don't mind the calf. Our poor landlady, lame as she is came with her apron full of barley straw – a present to her, because they say if she will eat anything it will be Barley . . . All the village came kindly to enquire about our dear cow – John Edwards' wife, the old man of Bala, the joiner, John Jones the little butcher, David the Miller, our Landlady, Edward Evans, his wife – all about her stable at the moment.

Wednesday May 27th   The old man of Bala ordered the cow to be brought to the field for half an hour and forbad her getting cold water. I declare I have more pride in recording the anxiety and attentions of these good and Simple People than if we had received Compliments from the first Nobility in the kingdom.

(The Journal)

Expenses

May 26   For the poor Cow 5d.

27 Sundries Also for the Cow 1s.
30 House and Servants Tax £2.12.0.

1790

Monday May 3rd Saw a family coming to occupy the Weaver's house. Enquired who they were. Blanche Moses. Not good people. Don't like such neighbours. Sent to our Landlord. He and his daughter-in-law John's wife came immediately. Said Blanche Moses and her sons should not stay there.

Saturday May 8th Brilliant. The Cuckoo and a Choir of Birds. Discovered a nest of cowslips by the pales. Transplanted them to the Bank of Primroses.

Sunday May 9th The Cuckoo, Linnets, Larks, Blackbirds, Thrushes, all about our window. John Jones of Chirk brought Thirteen plants of the Clove Pink, Slips of rosemary and Lavender. Saw above a hundred people up the field returning from Llansantffraid from the Dee side where an Anabaptist Clergy Man baptised two youths, one of fifteen, the other sixteen years of age.

Wednesday May 12th We went to Pen Street where our dear Margaret is boarded. The Pen Street are fields situated under the Hill over the new road of Llangollen Vechan. Those fields are beautiful and abound in grass and water but they are very distant from our Cottage. The fences are not good and Margaret is too apt to stray. Went into the new house which Richard Griffiths is building. The frightfullest, worst contrived piece of Architecture I ever beheld in the loveliest situation.

(The Journal)

Expenses

May 4   for Ivy Plants 6d.
     7   Molly's Wages to May Day £1.7.0.
     8   Mutton for Mr Chambre and Ourselves @ 4d halfpenny
        per lb £1.3.0.
        Smith cleaning the Jack 1s.
   12   Paint for Wheelbarrow and Melon Ground Spout 1s.4d.

13 John Jones's Son with Cowslips 1s.
25 Hand Waiter with a Carp from Mr Vaughan 1s.
27 One Quarter of our Pensions paid up to October last –
    reduced by deductions to *only* £18.4.4.
31 Tax Gatherer £2.1.3.
    David the Miller for 2 strike Potatoes 6s.

Receipts

TO STEW CARP

Clean and Gut the Carp well, wash the inside with red wine, which
save – Garnish the Bottom of your Fish Kettle with bits of Carrots,
Parsnips, a small Onion Sliced – Sprigs of Parsley – One Shallot
Stuck with Cloves – put the Carp upon these with Salt and Whole
Pepper, as much of the Blood as you can, a Sufficiency of red Wine,
a good bit of Butter and three Spoonfuls of Water. Stew it on a
middling Fire with Slices of Lemon – a Very little Thyme, a Bay leaf
– when the Fish is done Sift the Liquer, reduce it to the thickness of
a Sauce, Add a very little Butter, a little Flour, a few herbs shred
small – mix with the Sauce, set it upon the Fish with Fryed Bread in
and about the *Dish*.

TO STEW ASPARAGUS (Very excellent)

Cut them in small pieces – after they have had one Boil then put
them into a Stewpan with some Butter – Some Milk – Cream – Salt
– Pepper and Sweet Herbs – When done enough thicken with the
Yolks of Eggs – Some Milk and Cream.

GREEN PEASE SOUP

Take a quart of Green pease, boil them in a Gallon of Water till
tender, with a little Mint – Strain the pulp and Liquer through a

coarse sieve into a Sauce pan, Add to it a Cabbage Lettuce cut small, a handful of Spinach clean washed and cut small, a Quart of Young pease and a little Salt, Cover them and let it boil gently till it comes to 2 Quarts – the herbs must be very tender – Serve with a little fryed Bacon and a little Fryed Bread cut in Dice.

1791

Expenses

May 1   Ale from the Hand not fit to be drank 6d.

       3   Baillis for Whitewashing 5s.

       7   Baillis in full for white washing 15s.6d.

           Molly discharged 2s.6d. bounty to her. £1.2.6.

    11   Evans Boy planting Potatoes 3s.

    13   Brush for Carpets by Coach 6d.

           Poor Mary Green 2s.6d.

    14   Evans raising Gravel* 2s.6d. a Man do. 1s.2d.

           Evans drawing it 6d. Mr Appleyard Bookseller in full of all demands £26.13.6.

           Moses Jones Weeks Wages 10s.

    15   Trouts 1s.

    19   Box of Pills for Mary 4s.6d.

    23   To our Hair dresser from Chester 11s.6d.

    25   Corn Bill £6.4.0.

    27   Mr Hesketh in full £13.3.0.

           Malt Bill £16.14.6.

           Mary Green 2s.

    31   Mr Edwards of the Hand for our Carriage to Otley and Oswestry 16s.6d.

1793

May 18th   I have felt tho without presuming to complain of it, that you have been for some months past a less frequent correspondent than formerly . . . happiness is not the portion of a feeling heart in such a world as this –

---

* For the walks.

'Yet if she ever stoops
To visit Earth, one shrine the Goddess finds,
And one alone, to make her rich amend,
For assent Heaven – the bosom of a Friend.'

(Harriet Bowdler to Sarah Ponsonby)

1794

Expenses

May 7 Plate Powder 3s.6d.
  8 The Kitchen Maid discharged for having the Itch! 7s.
  9 Baillis' *Shameless* demand of £9.9s. reduced and still unreasonable £6.15.0.
  17 Clogmaker sent to Wrexham for Nothing 3s.
  Peggeen for Working while Molly was under cure for the Itch 3s.

1797

May 22nd Ah! how finely do you descant on the already commenced miseries of Ireland, and impending misfortunes of this country! What mournful beauty in that too just question 'To what part of Europe can we now turn our eyes, in which we shall not meet the embryo images of future woes?' Fatally spreads the pestilential taint of insubordinate principles . . . Oh! let us turn from the dark, the lurid prospect! . . . It gratifies me that your Ladyship shares my passion for surveying the living terrors of the desert. I wonder the sight of savage animals should not be as generally, and as much the delight of cultivated as of uncultivated minds. Last November, I hazarded breaking my limbs in ascending a booth in which they were exhibited. Mr Saville, who always hastens to such spectacles, tempted me by his description of the laughing Hyaena. Its expression of rage is a horrid laugh, exactly that of human insanity, only much louder than any human lungs are competent to produce. Never did I hear a sound so violent and appalling.

(Anna Seward to Lady Eleanor Butler)

Friday May 17th   William Jones sowing Hay and clover seeds.

Saturday May 18th   Cloudy morning. All the cows physicked.
William Jones cleaning the apiary.

Expenses

May 17   Man making the Waterfall 2s.
    18   The Cows Doctor 2s. Physick for them 1s.
    19   John Denbigh who brought a fine Cock 1s.

Thursday May 23rd   Superintending our workmen. The carrier
brought from Chester a noble Cheshire cheese ... The Waterfall
completed. A dam made below the flood gate. The garden front of
our house white washed. Walked on the summit of Penycoed and
home by the churchyard to behold the effect. Not to be seen. The
house so concealed by trees.

Expenses

May 23   Drink Money to David the Miller and our Workman at the
           Water 3s.
    24   Drink Money at the Water works 1s.

Saturday May 25th   Fine morning. Windy. One load of hot manure
from the Hand stables for cucumber beds. William Jones wheeling
it into the fruit garden. A clergyman came with (as *He* says)
compliments and enquiries from Lord Ormonde. Returned them to
Lord Ormonde but declined seeing the Reverend Gentleman.

Sunday May 26th   My better half and I went to Llantysilio church.
In the village met Lady Bellamont and a lady in a chaise and four, in
another chaise and four the three Lady Cootes. Spoke to Mrs Parry
about that Person who we suspect of having shot our Owls and
Pigeons and Blackbirds. Sat three quarters of an hour in the church
porch of Llantysilio conversing with the honest simple folks who
like us were waiting for Mr Roberts. Evening. My beloved and I
went to prayers in the village. Spoke to Ned of the Mill. Ned of the
Mill brought four little fish in a bowl. Put them in the dark deep Pool

above the Dam. Walked on the Corwen Road. Saw Mr Fortescue and Lady Ackland at some distance. Turned back. Miss Parry came with a message from Mr Pearson about mystery in the Pengwern wood.

Expenses

May 26   Ned of the Mill with Trouts to put in the Cuff Lyman 1s.
David the Miller for Do. 6d.

May 27th   While we were at the Mill a messenger came to announce the arrival of Mr Blair. Returned. Mr Blair is a Dentist. Native of Perthshire in Scotland. Served his time to Mr Bott of Nottingham. Is now settled in Leicester, but comes annually to Chester. Miss Page recommended him to us. He first cleaned the Teeth of my Beloved, then extracted the stump which had so long tormented her. He then cleaned my Teeth and drew two that were decayed. Brushes he recommended. Bought from him four Boxes of his Tooth Powder and Two Brushes. Gave him his demand. Three guineas.

Expenses

May 27   Mr Blair the Dentist for my tooth drawing etc. £3.3.0. Do.
for Tooth powder and Brushes 10s.
John Jones in the evening with Cucumber plants 2s.6d.

Tuesday May 28th   Superb summer's day. Harmony of birds. Rich foliage. Great heat.

Wednesday May 29th   William Jones riddling gravel, Edward's cart and team drawing it. Lawn mowed.

Thursday May 30th   Note from that twaddling Mrs Preston.

(The Journal)

1800

Wednesday May 20th   Mrs Wyn having informed us that you purpose returning to Bryn Bella* early in the ensuing month –

* Mrs Piozzi's house.

permit us to remind you of the Friends whom you seem to have forgotten – but who invariably think of you with Affection, Gratitude and Admiration – as some inducement to you giving this road the preference – we can with truth assure you that The Hand Inn under the new administration of *Mr Phillips* is the perfection of Neatness, Elegance and Civility – all the Parlours – all the Bedchambers – newly handsomely and completely furnished – the better for your Nocturnal Accommodation – as your Chicken and Asparagus will be prepared here – for indeed you *must* bestow at least one entire day – Upon, Dearest Mrs Piozzi

Your ever and affectionately Attached Eleanor Butler.

1802

May 17th   I know also that you will send me a few of your schemes for the maintenance of a family on two and a quarter acres, that is if I understood right in supposing you have printed some for distributing to do good. A few might perhaps be put into Welsh and circulated in our principality . . . Does planting of trees come into your plans for your own profit? We have been assured and our experience confirms that twenty thousand Larch would in twenty years be worth a guinea each.

(Sarah Ponsonby to Mrs Tighe)

1819

Thursday May 4th   . . . distant thunder at five in the Morning.

Friday May 8th   Painter's Son with a party of nine permitted to see this place; a Set of ill behaved fools. There is a Miss Fothergill rather pretty of Twenty Eight *Walking* alone all over Italy.

Friday May Twenty one   St Catherine's compliments to Lady Eleanor Butler and Miss Ponsonby. sends to enquire for them and hopes they are well – would have the pleasure of calling herself to see them – But as she is on her way to London and the very Short Time the coach Stops has prevented her from having that pleasure. Monday Evening – This must be the poor Madwoman at Bangor about whom Mr Cotton Wrote us.

Tuesday May Twenty five.   Took down the rotton Chimney piece in our room and put up the pretty little one of Shropshire Marble in the place . . . The Sopha from Shrewsbury purchased by Mrs Powys – Such a Horror and quite rotton . . .

(The Journal)

1821

Wednesday May 2nd   Poor Mrs Piozzi died this day at Clifton.

Saturday May 5th   On this day Bonaparte died at St Helena.

Monday May 7th   Mr and Mrs R. Wingfield arrived according to their promise precisely at eleven. To Breakfast, after which Mr Wingfield kindly administered the Sacrament to Mrs Wingfield, us and our two upper maids . . . Edward Hughes the Clerk obligingly assisted with the Communion Plate from the Church.

Tuesday May 8th   Wrote to Mr Wingfield on behalf of the poor Woman so cruelly oppressed by that Wretch of Wretches, Thomas Edwards, Oppressor and Grinder of the Poor.

May [undated]   Perhaps Mr Parker may remember it is now many years since he was so good as to rescue a poor woman then nearly four score years of age from the terrors of the Oswestry Palace of Vice and cruelty on her being content with one shilling per week to supply her with all the means and comforts of existence at a time of life when they are most necessary, to which we promised and have ever since paid her the addition of another every Sunday morning. We now understand from her that the Overseers of that Blessed Institution* have declared that she must now be content either to have her wretched pittance reduced to half (6d a week from her parish) or to be consigned to this dreaded and dreadful gaol of confinement.

(Sarah Ponsonby to Mrs Parker)

Thursday May 10th   Parcel containing 2 Bottles of Elixir which we had sent for the poor young woman of Pengwern Hall but did not find at all applicable to her case. We decided to send her Iceland Moss instead.

* The Workhouse.

Sunday May 20th   Mr Jones the Minister pro tem. drank Tea with us, as did the Ancient Housekeeper of Chirk Castle – for the first time for many years – with our Maidens.

(The Journal)

JUNE

1778

Wednesday June 24th   Lay at St Asaph – went from St Asaph over *Pentraso Bridge – Went to Denbigh* – Stop'd at Ruthin and proceeded Llangollen.

Thursday June 25th   Went to *Oswestry* and in search of Lodgings to Llanwryneck – a Small Village disagreeably situated on each side of the road and in the neighbourhood of*

(Account of a Journey in Wales Perform'd
in May 1778 by Two Fugitive Ladies)

1784

Saturday June 12th   I kept my bed with an headache – My Sweet Love.

* The Journal breaks off here.

June

Friday June 18th   Lovely Evening. Molly Jones went off like a Thief as she is.

(Eleanor Butler's Pocket Book)

1786

June 7th   We find by experience that the Smell of Musk is Obnoxious to Royal Personages – the Queen of G.B. was on the point of looking at some of my works – the Inscriptions in the Garden (have you got them?) and a Plan of our House, but was obliged to order them out of the Room – lest the Perfume should put us all into Mourning. this happen'd last Summer But We did not hear it 'till last week! We are busy *unsweetening* our Drawers.

Receipts

FOR A VIOLENT COUGH AND INVETERATE HOARSENESS AND ANYTHING THAT AFFECTS THE LUNGS

Take the four trotters of a sheep, let them be scalded so as to take off the hair. Split and wash them then put them into an earthen pan with two quarts of new milk and one of water – a nutmeg grossly powdered – tied down close with brown paper and let it stand in the oven as long as household bread. Then strain it through an hair sieve into a dry earthen pan. When cold take off the feet and white skin. Take a small teacup full warm the first thing in the morning and the last at night going to bed. To be kept in a cool but not a damp place.
NB   I recommend making only half the above quantity at a time as it will not keep (at least not at PN) more than four days.

(Sarah Ponsonby to Mrs Tighe)

1787

June 4th   I am sure you will forgive my writing but a short letter – when I inform you that His Majesty's Bounty has granted us a Pension of One Hundred a Year for which We are wholly indebted to the Interest of Lady Frances Douglas.

(Sarah Ponsonby to Mrs Tighe)

June 14th   Necessity alone could have influenced me to take such Measures for an increase of income, having found our utmost endeavours insufficient to Discharge our Debts from what we had before, though we have by Strict Economy reduced them very considerably . . . As for my Feelings, they are less Hurt by the Word Pension than the Horror of being asked by a Tradesman for his Honest Earnings without the power of acting Honestly towards him.

(Sarah Ponsonby to Mrs Tighe)

1788

June 3rd   The Taxgatherer came – paid him. At two retired to Powder and dress our hair, dined at half-past two, at three the Hand Chaise came. My beloved and I went to Hardwick thro' Chirk and Whittington to Halston. Lovely evening. The road new to us after Halston, fine verdure, large enclosures, well planted, cattle grazing, clumps of fine oak . . . Arrived at 5 . . . We went to the drawing-room, sat there some time, then went to the Dairy. *Mem* I like the Oval Table with the leaden cistern for cream, a plug in the middle by means of which the milk is drawn from the cream. Drank tea in the Cottage . . . Tea over we walked round the entire domain, one mile and a half, beautifully wooded . . . At nine we all dispersed, returned to our several abodes. Miss Vaughan to Oteley Park, the Venerable seat of the Kynastons. Our Barretts to their handsome mansion in Oswestry, and we to our quiet and delicious Cottage. What a night! And what a Country! The Lime Kilns blazing like so many volcanoes, glow worms on the Mountains.

Wednesday June 4th   At nine my beloved and I went to the dressing-room, the air being cold. We got a fire intending to write. Finished a letter to Lady Dungannon, and her letter to which ours was an answer lying on the Table we threw it in the fire. It blazed violently, and the flames communicating to the Soot the Chimney instantly took fire and roared internally with the most fearful noise Imaginable. Our agony at this is not to be described. We sent to the Village for assistance, but before we thought the intelligence could reach there we saw Mathew Morris and his wife, Jane Fisher, Harry Morris, his daughter, the Potter's wife, her son and two daughters, Simon, Peggy's father, his wife. Every one of these good people with a pail of Water on their head running to us. The potter's son had Perceived the flames from the field whither he had conducted his team and he ran to the village, gave the alarm, and having procured a ladder stripped to his shirt, mounted on the roof of the house and by pouring pails full of water down the Chimney at length extinguished the flames. This effected they got a long rope to which they affixed a Holly Bush and, having fastened a large stone at the bottom, let it down the chimney. By this means bringing down all the burning soot. This was the work of three agonizing hours to us. In the meantime all the village was assembled in the field before our Cottage and in our Shrubbery. But all was quiet, all concern. Silently and kindly affording their assistance, expressing their regret at our fears and comforting us by repeated assurances that there was no danger. When all was over they removed their Ladder, ropes, Pails, etc. We ordered them plentiful potation of Beer. They drank our Health, wished us long life and health. After returning thanks to the Almighty for our great deliverance we composed ourselves to rest, the Village clock striking two.

Expenses

June   4   Our neighbours for kindly assisting when our Chimney took fire 4s.

       5   Irish Woman 6d. Post 10d. Sweep Chimneys 2s. 6d.

Wednesday June 11th   We walked to the Joiner's. Found him and his wife sitting at dinner in the cleanest of all kitchens. A comfortable dish of boiled meat and new Cabbage, a large loaf of household bread, jug of Beer. Waited in the garden till their repast was ended.

Saturday June 14th   Compliments from Mr and Mrs Pope and Miss Saville desiring to see the Cottage and Shrubbery. They came. Saw from the State bedchamber window whither we retired till they were gone. Mr Pope tall gentlemanly handsome man, Mrs Pope in a green Capotte, Miss Saville scarlet habit. A beautiful large brown and white spaniel which they politely carried in their arms. They expressed the highest admiration of the place.

  Beautiful evening. Went to the Shrubbery. Then sat in our delicious seat over the Cyflymen . . . What a scene! On the side of the mountain immediately opposite our hall door, a crowd of people clustered like a swarm of Bees, were seated to behold a Stage play. The Stage erected under a clump of trees on the edge of the Precipice. A party of recruiting Soldiers, with drums beating and fifes playing, marching up the undulating path of the mountain to join them. Herds of cattle grazing above their heads and spread over the pasture beneath them. The Shouts of the happy multitude, echo of the drums and fifes, singing of birds . . . I returned to the Shrubbery. My beloved was returning to me when a pretty young woman accosted her and, presenting a neat Basket full of eggs, said: 'They were sent by poor Mary Green who daily prays for you and your companion' . . . Reading. Writing. A lad, quite breathless to let us know our Cow, our Margaret, had just calved in the fields of the Cilmedw. What an event! Sent to desire Mr Edwards of the Hand would dispatch some careful people to bring her and her calf thence. Sent to the old Man of Bala to know what we should give her. Had her Stable prepared for her, the Turkey Hen and her eleven chickens moved to the loft. About half-past eight Margaret arrived and her Great Son. Put them in the Stable, gave her a drench of warm ale, butter and sugar. Milked her, then at eleven gave her a mash. Delicious night, sun set in flames of crimson and gold. Moon rose calmly and cast her silver light on our Cottage and Shrubbery.

Expenses

June 14   Expenses of Margaret's Accouchement 4s. 6d.

Tuesday June 17th   Saw Edward Evans and his son coming down the field with sticks. Went with them to the place which had hitherto been appropriated to keeping Pea Sticks, slates, tiles etc. and was overgrown with nettles and thistles. Cleared all away . . . Edward Evans and his son enclosed with sticks and boughs of Ash Oak and hazel the whole place. While he was at work a man came to him to desire he would go to Mathew Morris, whose son was to be christened this evening and Edward Evans was to be one of the sponsors. We bade him go directly and leave the Messenger to work in his place. To say the truth, Edward Evans was so clumsy a Workman we were glad to get rid of him. Found we had made a blessed exchange – the one we preferred being active, diligent, modest and expeditious . . . When the fence was effectually made and the ground made level, brought the Turkey and her eleven young ones, the Bracket hen and her clutch into it with a good bedding of straw and a wooden house for them to retire to occasionally with water and corn. Their Transport at being liberated, their musical congratulation and delight, cannot be compared to anything but our own feelings at having made them so happy. Sent our new acquaintance William to the Spout for water for the Tub in the Melon ground. Then visited our Cow, saw her suckling her Son, and licking him with the most affecting fondness all the time. Went to the new garden, gathered gooseberries.

Sunday June 22nd A strange note from Mr and Mrs Sharpe desiring to see our Shrubbery and cottage. Consented. Retired to the State Bedchamber till they were come and gone. They did not stay long, thank heaven.

Tuesday June 24th Sat in the rustic Seat. disliked the appearance of the Stones over which the Water falls, thought it appeared too formal. Sent our workman to it with a Spade and Mattock.

Expenses

June 24   William Jones @ Gravel at Cufflimmen 1s.2d.

Saturday June 28th After our return from John Edwards' field a genteel serious-looking clergyman, very well dressed, presented a paper which he requested we should read. It contained an account of his distresses, setting forth that he had been many years a Curate in the Diocese of St Asaph, that a violent Asthma with which he was affected prevented his officiating any longer in that Capacity, by which he and five children were reduced to the greatest distress – Signed, Owen Jones. On the other side were a list of the most respectable names in this country who had contributed very largely to his relief, among the rest Mr Owen of Porkington besides pecuniary assistance gave him a gown. We had it not in our power to present him with such a sum as our *Heart* and our Pride would have led us to offer, but the little We did give was received in the handsomest manner.

(The Journal)

Expenses

June 28   A poor Curate to our Service *Only* 5s.

1789

[*Undated*]   List of Roses in the Garden '. . . taken when the pales were new painted . . .'

Provence; Maiden Blush; Frankfort; Childing; Blush Belgie; Rose Unique; Moss Provence; Double Marbled; White Damask; Thornless; Virgin Damask; Double Red; Red Austrian; Double Velvet; Red Belgie; Great Royal; Monthly; Double Musk; Rosa Mundi; Double Yellow; Miss Horts; Yellow Austrian; Singleton's hundred leaved; Double Apple bearing; Blush hundred leaved; Rose d'amour; Blush Provence; Dwarf Burgundy; Stepney; Pomponne; Double Burnet leaved; Scarlet Sweet Briar; Double Sweet Briar; Red Scotch; Evergreen Musk; Painted Lady; Tall Burgundy; Wright's; Blush Cluster; American double blush; Double Scarlet Sweet Briar; Small Pompadour; Large Sweet Crimson.

Tuesday June 2nd   My beloved and I went a delicious walk, round Edward Evans' field, by the Mill, the Pengwern lane, round our landlord's little croft under the Pengwern wood. The Bull bellowing not far off. Dark green shadows playing over the woods and meadows. Brilliant lights on the rocks. Every stream full to the brim. Evening, My beloved and I took a walk, down the Sycamore lane into the Vicar's meadow, thence to his corn field. Then by the brook side. Returned by the Pengwern mill. Sat on the huge rock on this side. Six children playing around. The eldest not six years old. One of them fell in the stream. They all plunged in, took the little thing up, wrung her cloaths. We brought them to Pengwern, got her dried and comforted.

Wednesday June 3rd ... *ran* the Home Circuit with the Barretts and Miss Wynne.

Tuesday June 9th Discharged Moses Jones from our service for repeated and outrageous Drunkeness. He had lived fourteen months with us in the capacity of gardener. For the last seven months he has been drunk three days in the Week. This morning he began to mow. He cut three Swards of Grass, laid Down his Scythe, ran to the Ale House. Returned, began to Mow. Then went again. But when he returned the third time, my Beloved and I met him, took the keys of the garden from him, paid him one-and-twenty pence, which was all that was due to him for one day's work, as every Saturday from the time we Hired him we paid him Ten Shillings.

Saturday June 13th My beloved and I went to the Potager hedge-clipping. While we were there Mr Sneyde of Belmont in Staffordshire and his two Daughters came, made an apology for Mrs Sneyde's not coming as she was so extremely fatigued. We went the Home Circuit with them. Mr Sneyde found our trees very much improved. We were delighted at having an opportunity of Consulting the first Botanist in England about our Trees and Plants. For the Dunmore Apricot, he advised that the Dying Branch may be immediately cut off because the Infected Sap will be apt to return to the trunk and injure the whole Tree. For the Peaches, he recommended the roots to be opened, a plug to be placed at the distance of 8 inches and covered with good soil. For the Nectarines, he advised the infected leaves to be picked off immediately, the soil removed from the roots, and the whole tree washed with soap suds before sunrise. For gooseberries, wool dipped in Soot tied round the Stem of the tree, the insects which all ascend from the bottom will get entangled in the wool.

Tuesday June 16th The sweetest softest silent night. Clouds to the West of a gleaming red. We leaned over the gate, admiring the solemnity of the scene and the profound Silence which reigned around as if we were the only inhabitants of this Sweet Valley.

Suddenly we heard a sweet pipe. Enquired who was the Performer. 'Thomas Jones the Glazier is playing on the Wall of the Church yard which is over the Dee.' We listened until the Village clock struck ten.

Thursday June 18th The Prince of Wales was drunk at the Birthday. He would not behave decently at either of the Ambassador's Galas because Mrs Fitzherbert was not invited.

Friday June 19th The evening being Beautiful we walked to the Abbey.* We were accompanied by the divinest Rainbow till we had passed the Green, when it began to rain. We took shelter in the farmhouse of Pendile. Found in the Kitchen a Beautiful young woman rocking a cradle. She appeared so young we could scarcely credit her being the Infant's mother, but the Ring on her finger convinced us of it. In an adjoining house a little woman was winding yarn, two pretty girls standing beside her. We made her Sing. She sang two Welch Songs, rested on her wheel, with such an expressive countenance accompanying the plaintive song she sang.

Monday June 22nd My beloved and I, Went to the room under the School house – In the Church Yard – had the Rubbish removed and there discovered the Mutilated Statue of Saint Cuthlin of which we had already some fragments – it is composed of the finest Alabaster by the fragments which remain. We could faintly trace the figure of a Bishop. but the face and inscription are entirely broken off. Went to the Joiners garden to see the Amunda Regalia or flowering Fern, which was behind the Abbey. the Joiner has given us the Plant.

Saturday June 27th Walked to the white gate, met a country woman going to market. Asked her if she came from Glynn. No – 'From the Pengwern hill where the Moon rose last night.'

Monday June 29th Letter from Lady Dungannon. Like everything she does, ungrateful and disagreeable.

Tuesday June 30th Saw the Bull standing with the cows, retired with precipitation – tho he was too far off and the field between us – yet We liked not his Aspect.

* Valle Crucis, which is nearby.

Company here Since the First of April 1789

Saturday April the 4th.   Frizzle, for a Moment.
Saturday April 27th.   Frizzle again for another Moment.
36 people 1st April–June 27th.

From Home April the First 1789

Sunday May the 17th.   Breakfasted dined and sup'd at Oswestry –
  drank Coffee at Halston.
Friday May the 22nd.   Breakfasted and sup'd at Oswestry – dined
  at Halston.
Tuesday June the 23rd.   Dined and Sup'd at Oswestry.

Books Read Since April the First 1789

24 Works Including –
Memoires de Madame de Metterniche 5 Tomes
Les Oeuvres de Jean Baptiste Poquelin de Moliere – 4 Tomes
Theatro du grand Corneille 12 Tomes
Theatro et Oeuvres de Racine 9 Tomes
La Divina Commedia Di Dante Algheri |sic| 2 Tomes
Opera de Signor Pietro Metastasio – 16 Tomi
Gilpins *Northern Tour* 2 Vols.
Grays *Works* 4 Tomes . . .

(The Journal)

1790

Wednesday June 2nd   Looked over the Journals of the Two last years. June 2nd., 1788, Miss Davies, Mrs Barrett, dine here. Mrs Price, Lady Dungannon's woman came here with a message from her Lady. Mr Bridgeman married Miss Byng. What a change have two years effected. Miss Davies, Mrs Barrett and we meet no more. The Barretts having manifested themselves ungrateful, unworthy, treacherous, and in every respect the reverse of what we so long thought them. Miss Davies violently their adherent. Lady Dungannon from Distressed Circumstances, Broken Credit, and many sore Trials has quitted this neighbourhood for ever . . . *June 2nd.* 1789, the weather was delicious. Tomorrow twelvemonth the Barretts and Miss Wynne dined here. Thank heaven we have found out who were and who were not our friends, in which number the Barretts had never a right to be included.

Wednesday June 16th   Dined under the shade of the Lime Tree by the door. After dinner we walked to Pengwern. Our Landlord and all his family sheep-shearing in the Barn. Our Landlady, with all her daughters, daughters-in-law and grandchildren, drinking tea. Went to see the Bridge and walk on the green. Found the River full of sheep washing, preparatory to their shearing to-morrow.

Sunday June 20th   Note from two men, stiling themselves Gentlemen, of the names of O'Reilly and O'Connor, desiring to see this place. Had great pleasure in refusing them. They walked in the field. Saw nothing in their appearance to make us alter our resolution of not admitting them.

Tuesday June 22nd   Intense heat. Walked to Pengwern. Our Landlord told us that a smith from Dimbraneth has been dreaming for more than a year past of Treasure at Dinas Bran. He has within this week begun to dig.

(The Journal)

1791

June 25th   I take it for granted that your Ladyp. has been informed of the flight of the King, Queen and Dauphin from Paris before my letter can reach you. I need therefore only assure you that the fact is so. We are as yet ignorant of the mode by which they effected their escape, of the success of their attempt, and of the place to which they are gone. Lord Gower's messenger left Paris on the Thursday morning. They left the Tuilleries on Tuesday morning at 2 o'clock. At 8 on Wednesday they were missed.*

(Robert Stewart to Lady Eleanor Butler)

Receipts

DRESSED SALMON

Chop some sweet herbs Shallot, Pepper and Salt – mix all these together with good Butter and lay some of them mixed with Crumbs of Bread in the Bottom of your Dish – put one or two Slices of Salmon upon it – the same again upon the Salmon – then a second Layer of Salmon with the same – Cover all with Crumbs of Bread and small bits of Butter. put it in the Oven till of a fine Brown Colour.

TO MAKE POMATUM OF ROSES

An equal Quantity of Hog's Lard and Beef Suet cut small and put into a Crock of water with a Handful or two of Salt – let it lie three or four hours, then take it out of the water and drain it well – Put Layers of this into a Jar, with a Layer of Roses between the Layers of Lard and Suet. Let it melt by putting the Jar into a Pot of Boiling Water – When the Pomatum is thoroughly melted Squeeze it well through a Cloth. Add a Very little Essence of Bergamot and put the Pomatum into your Pots.

1794

June 20th   Shall I congratulate you on the Naval Victory† or adopt the Mild Humanity of the People called Quakers – and find it impossible to rejoice in any advantage so dearly purchased by the Death and Wounds of so many fellow Creatures – Indeed none but Callous hearts *can* rejoice in days like the Present.

(Sarah Ponsonby to Mrs Tighe)

* This is in fact early news of the French Royal Family's famous flight to Varennes from the capital. They were apprehended and brought back to eventual execution.

† The naval victory of the Glorious First of June. It was the custom to congratulate friends at the news of victories or a peace.

June 24th   On this day in the year 1792 I was your happy guest –
too happy for this world . . .

(Harriet Bowdler to Sarah Ponsonby)

1796

June 25th   . . . we have had the additional vexation of pecuniary
embarrassments from the Civil List having stop'd payment – there
are six quarters of our pensions in arrears – and likely to continue
increasingly so – while the War endures.

(Sarah Ponsonby to Mrs Tighe)

1798

Expenses

June   1   Preparations for the Piozzis who dined here 7s.
       9   To the Llantysilio post boy guarding us from the Bull 1s.
      12   Evan of Blaen Bache who walked with dear Glory 1s.*

June 16th   Your mentioning want of money is a heavy blow to my
poor Spirits – I grieve to think that *I* add to that want and yet – if I
do not hear from Mr Palmer† as usual this month – it will be a
mournful addition to my distress.

(Sarah Ponsonby to Mrs Tighe)

June 19th   To attain lettered ease and tranquillity of spirit you fled
together, in early youth, from the otherwise inextricable mazes of
connection. The resolution of constancy with which the plan has
been pursued through nineteen years, rendered it, as I thought,
invulnerable to any long-enduring care, sorrow or solicitude, while
life and health were mutually lent you. Often have I said to myself,
picturing the little Eden,

> 'If e'er content deign'd visit mortal clime,
>   That is her place of dearest residence.'

But, alas! civil war is an omnipresent fiend.

(Anna Seward to Sarah Ponsonby,
sympathizing over the troubles in Ireland)

---

* The cow Glory had accompanied the Ladies and their friends on a picnic.
† Mrs Tighe's accountant, who paid the annuity to Sarah.

June 23rd   In passing through Llangollen the 27th of May – in Our way to Tower – the residence of Our Loved Mrs Bowdler – whom we call upon and accompany to Llantysilio Church every Sunday – Mrs Parker the Hand Landlady told us she *suspected* Lady Edward Fitzgerald* was in her house. We could not bear the idea of avoiding her in such a situation – therefore sent word that if the Lady was as we believed an acquaintance of ours and wished to see us . . . we were within call . . . She had an idea of passing the day here, but we persuaded her principally for her own sake and a little for ours, to proceed as fast and incognito to London, the mind of the people in this country being so exasperated against the Cause in which she was, I fear, too deeply engaged that we dreaded her being insulted.

(Sarah Ponsonby to Mrs Tighe)

1799

Monday June 3rd   Saw Muff and her four lovely kittens. We went away with David as an escort to guard us from the bull.

(The Journal)

Expenses

June 4   Simon's Wife with a present of Ducks 6s.
a Dozen China Oranges 2s. 6d.
The Turner for a new Spinning Wheel £1. 1s.
Do for eight Minnows to put in the Cufflymin 6d.

Saturday June 8th   David the Miller's boy brought three live Trouts. 'Ingurgitated' them in the Pool above the Cascade – Heavenly day – Spent the Morning under the shade of our Lime Trees.

(The Journal)

Expenses

June 9   Man who brought me a pair of Shoes 1s.
Llantysilio post boy guarding us from the Bull 1s.

Monday June 10th   Dined under the Trees.

Tuesday June 11th   Splendid day. Breezy wind. William Jones cutting pea sticks. Price washing the library ceiling. Writing under the trees.

* One of the leaders of the Irish Rebellion was her husband, Lord Edward Fitzgerald.

Wednesday June 12th   Walked with Mr Du Barry to Llantysilio. Perfect whirlwind on the bridge. Met Henley the Engineer on the road. Miss Jones not at home. The house, gardens, and environs silent, desolate, and exhibiting every appearance of Being the constant residence of dulness and ennui.

Friday June 14th   Mr Du Barry came while we were at Breakfast in the State Bedchamber. As we were looking over some Prints Lord and Lady Templetown and Mr Greville Upton arrived. Brought a letter from our charming friend the Dowager Lady Templetown. A large Liverpool party desired to see this place. Refused. Relented and said they might come to-morrow. Lord Templetowns landau being ready we accompanied Lady Templetown – the gentlemen walking – to the Abbey. A nasty prating woman, tiring us to death with her nonsense. A large party there at the time. Dined at four with the Templetowns. At five we came up here. The Parlour and Library in the utmost neatness and perfection. Coffee and conversation by lamplight.

(The Journal)

Expenses

June 17   Hair Powder 4s. 4d. Mrs Dubbin for 4 prs Gloves 2s.
      19   Simon with Glory to Pengwern Hall 6d. Simon and his Brother cutting Vistas 1s.

Sunday June 23rd My beloved and I went to Llantysilio Church. Pretty little girl from Oswestry School there with whom we had some conversation. Miss Fowckest in deep mourning, black Veil etc. swam up to her seat to our *Astonishment*.

(The Journal)

Expenses

Monday June 24 Simon and David the Miller for drink 2s.
          June 26 Simon and David at the Waterfall 1s.
          June 30 To Simon wearing his new cloaths bounty 1s.

Tuesday June 25th   Walked down the green shady lane of Pengwern Hall. Saw the Bull in the next field. Retired in Haste.

(The Journal)

Buxton June 15th   My dear Friend, Oh, no! no! It was indeed not
the answer which Lady E. Butler and her friend ought to have sent.
I am sorry, I am ashamed for them, in a much greater degree than I
am surprised. I am sure, however, that neither Miss Ponsonby's will
nor heart were in that message; but Lady E., who when pleased is
one of the most gracious of God's creatures, under a contrary
impression is extremely haughty and imperious. Her sweet amiable
friend who, when she has time can bend and soften that impetuous
temper, knows she cannot, and therefore does not attempt to,
assuage its *extempore* sallies.

On occasions, in some degree similar, I have seen Miss Ponsonby
sigh, shrug her shoulders and acquiesce. On these occasions Lady
E. always involves her by the words *we* and *us*. Accustomed to
incessant homage and compliance, a broken promise, and not even
apologised for, would, I know, be a sin in the eyes of both, which
scarcely any acknowledged repentance could atone. That sin was
your brother's; but I think Miss Ponsonby would not have sought to
avenge it by unjust rudeness to you. They were, you know,
unconscious of the family misfortunes and mental gloom which had
produced his breach of promise, and apparent cold neglect of them.
Lady Eleanor repents, as she often does on other occasions, her rude
injustice to you, and unites with Miss Ponsonby in unavailing
wishes for an opportunity of repairing it. Could they obtain that
opportunity, I know their reparation would be as ample as it might
be in their power to make it; and I am sure, should you ever again
travel through their Vale, and receive an invitation from them,
which I am sure they would send you, you are the man of all others
to say 'Repentance, which is enough for Heaven, is enough for me.'
Adieu!

(Anna Seward to Dr Whalley, *re* a social peccadillo perpetrated by
the Ladies. In the event, repentance was *not* enough for the touchy
doctor. Eight years later he had still not deigned to visit them!)

June [undated]   The trouble I have above alluded to in which we
have been so lately involved, and from which we are so recently
rescued – was no less than a new endeavour to terminate our
peaceful possession of this little mansion, which at one time . . .
threatened us with the absolute necessity of removing from a spot

so honoured by You – so dear to us – with Our furniture and Books – which a Common sized Satchel would not speedily convey, to seek a new habitation amid these mountains –

> (Sarah Ponsonby to Anna Seward)

Expenses

June 27   To Mr Wynne for the Legal and friendly comfort his Visit gave us £3.3s.

1803

June 20th   Our Gardens are overflowing with Green Peas and Strawberries, and Our Dairy with Butter.

> (Sarah Ponsonby to Mrs Tighe)

1819

June Four   Why is the Prince Regent like a Sequence? Because he is King . . . Queen . . . and Knave! Turned our Hay Eighteen times.

> (The Journal)

1821

June [undated]   A correspondent informs us potato water thrown upon gooseberry and other fruit trees will effectually destroy the caterpillars.

> (The Journal)

JULY

1783

St Omer, July 19th   A Lady of my acquaintance, about Forty, a widow without children, of a most amiable, entertaining disposition, *always* accustomed to genteel Life, having formed a *strict* Friendship with a Lady of a similar turn, who is just upon the point of going into a Convent, She not being of a Monastical turn, is now at a loss for a Retirement adapted to her taste. She is in France with her friend till she Enters. A Family lately from Ireland mentioned your Pleasing connection. Possibly a third added to your Small Community might vary the Scene, and render it not less agreeable . . .

(Mrs Paulet to Eleanor Butler)

[*August 1st*   Madam, I was this morning favour'd with your Letter. I must beg leave to say that Miss Ponsonby and I can only attribute the proposal you make us, to your being Totally Ignorant Who We Are – as you mention that you are Soon to come to England, a few enquiries on that Subject Will Satisfy you of the Very Great impropriety (to give it no harsher term) of such an application to us. I take the Liberty to add that We receive no Visitors with whose names Characters and Consequence We are not perfectly well acquainted. I am Madam etc.

(Eleanor Butler to Mrs Paulet)|

1784

Friday July the 16th   Read *The Faithful Shepherd* to My Love.

(Eleanor Butler's Pocket Book)

1785

July 30th   If I live two or three years longer* I will ask you for some Abortive Vellum but you have already supplied me with ample material for amusement during that period . . . I wish to devote all my Leisure to attempts at improving myself in Landscape Drawing (though almost hopeless of success) . . .

(Sarah Ponsonby to Mrs Tighe)

1786

July 3rd   . . . the Shrewsbury Wagon . . . has been robbed of Lord Berwick's plate . . . the two Dogs which Guarded it were intoxicated – We hope the thieves May not be Hanged, as they only made the dogs drunk – instead of poisoning them – as Cruel theives would have done.

(Sarah Ponsonby to Mrs Tighe)

1787

July 9th   . . . a profusion of wonderful fine Goose and Raspberries . . . and we want to make some into giam – or jam, for you . . .

(Sarah Ponsonby to Mrs Tighe)

---

* Early on in their life at Plas Newydd, Sarah was thought to be consumptive.

Tuesday July 1st   My beloved and I went to the quarry. As we were going we met a young man with a Spade on his Shoulder, asked him if he would come with us and assist our workmen. 'Aye, Sure, with all my Heart.' Thanked him and asked his name. 'William Evans, I was a servant at the Mill of Dee side when you came to settle here, and I was the man who ground the first batch of corn you had in this country.' . . . When our workmen went to dinner, as we were crossing the Bridge over the Cyflymen, saw a venerable grey-headed man assisting a youth (who proved to be his son) to walk who had just fallen from the roof of Pengwern Hall and broke his arm.

Expenses

July 1   John Hughes at the Quarry 1s.6d.
           Wm Jones do 1s.2d.

Thursday July 3rd   Writing. A little boy came to us with a present of five plants of White Foxgloves which he found in the Tanks [water meadows]. He took them up very carefully with soil about the roots. The boy's kindness in thinking of bringing them to us was more flattering than the gift was acceptable – the white Foxglove is a very great curiosity and Very beautiful Plant.

Expenses

July 3   White Foxglove 2d.

Saturday July 5th   Rose at six. Showery all night. Heavy clouds. We shall have more rain I fear. Got two plates of cherries, one white and the other the Orleans cherry, for breakfast. Got a bundle of Moss Rose buds. Threw them in a careless manner over the Library table, which had a beautiful effect. Nine the Bishop of St. Asaph, Mrs Shipley, two Miss Shipleys came. Went the home circuit with them. Sat in the new seat. Examined our vines, melons, and mushroom bed, our back yard, fowl yard, stable, dairy. Then returned to the Library. Looked over our books and drawing. They staid 'till one. We felt quite sorry when they took leave. Most charming and wonderfully accomplished family, perfect mistresses of Latin, Italian, French and painting.

Monday July 7th   The day was fine. Country in the highest beauty, well washed by the late rains. Verdure glowing, fields filled with Cattle or new mown hay. Saw several groups of Simple figures. No carriages. At two arrived at the Venerable mansion,* which never appeared more solemn. Poor Lady Dungannon was writing in the Parlour. Received us with open arms. Walked round the Lawn to the gate etc. Dined at four – at Seven with great regret bade her adieu, I fear for the last time. She thought and said so herself with Tears, which caused ours to flow.

Wednesday July 9th   Mr and Mrs de Luc dined and sup'd here. Went away at twelve. Showery and misty gloomy day. Mrs de Luc came first. Went the Home circuit with her. Every bough dripping. Walks soaking wet. Such weather! Sat in the library. Mrs de Luc gave us some sweet sonnets she had translated from Carlo Magi. Mr de Luc came before three. Continued rain 'till six, when it stop'd for a moment and Mrs de Luc and I went to the White Gate. Subjects of Conversation – A full account of Rousseau, his acquaintance and marriage with Mdlle Levasseur etc. – Haller† on hatching chickens – the small red speck in an egg the heart of the chicken . . . Travels in Languedoc – Dauphine – Switzerland – Herschel's telescope for viewing the moon, another for stars. Doubts whether spots on the moon are Volcanic or light reflected from some distant planet. Sun not a body of fire – Heaven – Experiments on Water – Voltaire – Marechal de Richlieu – their disgusting amours at Ferney – Voltaire's guilty terrors whenever he was ill . . . At Twelve this delightful couple went away.

Friday July 11th   Mrs Price from Brynkinalt came – brought Phillis, Lady Dungannon's little yellow Spaniel, which she has besought us to keep and cherish for her sake, she not being permitted to bring it to Hampton Court.

Saturday July 12th   Reading. Finished that *Emmeline*, a Trumpery novel in four volumes. If I can answer for myself I will never again

* Brynkinalt.
† Albrecht von Haller (1708–77), Swiss anatomist and physiologist.

undertake such a tiresome nonsensical piece of business. My morning and evening lost in perusing the stupid work.

Sunday July 13th The sun unexpectedly breaking forth and dispelling the mists gave us hopes of a fine evening, and being very anxious to know about poor Mrs Barrett, whose health we have reason to fear is very indifferent, we sent to order a carriage from the Hand – and having no other alteration to make in our dress than powdering . . . we set off. Weather delicious. Sighed as we passed the again desolate Mansion of Brynkinalt where we have spent so many, many hours – some agreeable – some the reverse. Arrived at Oswestry at half past six. Found the Barretts, Miss Davies, and Miss Jones of Finart in the Bedroom. Miss Jones departed as we entered. Mrs Barrett not at all well. Her throat still sore, glands swelled and inflamed, the Fever however happily abated . . . They showed us Various patterns they had received from London of Woodmason's new invented paper. Never more disappointed – Dingy. Wholly deficient in Colour, lustre and effect . . . Mrs Barrett related to us that she had been awakened on Thursday night by a most violent tumult among the Chickens, which disturbed her so much she came to enquire into the Cause of it. Found all the little Poultry mournfully exclaiming under the Cherry tree in which they roosted every Night. The Turkey hen lying dead among them (Supposed to have been killed by a Weazle) The Turkey Cock, now a Widower, at some distance joining in the Lamentations. From that time he has taken the charge of the Orphans to himself, watching them with the most affectionate attentions the entire day, at night Collecting them around him and sheltering them under his Wings. An Instance of Sense and Affection unparalleled in the Annals of the Feathered Tribe. At 12 we arrived at our peaceful cottage.

Monday July 14th What Tenderness – what attention – what anxiety did I not experience from the beloved of my Soul – She never quitted My bed Side for a Single instant reading to me to Soothe the pain Till it was abated – with difficulty I cou'd prevail with her to breakfast or dine, – when she did eat Still it was by my bed side . . . so soft so delicious, so tender a day.

Tuesday July 15th Our Landlord, his son John, their hind, all cutting hay in the field before this Cottage. A long conversation with them. Delicious day. Our Landlord said, 'The Springs begin to stir and gush freely, we shall have fine weather' . . . walked up the field. Met old Sarah of the Mill. Enquired for her husband. Answered with tears – very bad.

Tuesday July 22nd Rose at seven. Delicious soft grey morning. If it would but continue fair! Rooks cawing, sheep bleating, rush of waters. Weaver's loom. Village bell Tolling. Such an assembly of rural noises.

Wednesday July 23rd Letter from Mrs Tucker dated Parkgate the 17th. Col. and Mrs St George and Miss Stepney purpose settling in the neighbourhood of Llangollen if they can get a House. We shall take care not to be troubled with their visits.

Thursday July 25th My beloved and I walked in the delicious meadows under Pengwern Wood. Our Landlord in one of them like a Patriarch making hay surrounded by his entire household . . . Met the Vicar, invited him in. He stayed half an hour. Three Dinner boil'd corned Beef with all sorts of vegetables in profusion – boiled fresh salmon. Reading. Drawing. Fine sunshine, light and shadow. The Clerk's Harvest cart with scarlet wheels removing the Hay. My beloved and I walked in the beautiful mill fields.

[Written along the margin of the Accounts: 'for want of money from 19th July to 26th – from 26th to –']

Saturday July 27th My beloved and I walked in the lane and meadows – saw a little pale boy climbing over our gate with a bundle of sticks on his back. Where are you going? Home. Where do you live? With my Dad and my Mam. What is your name? Tommy, son to John Edwards. Have you any brothers? Yes, Bobby and Jacky and Neddy and Dick. What is your mother's name? Blanche. Sat on the rock which rises abruptly in the meadow. Returned by Pengwern Mill and our Landlord's, then walked in the little fold at the back of their cottage. John Edwards' wife came to Us with cherries. She was going to Visit her mother on the Mountains. Our Landlady came to us, walked to her Barn with Us. Met our Landlord returning from Llandyn. Spoke to him. Then the Venerable worthy old Couple walked home arm in arm.

Sunday July 28th   We walked to the new waterfall by the Mill – sat on the wall beside it and then returned to Pengwern. Our Landlady brought us cherries. Sat beside the great ash tree and made our Landlady sit with us and relate her Courtship and Marriage with our Landlord . . . My Beloved and I walked on the Lawn. Saw two Ladies (one in a black capotte, the other one in white muslin, short dress, Each with large straw bonnet) coming up the lane, guessed them to be our neighbours Mrs St George and Miss Stepney – noticed they walked round the clump before the pales, stared into the windows, and behaved with a degree of vulgarity peculiar to the stile and line of Life those Ladies have wilfully adopted.

Tuesday July 30th   Writing. Drawing. My beloved and I went the home circuit then visited the waterfall . . . Met a child gathering wild flowers on a bank. Looked in* a Cottage by the brook side. A young woman winding thread – a little boy beside her rocking a cradle. Three dinner – boiled mutton – Cauliflowers mushrooms – Potatoes.

Wednesday July 31st   Gathered vegetables – pulled apples. Went to the Dressing-room – frizzing – powdering. The operation over read 'till twelve. Mr and Mrs Mytton arrived – brought Johnson's Letters published by Mrs Thrale now Mrs Lynch Piozzi. Went the Home circuit. Sprinkling rain.

(The Journal)

1789

Receipt

OLIVERS BISCUITS

Try'd 1st July 1789 and found excellent.

   Take two pounds of Flour, put two Spoonfuls of Yeast in a little Warm milk – mix it in a little of the Flour and let it stand a quarter of an hour to rise, then melt a Quarter of a pound of Butter in a

---

* Well, well!

sufficient quantity of Milk to make it in a Stiff Paste – roll it out –
and Bake them in a Slow oven.
NB   The Above Quantity will make three Dozen.

Thursday July 13th   Letter from Miss H. Bowdler dated Bath the
11th. 'The Palais Royal is a scene of riot, murder, and everything
that's dreadful. The King* has been publicly insulted and has now
sent for a great number of Swiss troops who will be a very weak
support against an enraged nation.'

Tuesday July 14th†   Sky white. Millions of Rooks on the mountains
of Pengwern consulting I suppose about the weather. I wish they
could communicate their observations, or that I could understand
their language. Mrs Kynaston and Miss Mytton came. Never saw
Mrs Kynaston in greater beauty. Her hair surpasses anything I ever
saw in that way.

Friday July 17th   Letter from Miss Lewis dated Chester the 13th.
'Mr Keate informed me that Capt. Wilson from motives of gratitude
and himself from motives of Justice had proposed to several of the
East India Directors to acknowledge their obligation to the King of
the Pelew Islands for their friendly reception of Capt. Wilson and
his People in their distress, and for furnishing them with the means
of returning to Europe . . . no Impression could be made on any of
those Gentlemen, nor a Spark of gratitude kindled. Capt. Wilson
was sent to China charged with the commercial concerns of the
Company, with the liberty only of remembering his Deliverers but
without the power of making them any return for their generosity'.
And indeed I may be happy for those untutored Islanders if they are
permitted to remain in a state of nature in her Original beauty and
purity uncontaminated with, and beyond the reach of European
avarice and refinement. Our naked and painted Ancestors in the
days of Julius Caesar would have been ashamed to behave so to
their benefactors.

Thursday July 30th   Letter from Miss H. Bowdler, Teignemouth,
the 26th, with some lines enclosed so beautiful that I shall here
transcribe them:

* Louis XVI.

† Outbreak of the French Revolution.

Sigh not ye winds as passing o'er
The chambers of the Dead ye fly;
Weep not ye Dews for these no more
Shall ever Weep, shall ever Sigh!
Why mourn? The throbbing heart's at rest;
How still it lies within the breast!
Why mourn? Since Death presents us peace
And in the grave our Sorrows cease,
The Shatter'd Bark, from adverse winds,
Rest in this peaceful Harbour finds
And when the storms of Life are past
Hope drops her Anchor here at last!

'All is once more quiet in France, and Necker returned, but I cannot think these extraordinary affairs will end thus. The King is now no more than the Doge of Venice. He is waiting patiently to see what Power the States will give him. They have acted with wonderful moderation and good sense all things considered. A Polish Princess of the first consequence who happened to be in Paris took refuge in the Bastille as the safest place and was of course besieged in it and saw all the horrors which followed and the execution of the Governor who was her intimate acquaintance.' The Duc de Luxembourg made his escape from Paris literally without his shirt.

(The Journal)

1790

Sunday July 4th   Tried on the black habits made by Barker. Must return them the skirts horribly made.

Expenses

July   7   Old Woman for the Cruel Cock 1s.

Wednesday July 14th   The sky like a sea of Blood. Never beheld anything like it but once before – that was the evening of the fire kindled by Lord George Gordon in London. I tremble for France.

Expenses

July 16   A Mild and amiable Cock which came to offer itself 6d.

Friday July 16th   Went a delightful walk by the mill, to the beautiful solitary meadows under Pengwern on this side the Brook. John Edwards and his Hind mowing. Then went to the narrow deep and shady lane which goes to the mountain. The Hedges adorned with a profusion of Honey Suckle wild roses and elder – the Banks with Strawberries and blue Campanula.

Monday July 19th   My beloved and I went the Home Circuit. Met our good Landlady going to see the old woman of the Bache who was prayed for in Church. Made her come in. We then walked towards the Mill. Met two men who had something more the appearance of gentlemen than the Welsh gentry usually are endowed with.

Wednesday July 21st   The Dean of Chester's sons and daughters desired to see this place – From the Hand. Refused. [This was because the Hand was suspected of propagating the following squib:]

July

Saturday July 24th   GENERAL EVENING POST

Extraordinary Female Affection.

Miss Butler and Miss Ponsonby have retired from society into a certain Welch Vale. Both Ladies are daughters of the great Irish families whose names they retain. Miss Butler, who is of the Ormonde family, had several offers of marriage, all of which she rejected. Miss Ponsonby, her particular friend and companion, was supposed to be the bar to all matrimonial union, it was thought proper to separate them, and Miss Butler was confined.

The two Ladies, however found means to elope together. But being soon overtaken, they were each brought back by their respective relations. Many attempts were renewed to draw Miss Butler into marriage. But upon her solemnly and repeatedly declaring that nothing could induce her to wed any one, her parents ceased to persecute her by any more offers. Not many months after, the ladies concerted and executed a fresh elopement. Each having a small sum with them, and having been allowed a trifling income the place of their retreat was confided to a female servant of the Butler family, who was sworn to secrecy as to the place of their retirement. She was only to say that they were well and safe and hoped that their friends would without further enquiry, continue their annuities, which has not only been done but increased.

The beautiful above-mentioned vale is the spot they fixed on where they have resided for several years unknown to the neighbouring villages by any other appellation than *the Ladies of the Vale!*

About a twelve month since three Ladies and a Gentleman stopping one night at an inn in the village, not being able to procure beds, the inhabitants applied to the Female Hermits for accommodation to some foreign strangers. This was readily granted – when lo! in these foreigners they descried some of their own relations! But no entreaties could prevail on the Ladies to quit their sweet retreat.

Miss Butler is tall and masculine, she wears always a riding habit, hangs her hat with the air of a sportsman in the hall, and appears in all respects as a young man if we except the petticoats which she still retains.

Miss Ponsonby, on the contrary, is polite and effeminate, fair and beautiful. In Mr Secretary Steel's list of Pensions for 1788, there are the names of Elinor [*sic*] Butler and Sarah Ponsonby, for annuities of fifty pounds each. We have many reasons to imagine that these pensioners are the Ladies of the Vale; their female confidante continues to send them their Irish annuities beside.

They live in elegance, neatness and taste. Two females are their only servants.

Miss Ponsonby does the duties and honours of the house, while Miss Butler superintends the gardens and the rest of the grounds.

Saturday July 24th Wrote to Wood to forbid the *General Evening Post* for Very Essential Reasons . . . Ten 'till Twelve in the Dressing room Reading.

Beaconsfield July 30th My dear Ladies . . . They must be the most wicked probably, certainly the most unthinking, of all wretches who could make that retirement unpleasant to you. I have not seen the base publications to which you allude. I have spoken to a friend who has seen them and who speaks of them with indignation felt by every worthy mind, but who doubts whether that redress can be had by an appeal to the law to which the whole community as well as you are entitled . . . Your consolation must be that you suffer only by the baseness of the age you live in, that you suffer from the violence of calumny for the virtues that entitle you to the esteem of all who know how to esteem honour, friendship, principle, and dignity of thinking, and that you suffer along with everything that is excellent in the world . . .

(Edmund Burke* to Eleanor Butler)

Tuesday August 3rd Storm. Gloom. Heavy rain. What weather! Writing to the Right Honble. Ed. Burke, Beaconsfield Bucks. A Rabbit in the Shrubbery. Sent to the village for hounds to hunt it. No noses. Nor indeed Eyes. Could neither smell nor see the Rabbit which sat before them by the Library Window.

(The Journal)

1791

Expenses

July 8 4 Chairs by the Stage Yesterday 3s.6d.
Irish Woman for Plain Work 7s.
15 Peggeen winding Yarn 3s.6d.
22 Francis for bringing Wine 3s.
27 Tax Gatherer £2.4.3.

July 24th . . . the coach which passed through Llangollen a few hours since, brought intelligence that the Birmingham riots† had begun again – and though that town is ninety-one miles from hence

* The famous orator, politician and philosopher.
† The Birmingham Dissenters had antagonized the town by celebrating the anniversary of the French Revolution.

we are assured that the Inhabitants of Shrewsbury which is but thirty entertain serious apprehensions for their own safety on account of the many dissenters it contains and if a very numerous Mob should assemble so near us – have we not some reason, my dear friend, to tremble for the safety of Our Cottage?

(Sarah Ponsonby to Mrs Tighe)

Receipts

TO PRESERVE CHERRIES

The proportion of Sugar highly Clarified is three quarters of a pound to one pound of Cherries – which ought to be quite ripe. Cut the tails to half, put them into the Sugar, let them Simmer about five minutes the Pan being covered: *let the whole rest together* 'till next day – then add a quarter of a pound of Sugar prepared as at first to each pound of Cherries with a little red Currant Juice – simmer together 'till the Syrup is quite rich.

FOWL

Prepare a Fowl for roasting – make a force with the Liver One Sweetbread – Parsley – a bit of Butter, Pepper, Salt and Chervil – Stuff the Fowl with it: and roast it wrapt in Paper and Lard very thinly Cut. When three parts done, take off the Paper and Lard. Baste it all over – with Yolks of Eggs beat up with melted Butter – Sprinkle it with Crumbs of Bread in Abundance and finish the Fowl of a fine Yellow Colour. Make a Sauce with a bit of butter One Chop't Anchovy a few Capers – a little flour two Spoonfuls of Broth – Pepper and Salt – thicken it with a White Sauce.

A MELON TART

Take a Melon, Pare it and take out the Seeds – pound it in a Mortar – put to it half a pound of Sugar the Yolks of Six Eggs and whites of Three – mix with Your Melon and Sugar – put this paste round the edge and in the Bottom of your Baking Dish – Lay the Melon* in it and Bake it – Frosting it over with Sugar. Add a little Orange Flower Water.

* Presumably another melon!

1793

Expenses

July 24 Mr Crewe £1.1.0.
   27 Mr Crewe "
   28 A Walking Stick 6d.*

July 27th Tell the dear Sufferer how tenderly I feel for her – how anxiously I wish that her angelic patience may never again be so severely tried . . .

(Harriet Bowdler to Sarah Ponsonby)

1794

Expenses

July 6 little Molly – encouragement for going well dressed to Church 1s.
   16 Samuel Evans nailing and pruning the Fruit 14s.
   26 David of the Mill walking with Mrs Boys and us Over the Mountain 6d.

1795

Expenses

July 16 Samuel Jones finishing the Kitchen – at *last* completed 6s.
   18 Beer for Haymakers 6s.
     Molly's Mother and Sister Hay making 2s.6d.

---

* Eleanor had obviously had an accident of some sort. She tended to be accident-prone.

21 Poor little dancing Dogs 1s.
27 Lobsters 1s.
28 Trouts 11d. Edward Roberts making the Hay Stacks 2s.6d.

1796

Lichfield July 19th You heard of my purpose to have an Eolian harp, made upon the construction of Miss Ponsonby's, mentioned in my poem, Llangollen Vale. She was so good to give me an exact drawing of hers; which, being three times the size they are usually made, and with twenty two strings, instead of the usual number, six, far transcends, both in the quantity and quality of the tone, the general order of these airy instruments. Mine is at length finished and strung; but, being made to fit my only eastern sash-windows, no gale has yet blown from that point, strong enough to wake the sullen slumber of its many chords . . .

(Anna Seward to Miss Wingfield)

1799

Saturday July 6th The Hand chaise came. My beloved and I went to Oswestry. Arrived at Mrs Barrett's at nine. Breakfast. Then Price the Hairdresser cut Our Hair. Went to Church.

Monday July 8th Mr Wynne came. Paid him four pounds, being a year's rent for the Cyflymen field which we hold from Sir Thomas Mostyn.

Friday July 12th Rain, gloom and cold.

(The Journal)

Expenses

July 13   Simon's Daughter for Mushrooms 6d.
      14   Simon for burying My poor little Cat this Sunday 1s.
      15   Simon for bringing back poor Brandy's body and burying
           it! 1s.

1800

Expenses

July 2   Bread for the Harvest Supper 2s.
          to the Mother of the Boys whom we caught in our part of
          the Cufflymin, for Whipping them 1s.
      3   6d. to the one 6d. to the other, and 1s. to Mrs Davies Son
          John in compensation of our unjustly suspecting them of
          taking our Strawberries 2s.
      4   To the 4 Hay-making Women 1s. each.
      5   Market including our Hay-making Supper for 14 persons
          19s.3d.
          Simon's Wife for cutting thistles 1s.6d.
      7   Mr Wynne of Mold – for the Instrument which is to secure
          us from molestation* during the lives of John and Mary
          Edwards though he most liberally and earnestly refused
          any Compensation – £5.5s.
          To the Thatcher for Thatching our Haystack 2s.6d.
      9   David the Miller and Simon to drink success to the
          Waterfall 1s.2d.
          Simon's Wife bringing Moss for Do. 1s.
     17   A travelling Boy for the Kindness with which he gave us
          some Pinks 1s.

1801

July 30th   They will tell you of . . . the beauty and neatness of our
nine acres – as for their *paying*, it is a different affair. We shall make
a little by selling butter as soon as we can purchase a fourth Cow,
and if potatoes kept their last years prices (4s or 5s the measure) we
should make near £20 by what we shall have to sell of them, but
thank Heaven (for we are not yet sufficient farmers or *monsters* not

* The son of their old Landlord was trying to put up their rent, or else evict them.

to say 'thank Heaven' though we should starve or go to gaol for it)
we shall not make near a fourth of that sum, for we yesterday heard
that 20 measures of good ones had been offered for 10s . . . We have
only four fields, not much above 8 acres in the whole – *little Welsh
acres!* in which we think it doing very well to keep four cows in
pasture and hay. And we have now brought them to so fine a sward
with white Dutch clover and high manuring that we hope they will
never again be even *scratched* by a ploughshare in our time . . . Our
cows are vastly obliging in doing all in their power to increase our
heaps of Manure . . .

(Sarah Ponsonby to Mrs Tighe)

1802

July 3rd   My kind friend Mrs Goddard has bequeathed me as a
further proof of that regard to which I before owed so many
obligations, a legacy of one hundred pounds and an annuity of
thirty guineas a year for my life.

(Sarah Ponsonby to Mrs Tighe)

1803

Llangollen Vale Tuesday July 10th   Such assurances – Welcome at
all times from a dear and respected Hand must be so in a peculiar
degree to Spirits doubly Assailed by the Lofty exultations of the
dreaded Cotton Mills and the depression of the finest Crop of Hay
– nor Farming existence ever Witnessed – by a deluge of three days
incessant flood . . .

(Sarah Ponsonby to Mrs Piozzi)

1813

Brynbella July 7th   Shropshire hospitality delayed us next, and we
passed one week with our agreeable friends at Longar, where,
among other chat we learnt that Lady Eleanor Butler had fractured
her arm and dislocated her shoulder; a visit at Llangollen, in our
way home confirmed the account, But she is well and merry, and
was not confined to her bed an hour, it seems, so strong is her
constitution.

(Mrs Piozzi to Dr Whalley)

1819

July One   Turned our Hay – Eighteen times . . . The dowager Lady Donegal having mentioned that the PR* in consequence of the advice of his physicians had left off wearing stays – and his stomach had fallen down to his knees – Mrs Scott said it was a movable Feast! . . . Splendid Gorgeous day.

Tuesday July Thirteen   . . . a Glorious Splendid Blessed Day – Hay Stack made – Dinner under the Trees for all our kind neighbours – More than thirty . . .

Wednesday July Twenty Eight   . . . heat intense! – receipt for 'Ginger Beer' from that enchanting Lady Glynn.

(The Journal)

1821

Wednesday July 11th   Our three meadows cut before six o'clock in the evening by eighteen mowers!!!

Wednesday July 18th   Mr Lubbock very civilly called with a Grand Transparency† of Britannia which he was so good as to lend us for our Coronation transparencies to-morrow.

Thursday July 19th   Mr Lubbock in the morning assisting in placing our Transparencies, which were very successfully arranged. Our House (!) illuminated and much admired by Mr and Mrs Eyton, Miss Morgan, who drank tea with us, and all the Mob-ility of Llangollen.

Thursday July 26th   Shrewsbury paper with account of our illuminations.

1828

July [undated]   . . . In quarter of an hour I arrived amidst the most charming neighbourhood, driving through a very nice pleasure ground, at a small tasteful Gothic house, just opposite Castle Dinas Bran, to view which apertures had been cut through the foliage of lofty trees. I got out of the carriage and was received by the two ladies at the foot of the stairs. Fortunately I was quite prepared as regards their singularity . . . Both wore their hair, which is quite full

* Prince Regent.

† Oiled paper with coloured pictures, illuminated by a candle.

yet combed down straight and powdered, a gentleman's round hat, a gentleman's cravat and waistcoat, instead of the 'inexpressibles' however, a short *Jupon* and gentlemens' boots. The whole was covered by an overdress of blue cloth of a quite peculiar cut, keeping the middle between a gentleman's overcoat and a lady's riding habit. Over all this 'toggery' Lady Eleanor wore 1) the *grand cordon* of the order of the collar of Saint Louis round her waist; 2) the same order round her neck; 3) the small cross of the same order in the button-hole; *et pour comble de gloire*, a silver lily of almost natural size as a star on her breast – all this being, as she told me, presents of the Bourbon family . . . now imagine these two ladies full of the most *plaisante aisance* and the tone of great people of the *ancien regime;* obliging and entertaining without any affectation, speaking French at least as well as any noble Englishman of my acquaintance, and at the same time of those essentially polite *sans gêne,* and I might say *naif* and cheerful manners of the good society of that time, which it will almost appear have been carried to the grave in our earnest and industrial century of business life . . . I could not help but remarking at the same time, the uninterrupted and nevertheless apparently so natural and tender consideration with which the younger of the two was treating her somewhat infirm elder friend, and how she anticipated every one of her little wants. Such things reveal themselves more in the way they are done, in little insignificant traits, perhaps, but do not escape the sympathetic eye . . . a well furnished library, a charming neighbourhood, an even-tempered life without material cares, a most intimate friendship and community amongst themselves – these are their treasures . . .

(Prince Puckler Muskaus to 'Julia')

AUGUST

1784

Sunday August 7th   I took a dose of Caster oyl.

Tuesday August 19th   I ill of a head ach. My Sweet Love got magnesia from the Little Doctor's.

Thursday August 26th   Dark. Cold. Gloomy dispiriting day – a Fire in the library.

Sunday August 29th   After dinner went to Church – laugh'd Shamefully.

(Eleanor Butler's Pocket Book)

1785

August 21st   The 9th We had some Visitors – the 10th we were obliged to spend with Lady Dungannon – and the 11th our friends Miss Davies and Miss Bowdler came to spend a few days with us – Though they are both extremely agreeable – My B cou'd hardly

brook such continual interruptions to her Manuscript* in which She
has made considerable progress . . . We have been in possession of
a cow almost a week. She is a very amiable creature (we call her
Margaret) and we abound in milk, cream, butter and buttermilk.

(Sarah Ponsonby to Mrs Tighe)

1786

August 28th Company with whom I am not perfectly at ease
always gives me an *Emetical* Headach . . . I am grateful to Dr Dealtry
since my Friends *must* amuse themselves with Creating reports on
my subject, his was by far the kindest of many that I have been
surprized at – was it not better than my wearing out my dear B's
patience by cruel usage, and making it impossible for her to endure
me any longer – nay absolutely putting her in fear of her life by my
Barbarity etc. etc.? which I was said to do two years ago. I was
afterwards married at least half a dozen times, the last as Chief Baron
Yelverton told us not three Months since – the Bishop of Cork would
have dissuaded Mr and Lady Anne Talbot from coming this way as
they did soon after you *insisting* upon it that We had been returned
to Ireland some time . . .

(Sarah Ponsonby to Mrs Tighe)

1787

July – I mean August 4th We had a very comfortable drive from
Kinioge Waterfall† – and our Drivers being much More Harmonized
than their Predecessors We Stopt by the Waterfall and Walked part
of that Beautiful road. Staid half an hour at Aswern listening to old
Welch Tunes . . . saw the moon unveil 'her peerless light' over our
beloved Mountains and reached our Own Cot between nine and ten.

(Sarah Ponsonby to Mrs Tighe)

1788

Friday August 1st Half past eight Lord Kenmare, Madame la

* This was a meticulous hand-written copy of Lady Ann Fanshawe's memoirs for
Mrs Tighe.

† They had obviously accompanied Mrs Tighe some of the road on her way to Ireland.

Comtesse de Civrac, Mr Griffin, chanoine de Cambrai,* came, breakfasted, staid 'till twelve, then proceeded to Ireland . . . I asked Mr Griffin about Cambrai, sent my love to all in the Convent who remembered me. Went the home circuit . . . Heavy white clouds, but dispiriting as is the weather – we may thank God it is no worse – the Chanoine de Cambrai told us that the storms in France did more damage than the kingdom was likely to sustain from the internal feuds of which the English papers say so much.

Saturday August 2nd Donnes came, poor man related his melancholy story and the villainy of Pryce. Riots in London . . . Promised the poor man every assistance in our slender power towards discharging our account.

Wednesday August 6th Writing. Rap at the Door. Dean and Mrs Coote and the prettiest nicest little dog I ever beheld.

Thursday August 7th My beloved – her Nine Copies of Antique Statues from Rome finished with that Elegance and Minuteness which characterises all her performances.

Saturday August 9th I was Siezed with one of my Splitting head aches. My beloved with her accustomed tenderness and anxiety Made me go to the dressing Room, procured an Emetic which She administered herself. When I grew Easier She read to me Till I was entirely relieved from the splitting pain. [Upside down is written:] a Cottage August the 13th – the having but one Heart between my beloved and –

Sunday August 10th Brown the Wrexham grocer came with his little Bill. Paid him – thank heaven. Holiday, the Chester hairdresser whom we sent for to Wrexham, he being at the assizes there, came. Cut and powdered our Hair, dress'd it. Got slides and a pot of Rose Pomatum. Holiday is a Roman Catholic born at Preston in Lancashire . . . Lady Mostyn going to send Holiday's son to College, offered to send him to Lisbon or Valladolid which he preferred. Lancashire servants the best in England, preferred to any others. William Holiday a Lancashire man.

Monday August 11th Rose at four. Holiday dress'd our hair. Went in the Hand Chaise and four. Morning chill and grey. Arrived at

* Eleanor had been educated at the Convent at Cambrai.

Ruthin at seven. Did not get out of the Chaise while the Horses were resting. Enquired for the Suttons of the Maid of the Lyon, she informed us they had quitted their old house and removed to the Churchyard. Arrived at the Palace of St Asaph at half past nine. We were received at the Hall Door by the most benevolent and Reverend of all Prelates in his gown and black velvet cap. Mrs Shipley and her two sweet daughters who all exclaimed at our expedition. Found breakfast ready . . . *Mem* the Country in most astonishing beauty, several new cottages built near the Bwlch – corn cutting near Ruthin, the great appearance of industry in the Vale of Clwyd, large fields well enclosed of corn, turnips, french or black wheat, potatoes. Reapers and Haymakers all employed on either Side of the Road. Hedgerows of tall Poplars, fine lime, elm and oak trees. Mountain ash in full berry. Charming view from Pontruffydd bridge. Hanging woods, fine meadows, the Spire of the Cathedral rising amidst trees. The Bishop related his having found, when Dean of Winchester, the Body and Ring of Cardinal Blois, brother of King Stephen, son to the Comte de Blois and grandson of the Conqueror by his daughter Adela, The Ring the finest saphire . . .

Saturday August 16th At half-past seven went in the Hand Chaise to Halston. Met a multitude of waggons, coal carts, one caravan – a young couple in it who appeared innocent and interesting. Arrived at Halston precisely at nine. Mrs and Miss Mytton in the beautiful parlour with a little old Frenchwoman who is come to Halston for the purpose of instructing Miss Mytton in the French and Italian languages . . . At two went in the carriage to Hardwick – our dear Barretts and Miss Davies there. We found Mrs Kynaston sitting on a sopha in the drawing-room unable to move without assistance from the sting of a wasp . . .'

Wednesday August 20th Breakfast over, we were agreeably surprised by the appearance of Butler* who told us his brothers Wandesford and James were coming, as they did while he was speaking, and brought with them his Picture beautifully done by Downman. Butler is, we think still handsomer than when we saw him last and from every word he spoke we have reason to believe he will do honour to his ancestors. Wandesford tall, well made, good hair, plain face. James the image of his grandfather. I trust he will

* Eleanor's nephew.

resemble him in his mind as he does in his person and then indeed his family may be proud of him. Tho' straiten'd for time they staid with us till half-past twelve and then posted on to the Hand. My Beloved and I sent for the joiner, hung up Butler's picture beside Lady Anne Wesley's. Mrs Ponsonby next him.

Sunday August 24th   One of the Llannest drivers came to let us know that Butler and his Brothers had left their keys in the pockets of Mrs Mousley's Coach at the Eagle.

Monday August 25th   Compliments from Mr White desiring permission for himself, his Son and Daughter to see this place – permitted. They came. An old man with spectacles, a flaunting Daughter in a brown and gold Capotte, a school Boy. He left a Poem (which please God I shall not read) signed Samuel White. When they were gone went to the Library . . . the Bishop of St Asaph, Mrs Shipley and the two charming Daughters arrived. They dined, sup'd and staid 'till eleven. We walked to the Lyon with Miss Louise, delicious night – Bell tolling, river murmuring – Harper playing in the Hall of the Hand.

Friday August 29th   Damp – heavy and still. A Toad on the Cellar window – a frog on the steps of the Hall door – a certain sign of rain.

Saturday August 30th   Message from Mr Crewe, will come in an hour. Message to him, He shall be welcome. Sitting in our parlour window we beheld a very affecting sight – at least the burial of our old neighbour Mathew the Miller was to us an affecting sight. The Funeral was preceded by the Vicar and the head farmers of the Parish, then came the clerk and all the members of the Club to which the poor Miller belonged, bare-headed, each bearing a Staff and singing a solemn Dirge – immediately after was the Body borne on a Bier, his old widow habited in black and in the most piercing afflictions close behind it. Many women accompanying her. This mournful procession came slowly along the undulating path through our field, the passing Bell solemnly tolling all the while – it drew many tears from us and left an impression of tender melancholy which we would rather cherish than seek to dissipate.

(The Journal)

1789

Saturday August 1st   Mr Edwards of the Hand came up with his Bill. Exorbitant to the last degree. A fearful madman came to the Lyon in a Carriage with two men to guard him. He appeared no better than a common man, a labourer or under farmer.

Monday August 3rd   Letter from Miss H. Bowdler dated Teignmouth the 31st. 'Sir Robert Herries is returned to London and brings sad Tales of Horror which he learned at Dover from Mr Hinchcliffe. The Duc de Brissac and the Abbesse de Monmartre are executed and many others, and much worse was expected. I hope it will please God to still the madness of these People, for all earthly power is Vain' – *General Evening Post* This Paper contains accounts of the Horrors in France which I Trust in the all merciful Being are Exaggerated.

Tuesday August 4th   My beloved and I went to the white gate – gentle wind – burning air – high white clouds in an azure sky.

Wednesday August 5th   Sent for Mr Edwards of the Hand. Taxed him with what his odious Brother-in-law said. He offered to take his oath. Drawing a buckle found in a field near Valle Crucis and sent by Mrs Lloyde of Tower. While I was examining it Our poor Dear little Gipsey . . . suddenly fell into a fit. We held her – she came to herself but deprived of all power of Using her hinder parts . . .

Thursday August 6th No newspaper – how provoking at this Critical time for France.

Friday August 7th Light airy Clouds – purple mountains – lilac and silver rocks – hum of Bees – rush of Waters. Goat. Sheep. Cattle. Melody of Haymakers. What weather! What a country! We sent to Mr Lloydde of Trevor to request he would permit our *little* Household to sit in one of his Pews at Church, as we have determined never to allow anyone belonging to us to Sit in the Hand Seat after the great offence we have received from that ungrateful House. Mr Lloydde complied in the handsomest manner. Mr Edwards of the Hand came up at nine to entreat we would relent, but his submission came too late.

Monday August 10th Letter from Miss H. Bowdler dated Teignmouth the 6th. The accounts from France are very favourable. The return of the Guardian Angel* of the land has restored tranquillity for the present, but knowing ones seem to fear that even his gentle influence cannot long preserve it. The last time the King and Queen showed themselves to the people at a Balcony there was a Very loud cry – '*Vive le Roi, mais à Bastille P!*'†

Wednesday August 12th Two Mr Watkins desired permission to see this Cottage. Did not refuse them. Two ungainly maypoles. One of them in the Church.

Expenses

August 17 Mr Edwards of the *Hand in full* £52.6.7 halfpenny.
  Seeds for the Cow 6d. Salmon 8s.
  19 Our poor dear, *dear* little Gypsey 4s.6d.

Wednesday August 19th Our Dear Gypsey, our beautiful our faithful companion, died last night. We shed many, many tears over her and interred her beside our dear Flirt and Bess, her mother and sister. Poor little Thing, her affection was disinterested and sincere and we repaid it with attention, indulgence and great tenderness. Visited the grave of our dear Gypsey. A rap at the Door. To our agreeable surprise Mr Burke came whom we had not seen these five

* Necker.
† *Putaine* – the Queen.

years. Just returned from France. Had been in Paris in all the Riots. Mrs Burke at Bath, goes to Ireland in a fortnight. We dined, went the home circuit with him. Then at 5 walked with him to the Lyon Inn.* Met the Vicar at the Burial of a child. Lovely, lovely evening.

Friday August 21st   Rose at seven, dark morning. At nine my beloved and I set out in the Lyon's Chaise for Halston. Air temperate and soft, views excellent. Met carts, horsemen, pedestrians, flocks of sheep, some cattle going to the fair at Llangollen. Baskets of fruit carried by boys and girls, who ate of them as they tripped merrily along. The Stage coach loaded, a young woman in a riding habit, hat and feather, riding single, attended by her maid in a bonnet and cloak, riding also single with a cotton valise before her. Left a letter for Mrs Lovett as we drove through Chirk, arrived at Halston at half past ten. Mrs and Miss Mytton, Miss Bell Pigott, waiting for us on the steps. Breakfasted, then we all went on the water. Thompson and the Coachman rowed us twice round the piece of water. Overtaken by a sudden shower. Rowed into the Boathouse. When the Shower was over walked in the wood to the farm yard. Cottage. Drank of the Spring – a strong taste of Copper. Next to the Butts. Visited the Dairy. Returned.

(The Journal)

* Instead of the defaulting Hand!

1790

Expenses

August   4   Our Neighbour* but no Object of Charity 1s.
           5   2 pair Ducks 2s.6d.   Ruth for plain Work 1s.4d. A
               poor Woman 1s. a ditto 2s.

Monday August 9th Note from Mr Walmsley an artist from London, desiring to see this place. Desired to be excused. We have appeared in the Newspapers – Will take care not wilfully to be exhibited in the Magazines.

Tuesday August 10th My beloved and I set out in the Lyon Chaise and four. The village of Mountford very neat and picturesque on the banks of the Severn with gardens before the houses. Stop'd at the Talbot. Got a Hair Dresser. At one set out for Berwick. That charming woman Mrs Powys and her daughter in the drawing room – an apartment fitted up with perfect elegance and taste. They went with us through the grounds – the Severn winding through them. Finely wooded. Clumps and single trees of an immense size, beautifully scattered on the lawn, terminated in the front by the Town of Shrewsbury with all its towers and Spires. At our return found Mrs Mytton, Miss Mytton, Miss Pigott, Miss Fanny Pigott, Miss Webb, Mrs Powys' Mother. At eight our carriage came. Stop'd at Whittington. Sat in a very neat Parlour by a Pair of Candles. Grew tired of it. Went for a walk. The woman of the house† followed us with a candle. She showed us the house of Doctor H. Walked to it. Examined it. Heard somebody sneeze. Went to the Castle. Examined that. Horses harnessed – proceeded on our way.

Tuesday August 17th My beloved and I went the Home Circuit. Walked to the Gate. Met the Vicar. Invited him to coffee. The good man more stupid than ever, incredible and impossible as that appeared the last time we saw him.

Saturday August 21st Rose at four. Turner dress'd our Hair. Morning delicious. My beloved and I set out in the Lyon Chaise and four. At the Hand door a chaise standing with two frightful men in it. One in a nightcap as if he were sick, the other ferocious and like

* The weaver.
† The inn.

a madman. Windy and misty before we got to the Turnpike. Lime carts without end from there to Whittington. Did not get out of the Carriage. Sent our compliments to Mr Lloydde of Aston by the man of the White Lyon who is a schoolmaster and goes every Saturday to Aston to teach the little girls to write. From Whittington to Ness wind and rain. One carriage – a dull couple in it – standing at the door of a public House near the Road. Gave the horses water at Ness Cliff. In the parlour of the Inn a Dancing Master teaching all the Farmer's sons and daughters French Dances. I think a melancholy sight. We were directed to go to Boreatton by the Hostler who told us to turn up the Right by the next House. We did so, got on a wild Heath under the Wood and cliff. Prospect beautiful. Drove through a farmyard, then got into a cornfield, from thence to a field of French wheat. Found it almost impassable. Alighted. A prattling old woman directed us to the village of Ruyton thro' a narrow lane, so very narrow we were under a necessity of taking off a pair of Horses. With the utmost difficulty got to the end of it. From thence got into a narrow Road under a wood. An old woman directed us to Ruyton thro' the wood, a little Boy to Boreatton thro' the field. Followed the latter. Came to three gates. A little girl then appeared and conducted us through meadows, cornfields, ploughed fields to a Bridge and Mill, from whence the Road was direct to Boreatton. Received most hospitably by Mr and Mrs Hunt and five of the Loveliest children I ever beheld. We breakfasted in the Tent. Mr and Mrs Hunt accompanied us horseback, to the Park . . . we went away Mr Hunt sent his coachman to show us the way from the village of Ruyton to the Shrewsbury road. Returned by a splendid moon to Whittington. Fed the horses. My beloved and I did not get out of the carriage. Being saturday all the neighbouring Farmers had assembled there to pay their Reapers and spend the evening, or rather night, in mirth and conviviality. They sang many Songs, all applicable to their Situation in praise of a Farmer's Life, some Hunting songs, and one on Lord Hawke. We are quite delighted at the Excellence of their Voices. Returned home by a delicious Moon. Arrived at one.

Expenses

August 21   Turnpike to Boreatton 4s. To Guide when we lost our way 9d. Driver 6s. Mr Hunt's Coachman 2s.

|August 14   The Quarter of our Pensions due in April reduced to
£13.3.8. |

Monday August 23rd   Compliments from Mr Fielden and the Miss
Sheperds desiring to see this place. Permitted. They came – one of
them so affected by a fearful accident in this village that she was
obliged to get a glass of water. The Accident was a Child, son to the
Blacksmith, aged six years, killed on the Spot by the Stage Coach
going over it.

(The Journal)

1793

August 3rd   I intreat you my precious friend to employ all your
authority to prevent her indulging me with a single line 'till it can
be done without the slightest degree of pain. Let her sing French
Songs as Much as she pleases, but lock up her pen and ink.

(Harriet Bowdler to Sarah Ponsonby)

A Cottage 7th August   ... my precious patient is in as fair a way
towards speedy and perfect recovery as we could possibly wish. Her
excellent natural constitution, sweetness of temper and temperate
way of life have enabled her to resist the consequences of an accident
which I am convinced would have been attended with the most
serious and lasting ill effects to many other subjects.

(Sarah Ponsonby to Mrs Tighe)

Expenses

August   3   Mr Tudor Upholsterer in full £19.14.6.
       5   Carriage of Bed 6s.6d.
       8   Lobsters 1s.6d. Mushrooms 8d.
     10   Nancy our Old Servant 3s.
     30   Gardener for his disappointment 2s.6d.
         Little Girl 6d.
     31   Mr Rosedale Harper and Organist 10s.6d.
         Pencils and Paper 12s.
         That most Ungrateful and *mean* Ed. Parry 5s.
         A magnifying Glass 5s.

August

1794

August 7th   I have anxiously waited day after day, in hopes of a letter from my beloved friends, but none arrives. Forgive my anxiety and indulge me with a line to say that you are well and have not forgotton me. I wrote to my Viellard on the 17th of July, and to you, my ever Dear Friend, on the 25th, but have no answer to either of these letters. Tell me why is this?

(Harriet Bowdler to Sarah Ponsonby)

August 10th   I heard from our dear Margaret that you looked remarkably well (wch removed one cause of anxiety) that your Place is more lovely than ever, that there is a new door to the library wch is the most beautiful ever seen, that she spent some delightful hours in your sweet society and etc. and etc. and etc. All this I can know from her, and I leave you to imagine the pleasure it gave me; but it is only from your own dear hand that I can learn what I most wish to know – that you still love me . . .

(Harriet Bowdler to Sarah Ponsonby)

Receipts

SOUP MAIGRE

Take Celery, Beet Leaves, Cabbage, Lettuce, Sorrell, Young Onions and Cucumbers, chop them very small – put them in a Stewpan, with a quarter of a pound of fresh Butter – let them stew slowly till quite soft, then add gradually a Spoonful of Flour, mix them well together, add to this three pints of Boiling water, a little Salt and Cayan Pepper a little Nutmeg, a spoonful or two of Mushroom Catchup, Let them all Stew together 'till they are tender, before you Dish it up add the Yolks of five Eggs, and a quarter of a Pint of Cream, and put this to your Soup mixing them well together, put on some Fry'd Bread and serve it up.

A GREEN PEACH TART

Cut them in halves – Boil them a moment in water that you may peel off the skins – then stew them gently in Clarified Sugar – lay them gently in your Patty – Cover with nice Pastry and Bake them a fine Colour.

A VERY PRETTY CRUST FOR TARTS

Take three Eggs and beat them well together, put to them three Spoonfuls of Cold Water, then break in a Pound of Butter – while you are working it all together, let some Flour be shaked in, and work it together, still strewing more Flour 'till it is a pretty stiff paste. then roll it out for Tarts – It Keeps crisper and longer than Puff Crust for most Uses.

1795

Expenses

August 13   Thos. Simon for killing his Cat 1s.
       16   Harpwoman for Mr and Mrs Ormsby and Miss Seward 3s.

August 20th   By their* own invitation I drank tea with them thrice during the nine days of my visit to Dinbren; and, by their kind introduction, partook of a rural dinner, given by their friend Mrs Ormsby, amid the ruins of Valle-Crucis, an ancient abbey, distant a mile and a half from their villa. Our party was large enough to fill three chaises and two phaetons.

We find the scenery of Valle-Crucis Grand, Silent, Impressive, Awful. The deep repose, resulting from the high umbrageous mountains which rise immediately around these ruins, solemnly harmonizes with their ivied arches and broken columns. Our drive to it from the lovely villa leads throu one of the most picturesque parts of the peerless vale, and along the banks of the classic river.

After dinner, our whole party returned to drink tea and coffee in that retreat, which breathes all the witchery of genius, taste, and sentiment.

(Anna Seward to The Rev. Henry White, of Lichfield.)

* The Ladies'.

Expenses

August 20   Abbey Expenses and Moses driving us home 5s.
        25   Mr Lloyd of Aston's Son with fine fruit 2s.6d.
        30   Margaret the Harper 3s.6d.

1796

Buxton August 7th   I now sit writing by a good fire, in very commodious lodgings. My neat light parlour looks backward, is on the first flight of stairs and, from its aspect, is quiet and silent. When I close one of the sash windows, that looks on the superb stables, which are built on the rise of the hill, above this splendid, this golden half-moon, the other window shows me only a sloping range of bare fields, without hedge or tree, and intersected by stone walls they present a perfect picture of a barren country, of rudeness, silence, and solitude . . . You have taken an infinite deal of obliging trouble, in transcribing for me Mr William's translation of the Runic poem, which I paraphrased in my late publication. I am shocked to think that my curiosity should be gratified at such an expense of time, precious as Miss Ponsonby's – but what an admirable specimen of perfect skill in penmanship is this transcript! – the modern print-hand, that of the ancient black-letter type, and the Roman, are proofs of very uncommon skill. The poetry of this translation does not please me.

                                  (Anna Seward to Sarah Ponsonby)

Expenses

August 3   Our Hay from the little Meadow ending in a dance 3s.
        21   5 numbers of that odious Baker's publication 12s.6d.
        23   Man from Mr Crewe with Apricots 1s.
        27   At the Aqueduct with Mrs Barrett 6s.

1798

Expenses

August 15   Irishwoman to Peggeen for going in wind and rain to inquire after dearest HB 2s.*

                  * Harriet Bowdler.

28 Excursion to Mill with dearest Glory* and Mrs Barrett 2s.

29 Dinner at the Abbey with Lady Henley in the Evening 4s.

30 Expenses at Oswestry – Dear Dear HB left there 16s.

1799

Expenses

August 3 Woman of the Workhouse who brought Straw 1s.

4 Man of the Ton House for stuff to deter the Cows from breaking the Hedges 1s.

5 Dolly Kendrick for 6 Ink Pots 4s.

9 Barking Cups – a pound of Flax and Sundries 3s.
Cadwallader for hire of Hurdles 3s.

12 Thatcher for thatching our Haystack incomparably 2s.6d.

22 Sundries Mr Chappellow coming for 2 or 3 days 7s.

29 Pair of Turkies in expectation of Miss Seward the 4th Sept 10s.

1799

Llangollen Vale 29th August We are doubly pained Dearest Madam by the apprehension of suffering a little in Your and Mr Piozzi's opinion . . . from the inevitable necessity we are under of postponing the honour and happiness of our proposed Visit to Bryn Bella . . . The *true* reason (which is always best to be given) for this apparent inconsistency – is that our Friend Mrs Barrett positively will not encounter the Steep and dreary hills between Llangollen and Ruthin in our return without the comfort and protection of a favourable Moon. A too late inspection of the Almanack informed her that that must not be hoped for on the Day . . .

(Lady Eleanor Butler to Mrs Piozzi)

* It appears that Glory the cow walked to the mill with them.

Expenses

August 18   Little John Davies for a little of his Company 6d.

Brynbella Wednesday August 27th   And how did our Dear Ladies get home? Safely I hope – it could not be a more beautiful Evening, and before your Chaise had reached Ruthin . . . There was an outline of Snowden discernable . . . I could not last Sunday express my Concern about the Difficulties with Regard to that dear and celebrated Cottage – which never *never* must slip from the possession of Ladies which have made its very Name Immortal. Miss Ponsonby mention'd *Ten years* as secure I think?

> (Mrs Piozzi to Lady Eleanor Butler, sympathizing with them in their struggle to keep Plas Newydd from their new landlord)

1802

August 23rd   . . . having had a most favourable hay harvest, though few of our neighbours have been so fortunate, we humbly trust that we shall have an equal success in our crop of barley, which consists of about as much as will employ one man to reap in about three hours. It is then to be malted and made into ale . . . our cows are so fine that our neighbours are glad of their male as well as female progeny to rear and increase the species . . .

> (Sarah Ponsonby to Mrs Tighe)

1803

August 4th   We do not feel quite easy under the knowledge that every human Male in our neighbourhood will be armed next Sunday evening for though many may be too old and many too young to do good, all ages are capable of doing *Mischief* if its implements are placed in their hands . . .

> (Sarah Ponsonby to Mrs Tighe, commenting on arming the male population against the expected French invasion)

1806

Holyhead August ye 12th   Till Llangollen my journey was without
a rub . . . When I came to Llangollen there were no horses to be had,
and there I was forced to remain for four and twenty hours in a dirty
inn the worst on the road, with the rudest, most perverse people
from the mistress to the stable-boys, that can be imagined . . . As I
was to stay so long in Llangollen I felt a little wish to see the Irish
Ladies' place, and after walking round it on the outside, begged
leave to come in, and they received me themselves. I went to church
with them, and afterwards walked all over it. The house is a very
pretty and comfortable cottage, with beautiful views from the place,
but I think it laid out in very bad taste. The prettiest thing I saw was
a walk by the brook (for their river is not the Dee) with a long birch
avenue, something like that at Bothwell in miniature, and a view of
two mills at the same time. From the Ladies, or rather Lady Eleanor
– for Miss Ponsonby only seems to assent to what she says and
speaks little herself – I had many messages to you, that they
positively expect a visit some time or other. Lady Douglas had told
them that part of your heart was in Wales and that you had a passion
for the Spanish language. They had a charming library, and I was to
tell you a good part of it was Spanish. I think Lady Eleanor very
clever, very odd, and the greatest flatterer I ever met with, for she
not only flatters in her own name, but repeats so many flattering
things said of one by others that she quite astonished me . . .

(Lady Lonsdale to Lady Louisa Stuart)

1807

Thursday August 6th   In the evening Mr Wingfield and we went
in our chaise to Wynnstay . . . Staid an hour. Returned. Raining
hard. Supper to the Vicarage. At twelve returned. Driver quite
drunk. Rocking and sleeping on his horse. But for little Will who sat
in front and kept him awake we should have been overturned into
the Canal. Walked from the Hand stables home. Streets dirty from
the late deluging rain. Night rather dark and cloudy.

Sunday August 9th   Note from Mrs Griffiths desiring to see this
cottage. We desired to be excused. But were obliged to repeat this

refusal as this Welch Lady was driving her gig full of Boys and Misses.

Sunday August 23rd   The Hostler of the Hand came up with message from Lord Spencer. Overheard carriages enter the village. Sent to enquire. Sir William Jerningham. Saw Sir William, Mr Edward Jerningham and Lady Bedingfield coming up the Lane. Went with them to the Hand to see Lady Jerningham. Staid half an hour. Brought up dear, dear Lady Bedingfield with us. Put her in possession of the apartment allotted for her. Night lovely. Walked with her by moonlight. Sat up with her 'till three.

Tuesday August 25th   Rose at six. Found our charming guest Lady Bedingfield in The Tent. Brought her the Home Circuit. The Mill in particular beauty, water foaming and dashing over the wheel. Breakfast over the Carriage drove up . . .

Thursday August 27th   At 8 in the Hand Chaise, my Better half and I set out. Where the Canal had burst the road was covered with water. Stopped at the Turnpike . . . Then, taking Mrs E.W. in our chaise, went to the Grove. All the party assembled there with their Bows and Arrows. The Butts and Targets prepared. Great shooting. Dinner cold. Two Tables. After dinner returned to the Butts. Such a canting odious detestable Boasting woman under the trees. Then cards. After a most agreeable day we returned home.

(The Journal)

1813

August 13th   . . . my beloved Lady Eleanor's having last Sunday three weeks dismissed all her bandages and now enjoying passably as ever the use of her late dislocated and broken arm, which was much more than our surgeon dared hope at the time the dreadful accident happened . . . the poisonous reptile of a Woman and drunken Idiot of a Man, by whom the Hand Inn at Llangollen is Kept (and for the general accommodation of Travellers I must in justice say – very well and neatly kept also) . . .

(Sarah Ponsonby to Mrs Tighe)

1819

Wednesday August Twenty Five   Letter from Mrs Butler – anything but comfortable.

Friday August Twenty Seven   The Sale Stopped of that horrid *Don Juan** – delicious Rain all night. Evening Venison Pasty and receipt for chicken Sallad ... *Mem* Cutlers Shops not lighted with gas because the oil which exudes from thence infuses the Steel – gas sometimes and not infrequently has an obnoxious smell ...

(The Journal)

1825

Elleray August 24th   At Llangollen your papa† was waylaid by the celebrated 'Ladies' – viz. Lady Eleanor Butler and the Honourable Miss Ponsonby, who having been one or both crossed in love, forswore all dreams of matrimony in the heyday of youth, beauty, and fashion, and selected this charming spot for the repose of their now time-honoured virginity ... We proceeded up the hill, and found everything about them and their habitation odd and extravagant beyond report. Imagine two women – one apparently seventy, the other sixty five – dressed in heavy blue riding habits, enormous shoes, and men's hats, with their petticoats so tucked up, that at the first glance of them, fussing and tottering about their porch in the agony of expectation, we took them for a couple of hazy or crazy old sailors. On nearer inspection they both wear a world of brooches, rings etc., and Lady Eleanor positively *orders* – several stars and crosses, and a red ribbon exactly like a K.C.B. To crown all, they have crop heads, shaggy, rough, bushy, and as white as snow – the one with age alone, the other assisted by a sprinkling of powder ... But who could paint the prints, the dogs, the cats, the miniatures, the cram of cabinets, clocks, glass cases, books, bijouterie, and whirligigs of every shape and hue – the whole house outside and in (for we must see everything to the dressing-closets) *covered* with carved oak – very rich and fine some of it – and the illustrated copies of Sir W's poems, and the joking simpering compliments about Waverley, and the anxiety to know who MacIvor really was, and the

* By Byron.
† Sir Walter Scott.

absolute devouring of the poor Unknown . . . Their tables were piled with newspapers from every corner of the kingdom, and they seemed to have the deaths and marriages of the antipodes at their fingers' ends. Their albums and autographs, from Louis XVIII, and George IV, down to magazine poets and quack doctors, are a museum. I shall never see the spirit of blue-stockingism again in such perfect incarnation. Peveril won't get over their final kissing match for a week. Yet it is too bad to laugh at these good old girls; they have long been the guardian angels of the village, and are worshipped by man, woman, and child about them.

(John Lockhart to his wife)

SEPTEMBER

1784

Saturday September 3rd   Mary dined at Brynkinalt.

September 25th   At night little Bishop attempted to exhibit an air Balloon in our field. Fail'd.

(Eleanor Butler's Pocket Book)

1785

Thursday September 15th   A lovely morning. Rose at six, awakened by the village bells ringing for the return of young Myddelton to Chirk Castle. Sounds of joy ill suited to our present feelings. The Clerk's our Landlord's and Richard Griffith's cows put to graze in the field before our Cottage. After breakfast, My Sally and I Spent Some hours in the Shrubbery with very different Sensations from what we had hoped to have at this time.* This being the day on which We expected those Dear Friends from Whom We parted last Night . . . From 8 'till nine My Beloved and I Walked in the Shrubbery.

* An instance of excessive sensibility at parting from friends.

The Moon in all her Splendour – an Enchanting Scene – Nine till Ten look'd over Warton on Milton.

Saturday September 17th   Spent the Evening in 'Converse Sweet' with the darling of My Heart . . .

Sunday September 18th   Rose at Seven. Soft morning inclined to Rain. Went the Rounds after Breakfast. Our Shoes from Chirk – Vile. Scolded Thomas for growing fat . . . began Warton on Milton – in the Shrubbery 'till Eight. – Violent Rain. Powell returned from Wrexham – No Letters. Eight 'till nine, read *L'Esprit des Croisades* – paper'd our Hair – an uninterrupted delightful day.

Monday September 19th   My Beloved and I Went out at five. Walked to Pen a brin and on the Terrace over the Dee till seven. Saw the Moon rise in 'Clouded Majesty' behind the Trevor Woods Emerge in full lustre and Shine upon the Water – an August Scene . . . Margaret permitted to Spend the Night in the field before our Cottage – Nine 'till Eleven Walking by Moonlight – a Silent happy day.

Tuesday September 20th   A lovely day. In the evening the Barretts accompanied us in a charming walk beside the Dee to visit Mrs Whalley at Tower, two miles from this cottage in the neighbourhood of the Abbey. A small farm House, on an eminence in a most delightful situation. Dinas Bran, Eglwyseg rocks in front, a wooded dingle on one side with a rapid stream gushing through it. At the back of the house beyond the Dee the Berwyn mountains. From the garden a view of the village. This sweet spot is entirely in a state of nature, with every disadvantage of dirt and negligence. The house however is comfortable and clean. A remarkably pretty milk-white goat lying on the green under the Parlour window. Found Mrs Whalley at home with her two sweet boys. Prevailed on her to return with us. Met Mr Whalley on the Bridge. Her innocent Joy at seeing him . . . Miss Leslie came – *un*graciously received.

Wednesday September 21st   Rose before seven. awakened by Barbara Churning – a heavenly morning . . . Powell at work in the New kitchen garden . . . from Seven 'till Nine Walked in the Shrubbery – faint Moon glimmering through the Trees. Twelve flashes of Lightning – Some of them Sublime, a gloomy Night suited to our feelings and the recollection of our Melancholy parting with dear Friends this night Sen'night.

Thursday September 22nd Up at Seven. Dark Morning, all the Mountains enveloped in mist. Thick Rain. a fire in the Library, delightfully comfortable, Breakfasted at half past Eight. From nine 'till one writing. My Beloved drawing Pembroke Castle – from one 'till three read (Warton) to her – after dinner Went hastily round the gardens. Rain'd without interruption the Entire day – from Four 'till Ten reading to my Sally – She drawing – from ten 'till Eleven Sat over the Fire Conversing with My beloved. a Silent, happy Day.

Friday September 23rd Went the rounds, Powell howing Onions planting Endive in drills and Earthing Celery . . . Took a sublime walk on the Banks of the Dee (never saw it so full or so Tremendous) Ascended the mountain, endeavoured to get Birch Bark. Trees too old and too tall. Returned to Penlan and Bache. Almost dark when we came home.

Saturday September 24th . . . a Violent Storm in the Evening – Read Madame de Sevigné. My Love drawing. From seven 'till nine in Sweet Converse with the delight of my heart, over the Fire. Paper'd our Hair . . .

Tuesday September 27th After dinner Walked in the Shrubbery. Powell Scuffing and digging in the Kitchen garden, planted a large Bed of Doucettes for Winter and Spring Sallads . . . from 5 'till 7 read to My beloved – She drawing a map of the World – Stereographic Projection on the Plane of the Horizon, with her Patagonian Compasses.

(The Journal)

Tuesday September 27th . . . We are however return'd with encreased delight* to Our former Amusements which will now be free from interruptions . . . We are now going to eat our dinner – I shall then set about Bess's† Map – and My B will read White's Sermons to me.

(Sarah Ponsonby to Mrs Tighe)

Thursday September 29th Walked to the Birches. While we were

---

* After a visit from Harriet Bowdler.
† Mrs Tighe's daughter.

admiring the fall of waters saw a funeral Procession coming by the Dee side, attended by the Vicar, and all the Principal Farmers of the Parish. A most Picturesque Scene. We followed it to Churchyard of Llantysilio. Went into the Church, heard the Vicar by his snuffling, Lisping, and Vile reading spoil the most awful and Solemn Service. Nothing in the Church which could attract a moment's attention except a Squat, Tawdry, Clumsy monument belonging to the Family of Eyton.

Friday September 30th At Ten we set out from hence. The Roads delightful. Country Charming. Went to Halston ... at five Mrs Barrett, Mr Kynaston, his two daughters and we walked to Porkington. A fine still grey evening ... My Beloved, Mrs Barrett, Mrs Kynaston, little Mrs Jones play'd at whist 'till supper. The girls at work. The men sauntered about the room. Madam Bess and I sat on the sopha and had our own Fun.

(The Journal)

1788

Thursday September 4th Very kind and flattering letter from Lady Uxbridge – a very civil one from us. The Lady Pagets came up – prevented by the Tooth ache from seeing them ...

Saturday September 6th Celestial day. Compliments from Lord Scarborough desiring to see this cottage and shrubbery. Permitted with our compliments. Retired to the State Bedchamber 'till he was come and gone. Observed him from the window. Brown, thin, military-looking man with short hair.

Monday September 8th The Barretts and Miss Davies came ... After dinner the Barretts went away, left Margaret with us. At nine we walked in the shrubbery admiring the Moon and the sweet sound of a Pipe on the Mountain.

Tuesday September 9th After breakfast Margaret took out her work, my beloved her drawing, and I read to them 'till one ... At two compliments from Mr Crewe – he was just arrived – would wait on us either before or after dinner whichever was most agreeable. Silly message – our politeness took place of our inclinations – invited him to dinner – Crewe came – tiresome enough the Lord knows.

Thursday September 11th   Influenza.

Friday September 12th   Met the Vicar, gave him two mushrooms which we found on the Green – I hope they are not poison . . .
After supper adjourned to Margaret's room – Sat there 'till one, then
when all our household was in bed we went with Margaret to the
Kitchen – admired its neatness – opened the window – Contemplated
the Moon then retired.

Saturday September 13th   Parcel from Halston containing a poem,
written during a shooting excursion in Northumberland by Green-
wood with a letter from this gentleman who is travelling Tutor to Mr
Mytton. Neither Letter nor Poem do much honour to his imagination,
his genius or his Modesty . . . At six the Barretts went away and to
our infinite regret took Miss Davies with them. After they were gone
my beloved and I went the home circuit, then retired to the Dressing-
room for the Night, quite pensive and sad for the departure of our
Dear Margaret.

Sunday September 14th   Sent to enquire how our Landlady
was? Something better. All her old neighbours were coming to ask
how she did. Among them a little old woman aged fourscore-and-
eight who was perfect in health and intellects. She has thirty
grandchildren, and eight great grandchildren. She was twenty-
seven when she married and from the Night of her Marriage to that
of her Husband's Death (she said) they lay side by side Forty-seven
years – she had been a widow fifteen years. She holds a farm for
which she pays one hundred pounds a year Rent.

Monday September 15th   The Woman from the Bache came with
the Leeches – Linnaeus denominates them Intestine Worms – Never
Saw any before – Think them very beautiful. She Collects them in a
Lake near the Bulkely Mountain.

Expenses

Sept. 15   Woman Who applyed Leeches to My Temples 2s.6d.

Thursday September 25th   Our Habits from Donnes, by the Holyhead Coach from the George and Blue Boar, Holborne.

Saturday September 27th   Letter from Mr Chambre Brabazon

Ponsonby . . . a letter from a Brother worthy of such a Sister as my Sally.

(The Journal)

Accounts

Sept 27th   By a Bill on London a *Gift* from C.B. Ponsonby £50
Our Half Years Rent due since 1st May £11.7.6

Receipts

TO STEW CUCUMBERS

September the 27th 1788 – Saturday

Pare and Cut them in Slices, put them in a Stew pan with Pepper, Salt, Chopped Parsley, Vinegar – Very little Butter. Stew them in a gentle fire, and when ready to serve thicken them over the fire with a little Cream and the Yolk of an Egg. – Very Good.

TO STEW CUCUMBERS

Sunday September 28th 1788

When Pared Cut them in four. take out the Seeds put them to Soak with Salt, Pepper and Vinegar – leave them for half an hour, then put to them a pint of Good Gravy – Let them Stew on a gentle fire. When done – Add some rich Gravey and Carve them – extremely Good.

OXFORD SAUSAGES

Three pound of a Leg of Veal. Three pound Leg of Pork. One pound Beef Suet: Parsley, Thyme, Sage, Egg to every pound.

1789

Tuesday September 1st   The field before our Cottage a beautiful and busy scene. Binders, gleaners, reapers, the harvest in the midst. Anne Jones and her Son drank tea in the kitchen.

Wednesday September 2nd   Eat plums and Apricots – Went to the White gate.

Thursday September 3rd Discharged Betsy Haynes the kitchen maid for Idleness, dirt, and *Such a Tongue!*

Friday September 4th . . . a day of Such Sweet retirement and So perfectly enjoyed!

Saturday September 5th Carpets and cheese from Kendal, not in the least resembling the pattern we bespoke which was a Modest Blue tinged with Black – these have every fiery tawdrey Colour in Worsted, green and blue – Red and purple and yellow – huge roses and Tulips and Poppies Sprawling about – the Cheese which We particularly ordered might be the best (Berkeley hundred) proves no better than a Common Gloucester. *Mem* Never again to deal with Mr Kendal* for any Article Whatsoever.

Tuesday September 15th Reading. Drawing. Compliments from Lord Belmore on his Road from Corwen. He dined at Lord MtGarretts the other day with Wandesford. All the family at the Castle† well – as if I cared.

Thursday September 24th Walked in the stubble fields near the Mill. The Country heavenly and peopled with happy busy industrious beings – every hand employed about their Harvest. This delicious day is worth a million.

Friday September 25th Three dinner – Mutton and Potatoe Pie – Roast Duck. We retired to the dressing-room – powder'd, changed our Habits and came to the Library. Note from Mrs Parry of The Ship humbly entreating permission for some friends of hers to see the Shrubbery. We sent her word that we were extremely concerned to deny her but for the present it was impossible as we expected company, but to-morrow morning She and her Friends should be welcome to see the cottage and garden.

Wednesday September 30th Message from T. Kavanagh, my pretty nephew just come from France. He came looking prettier than ever. Has had leave of absence for some months, the regiment going to be reformed. He purposes going to Spain. We made him send for his Luggage to the Inn and accept of our State bedchamber. We passed

* This is the same Mr Kendal who was described in the entry for February 17th, 1789, as 'an honest plain Yeoman, a character I revere'!

† Kilkenny Castle, Eleanor's home.

a very agreeable day, talking of all the things in the World – but most particularly poor France.

(The Journal)

1790

Wednesday September 1st   Field under our windows full of Reapers, Binders, Gleaners. Pale sky. Soft tender air.

Sunday September 26th   Mr Edwards of the Hand came. Saw him. Accepted his apology.* A day of sweetly enjoyed Retirement.

1791

Expenses

Sept. 2 Mr Wynne of Mold on the renewal of our Lease £1.1.0.
            Lame handed woman with pound of Mushrooms 6d.
         3 Lion for Salmon 7s.
         5 A Crock for Pickling Walnuts 3d.
            3 Quarts Ale 1s.3d.
         7 Anne Jones 6d. daughter 1s.
            Mason and Labourers opening the beautiful new Vista 3s.
        14 Sundries. *Moses Jones discharged*† 2s.6d.
        15 Thos. Jones for Mary's foot 2s.6d.
            Poor Irish Boy 6d.
        22 Edwards Hand Ostler's Mother 1s.
        24 Thos. Jones giving Mary an Emetick the 24th 3s.6d.
        26 Paid our Rent due the first of May last £11.7.6.
        30 Our precious and never to be forgotten little Sapho's *last* expense 4s.6d.

1793

Expenses

Sept. 1 Moses Jones Weeks Wages 10s.

---

* This signals the end of the grand vendetta with the Hand Inn.
† Discharged yet again.

September 12th   My Viellard has forsaken me, not having so much patience as yourself with a dull Correspondent, and such I confess I have lately been, even to an *unusual* degree, but pray tell him* I hope he has received the Drawings from Lord Fielding, and that he will think it civil to tell me so, and then I shall be greatly over paid.

(Harriet Bowdler to Sarah Ponsonby)

1794

September 6th   I dare say my profligate Viellard is gone off with some new favourite, and I must as usual wait patiently 'till he is pleased to return.

(Harriet Bowdler to Sarah Ponsonby)

September 18th   I am still more gratified by her† approbation of *my marriage*,‡ for her judgement has more weight with me than a whole Theatre of others. Indeed as far as I have had an opportunity of knowing the Opinion of the world, I find that everybody thinks as she does on the subject, and I receive the kindest and most flattering congratulations from all quarters.

(Harriet Bowdler to Sarah Ponsonby)

1795

Barmouth September 7th   I resume my pen, to speak to you of the enchanting unique, in conduct and situation, of which you have heard so much, though as yet, without distinct description. You will guess that I mean the celebrated ladies of Llangollen Vale, their mansion, and their bowers . . . It consists of four small apartments, the exquisite cleanliness of the kitchen, its utensils, and its auxiliary offices, vieing with the finished elegance of the gay, the lightsome little dining-room, as that contrasts the gloomy, yet superior grace of the library, into which it opens. This room is fitted up in the Gothic style, the door and large sash windows of that form, and the latter of painted glass, 'shedding the dim religious light'. Candles are seldom admitted into this apartment.

* Eleanor!
† Miss Shipley's.
‡ Presumably to Eleanor – all part of an elaborate flirtation.

The ingenious friends have invented a kind of prismatic lantern which occupies the whole elliptic arch of the Gothic door. This lantern is of cut glass, variously coloured, enclosing two lamps with their reflectors. The light it imparts resembles that of a volcano – sanguine and solemn. It is assisted by two glow-worm lamps that, in little marble reservoirs, stand on the opposite chimney-piece, and these supply the here always chastised day-light, when the dusk of evening sables, or when night wholly involves the thrice-lovely solitude.

A large Eolian harp is fixed in one of the windows, and, when the weather permits them to be opened, it breathes its deep tones to the gale, swelling and softening as that rises and falls . . .

This saloon of the Minervas contains the finest editions, superbly bound, of the best authors, in prose and verse, which the English, Italian and French languages boast, contained in neat wire cases. Over them the portraits, in miniature, and some in larger ovals, of the favoured friends of these celebrated votaries to that sentiment . . .

The kitchen garden is neatness itself. Neither there, nor in the whole precincts, can a single weed be discovered. The fruit-trees are of the rarest and finest sort, and luxuriant in their produce, the garden house and its implements, arranged in the exactest order.

Nor is the dairy-house, for one cow, the least curiously elegant object of the magic domain. A short steep declivity shadowed over

with tall shrubs, conducts us to the cool and clean repository. The white and shining utensils that contain the milk, and cream, and butter, are pure 'as snows thrice bolted in the northern blast'. In the midst, a little machine, answering the purpose of a churn, enables the ladies to manufacture half a pound of butter for their own breakfast, with an apparatus which finishes the whole process without manual operation.

The wavy and shaded gravel-walk which encircles this Elysium, is enriched with curious shrubs and flowers. It is nothing in extent and everything in grace and beauty, and in variety of foliage, its gravel smooth as marble. In one part of it we turn upon a small knoll, which overhangs a deep hollow glen. In its tangled bottom, a frothing brook leaps and clamours over the rough stones in its channel. A large spreading beech canopies the knoll and a semi-circular seat, beneath its boughs, admits four people. A board, nailed to the elm [*sic*] has this inscription

O cara Selva! e Fiumicello amato!

. . . You will expect that I say something of the enchantresses themselves, beneath whose plastic wand these peculiar graces arose. Lady Eleanor is of middle height, and somewhat beyond the *enbonpoint* as to plumpness; her face round and fair with the glow of luxuriant health. She has not fine features, but they are agreeable; – enthusiasm in her eye, hilarity and benevolence in her smile. Exhaustless in her fund of historic and traditionary knowledge, and of every thing passing in the present eventful period. She has uncommon strength and fidelity of memory; and her taste for works of imagination, particularly for poetry is very awakened, and she expresses all she feels with an ingenuous ardour, at which the cold-spirited beings stare . . . Miss Ponsonby, somewhat taller than her friend, is neither slender nor otherwise, but very graceful. Easy, elegant, yet pensive, is her address and manner:

'Her voice, like lovers watch'd is kind and low.'

A face rather long than round, a complexion clear, but without bloom, with a countenance which from its soft melancholy, has peculiar interest. If her features are not beautiful, they are very sweet and feminine. Though the pensive spirit which permits not her lovely dimples to give mirth to her smile, they increase its sweetness, and consequently, her power of engaging the affections. We see, through their veil of shading reserve, that all the talents and accomplishments which enrich the mind of Lady Eleanor, exist, with equal powers, in this her charming friend . . .

> (Anna Seward to The Rev. Henry White, of Lichfield)

1796

Expenses

Sept. 11 Price of Our New Cow £11.5.0.
        to John Roberts for his trouble in bringing it to us 5s.
    12 Simon's Son rolling the lawn 3d.
        paid at different times for medecines for the sick Cow 6s.
        The joiner's Mother and other poor people in the last 4 weeks 16s.
    17 Paid Mr Edwards of Pengwern for two loads of Muck 15s.
        Samuel the Cooper in pt. payment for Hurdles £3.3.0.
    25 Price the Nailer with a Salmon from Mrs Ormsby 1s.

September 26th Were we, my dear friend, to mortgage Our Pensions at present, I do not believe any person would be absurd enough to advance half a Crown in the pound upon that Security – And it would be an act of Criminal extravagance in us to do so for the very trifling Sum that would retrieve us from all Our oppressive embarassments – for if the Nation does not become *Bankrupt* from Invasion or Insurrection – they will in time be paid . . . It would then be absurd to Sacrifice a future £200 for a present £50, if we could so obtain it, though that £50 would certainly restore the sleep of which our pillows have so long been deprived . . . I think being in debt, very often makes people look thin and feel apt to take cold . . .

> (Sarah Ponsonby to Mrs Tighe)

Expenses

Sept. 28 Poor people in Our Walk with Mrs Ogilvie and Miss Dundas 1s.6d.

1797

Expenses

Sept. 7 Simon and John Roberts Boy corn for the new Cow *Glory*
2s.

      9 Minstrel £1.3s.

   16 John Roberts Butcher for the new Cow Glory £12.9.6.
Mr Lloyd of Trevor's Man with Partridge 1s.

1798

Expenses

Sept. 28 My poor little Phillis's Distress. Dear HB gave a like sum
10s.6d.

   29 Expenses in our disastrous Journey this Evening with
Dear HB 3s.6d.

1799

Expenses

Sept. 2 David the Miller assisting Simon to repair the Cufflymen
bank 2s.

      3 Carriage of Port Wine from Mrs Worrall 1s.6d.

      4 A Salmon weighing ten pounds at 6d.

      7 Simon's Wife to Chirk Castle and their Daughter for a
Hare and Mushrooms 3s.

   20 Messenger from Lord Dungannon with Venison and
Partridge 2s.

   28 For the Vilest of all Michaelmas Geese 4s.6d.

Receipts

TO STEW VENISON

Cut in pieces, put it in a Stewpan with a little bit of Butter, a faggot
and a Bay leaf – One Onion and two or three Glasses of red Wine,
some Broth and a little Flour – Add Pepper and Salt – Stew and
serve it.

HARE À LA SUISSE

Cut it in pieces, put it to Stew in a Toss pan with some Broth – Salt
– Pepper – a Small Sprig of Thyme, a Bay leaf, and a Glass of Brandy.
Let it Stew together – then take the inside of the Hare, mix it with
Flour – the size of a Nut of Butter – and some red Wine – thicken
this Sauce over the Fire. then pour it over the Hare and serve it.

APPLES WITH CREAM

Peel and take out the Cores without breaking the Apples. Half stew
them with Sugar and lay them neatly in a dish – Make a Cream with
Six Yolks of Eggs a little Flour – Orange Flower Water, dryed Citron
cut small, Some Cream and Sugar – Let it thicken a little over the fire
– put it over Your Apples, Garnish it with powder Sugar – Bake it in
an Oven to give it a fine Colour and serve it hot.

1800

Expenses

Sept. 3   Our Half Years House, Window, New House, Servant and
Dog Tax in all £3.8.0.

September 24th   Yet I think if You had received My melancholy
history of Terrour and taxation we have been Martyrs to – You would
not have passed it unnoticed by . . .

(Sarah Ponsonby to Mrs Tighe)

1807

Wednesday September 16th   David the Miller putting up the fence
in Edward Evans' copse to defend us from the new neighbours
whoever they are . . . Evening. Pales and posts finished to secure us
from the lord only knows who.

Sunday September 20th   All went to Church. Letter from Mrs
Williams Wynn. All hurry and bustle. Carriage sent for to the Hand.
Miss Shipley's maid set off in it for Wynnstay. At eleven Miss
Shipley's maid returned, having been obliged to walk three miles
owing to the inebriety of the Postillion.

177

Thursday September 24th Clouds and rain and tempest. At eleven my Better half and I in the Hand chaise – Patrick, driver – went to Chirk Castle . . . Staid an hour. Then set off for Marchwiel where we arrived at three after losing our way and enquiring of everybody the right road. Everyone speaking English and civil. Company besides our dear Miss Shipley who was the great magnet of attraction, was Sir Foster, Lady Cunliffe, Miss Hayman, Mr Bedford. Miss Hayman played divinely on the piano. Full moon. Set out by the light of it. Home at one. In our absence three nameless ladies to see the place, two foreign gentlemen, and Humphries of Shrewsbury forsooth!

(The Journal)

1819

September [*undated*] . . . a Luncheon of Grouse Sandwich – Pine apple – Peaches and Apricots. Ruabon Vicarage – refreshments under the Trees – So Convenient – The Seats under the clumps of Oak – So happily disposed – the Tent for Dinner so well ordered – *So* plentiful – Such a profusion of fruit – the Weather so delicious – Every person so well pleased . . . an Affrican from the Kingdom of Morocco came to sell spices – made him Sing . . .

(The Journal)

1820

Oswestry September 4th The dear inseparable inimitables Lady Butler and Miss Ponsonby were in the boxes here on Friday. They came twelve miles from Llangollen, and returned, as they never sleep from home. Oh, such curiosities! I was nearly convulsed. I could scarcely get on for the first ten minutes after my eye caught them. Though I had never seen them, I instantly knew them. As they are seated, there is not one point to distinguish them from men: the dressing and powdering of the hair, their well-starched neckcloths; the upper part of their habits, which they always wear, even at a dinner-party made precisely like men's coats; and regular black beaver men's hats. They looked exactly like two respectable superannuated old clergymen. I was highly flattered, as they never were in the theatre before . . . I have to-day received an invitation to call if I have time as I pass, at Llangollen, to receive in due form from the dear old gentlemen called Lady Butler and Miss Ponsonby, their thanks for the entertainment I afforded them at the theatre.

(Charles Mathews, the actor, to Mrs Mathews)

1821

Sunday September 9th   The King's Groom, attending His Majesty's Horses, permitted to see our Grounds.

(The Journal)

1823

September 23rd   May I beg You my Dear Madam to assure your friend with my best Compliments and a thousand thanks – that I am quite as Grateful for her offer of a Lock of Bonaparte's Hair – as if my Allegiance to the Bourbon family did not prevent the possibility of My availing Myself of it . . .

(Lady Eleanor Butler to an unknown correspondent)

1824

Rydal Mount Saturday 18th September   My letters have been from Dora, who gives a most lively account of what she has seen, especially of the ladies of Llangothlin (I cannot spell these Welsh names), with whom they spent an evening; and were well pleased with *them* and their entertainment.

(Dorothy Wordsworth to Lady Beaumont)

Hindwell, Radnor, September 20th   . . . Called upon the celebrated recluses, who hoped that you and Lady B had not forgotten them; they certainly had not forgotten you, and they begged us to say that they retained a lively remembrance of you both. We drank tea and passed a couple of hours with them in the evening, having visited the aqueduct over the Dee and Chirk Castle in the afternoon. Lady E has not been well, and has suffered much in her eyes, but she is surprisingly lively for her years. Miss P. is apparently in unimperilled health. Next day I sent them the following sonnet from Ruthin, which was conceived, and in a great measure composed, in their Grounds –

Glyn Cafaillgaroch, in the Cambrian tongue,
In ours the Vale of Friendship, let this spot
Be nam'd where faithful to a low roof'd Cot
On Deva's banks, ye have abode so long,
Sisters in love, a love allowed to climb
Ev'n on this earth, above the reach of time.

(William Wordsworth to Sir George Beaumont)

OCTOBER

1784

Monday October 4th Cold Wett day. Staid in our Library the Entire day. reading – writing, and sharing a delicious day.

Tuesday October 5th You will be surprized to hear that We have infringed our resolution, of never passing a night from our Cottage – And were tempted by the Kind Solicitations of the Bridgeman family to pass two days Since I wrote last, at Weston. Our Reception and the Society there, was such, as will make us ever remember that visit with pleasure though it has if possible Added new Charms to our Retirement.

(Sarah Ponsonby to Mrs Tighe)

Monday October 11th Fine grey day. Load of dung for the mushroom bed.

Monday October 18th Lovely day. Finished the Copings round the garden walls.

Thursday October 28th I kept my bed all day with an headache. My Sweet Love all kindness as usual.

(Eleanor Butler's Pocket Book)

1785

Saturday October 1st Charming Comfortable fire in our Library. Sat over it with a Satisfaction and delight 'unknown to Vulgar minds' – read and wrote 'till Ten – a happy day.

Tuesday October 4th Rose at Seven – a Brilliant Morning – Present from the Hand of a Cock and some oysters . . . Went the Rounds. Scolded Powell. made him clean the Kitchen garden. Fine grey day. Mr Lloyde's Hounds hunting opposite our garden in the Pengwern wood and on the mountain above Pen-y-Coed. Charming night. At eight Mr Lloydde's Huntsman came with a Hare from his master, probably the same poor animal who made so free with, and was so welcome to, our Cabbage last winter . . . I should stile this an happy day but for the perpetual interruptions.

Wednesday October 5th At two a Servant came from Wynnstay announcing Sir Watkin and Lady Williams Wynne. They arrived soon after accompanied by Mr and Mrs Sheridan.* They staid two hours. Lady Wynne as agreeable and well bred this time as she was deficient last summer. *Mem I* was disappointed in Mrs Sheridan's beauty.

Friday October 7th At nine sent for the little doctor for poor Bess – the Habits We have so long expected arrived by the Stage Coach – that detestable Donne instead of the dark pitch Colour Which We so expressly ordered – he sent a Vulgar ordinary Snuff Colour like a Farmer's Coat – and in place of the plain Simple Buttons Which We Chose – has sent a paltry, devlish, Tawdry three colour'd thing like a Fairing – Just look'd at them obsessed with fury, the total Mistake of our orders – pack'd them up. and return'd them to him by the Same Coach in which they came – a perfect Hurricane – thick mizzling rain. Reading Rousseau to my Sally. She drawing her map upon Vellum made a great mistake in one of the tropics which spoil'd her morning's Work . . . Incessant rain the entire evening.

---

* The playwright and his wife.

Shut the shutters, made a good fire, lighted the Candles . . . A day of strict retirement, sentiment, and delight.

Saturday October 8th – at eight o'clock our poor little Sweet Bess died. Without any violent anguish – after lingering Since Tuesday last (Unable from extreme Weakness to Whelp!). We buried her Between her dear Mother (Flirt) and her Brother (Rover) under the Cypress Tree by the Parlour Window . . . Spent the Evening in Tears and regret for our dear faithfull little Bess.

Sunday October 9th . . . at Six I awoke with a Violent head ache – kept my bed all day. How can I sufficiently acknowledge the kindness and Tenderness of My Beloved Sally Who never for one Moment left me, but Sat reading and drawing Till Ten o'clock at night.

Monday October 10th Powell mowing the Lawn . . . This day our Landlord, Richard Griffiths and the Clerk began to plough the land before the Cottage for Wheat . . .

Wednesday October 12th Went the Rounds. Mild damp evening. Staid in the Shrubbery 'till it became quite dark. an excellent fire in the Library – candles lighted and an appearance of Content and chearfulness never to be found but in a Cottage – Margaret extremely Indelicate . . . the Cufflummin Roaring Loud . . .

Thursday October 13th Rose at Eight – a Violent Storm at night – Showery, Cloudy Morning. Powell mowing the Lawn the third time as he fail'd in his former attempts . . . the complexion of the Rocks a dark purple – a certain indication of bad Weather . . . returned White's Sermons to Mrs Mytton – *Mem* never again to keep a borrowed Book so long a time.

Saturday October 15th Mr Whalley came – staid 'till Two. Melancholy – Languid and interesting – gave him a Melon and a Pencil . . . Walked for two hours above the Cufflummin – the Sweetest pensive Moon light illuminating this most Enchanting Vale – No Sounds but the Rush of the Brooks and the hooting of Two Owls. the ancient inhabitants of Dinas Bran and Pengwern Wood – Mr Lloydde of Trevor Sent us a large Basket of Walnuts . . . paper'd our Hair – an Idle day.

Monday October 17th   Four quires of Writing paper from Wood of Salop. ill cut. Wrote to Scold him for it . . . Spent the Morning in the Shrubbery. Powell Clipping and Edging the Lawn and Verges . . . My Love and I spent from Five 'till Seven in the shrubbery and in the Field endeavouring to talk and walk away our little Sorrows. Sent the woman of Pen-y-coed to Ruabon for our Winter provision of groceries. At seven walked to the Hand to see Mrs Myddelton.

Tuesday October 18th   At nine Mr R. Myddelton came and break-fasted here. The country divinely beautiful. Mr Lloydde's Hounds hunting in the fields above Dinas Bran, and among the Ruins of the Castle – a charming Lively Scene . . . At six o'clock Col. and Mrs Myddelton, Mr Mrs and Miss Carter came . . . Mr Carter brought his great dog Bob from whom Tatters had a miraculous escape. Our poor little people obliged to be locked up from him. *Mem* the only dog I ever hated or wished out of the world. At nine o'clock we all walked to the Hand . . . after Supper Miss Carter sang. Col. Myd-delton Smoked and We ran off Sick to death.

Thursday October 20th   Brewed again – all our Beer proving Sour owing to the dishonesty or negligence of the Vestal whom for her malpractices we discarded last August. Went the Home Circuit – Powell scuffling the Shrubbery . . . Went to the Garden got some Endive. Made Mary Stew it with Cream for our Dinner. We thought it Very good.

Friday October 21st   Bought Herrings and Oysters. Loud and violent altercation between Mary and the Fisherman. Mary Trium-phant.

Sunday October 25th   My Beloved and I went to Tower to see Mrs Whalley. Soft. Mild Evening. drank Tea with them. at eight Thomas came for us with a Lanthorn. the night Very dark. the Dee roaring, fearfully Loud. When Shall We be quite Alone?

Tuesday October 25th   Violent Squalls of Wind at times a perfect Hurricane – inexpressibly Comfortable in the Library – from one 'till Three reading Rousseau to the Joy of my life. She drawing – Lady Dungannon Sent us a fat duck and some Saffron cakes by Mrs Pryce – Edward Evans brought us a present of yellow Turnips.

Friday October 28th   . . . a violent Storm all day from Six in the afternoon 'till Eleven – a fearful Tempest Blustering and Bellowing among the Mountains and Sweeping with the utmost violence Through the Valley – Torrents of Rain – wrote to Lady Clifden and Mrs Lowther – at nine paper'd our Hair – a day of Peace and Quiet.

Saturday October 29th   Rose before Seven – a perfect image of Winter – Cold Wind, dark Sky. heavy Showers of Hail. Sleet and Snow. an Excellent Fire in the Library When we Came down (which was before Eight). Every thing in neatness, Comfortable and Cheerful . . . Powell Cleaning the Shrubbery repairing the Walks cut by last nights Rain. From nine 'till two writing without ceasing . . . At two O'clock Mr Whalley and his eldest son came. Staid half an hour. Let them go away in a heavy shower. La vie est trop courte pour se gêner.*

Sunday October 30th   The Barretts came before Ten . . . Madam Bess astonished me with relating a conversation which pass'd in private between me and Mrs Kynaston the day we dined at Halston relative to the Kynaston's of Grosvenor Place. *Mem* Our sage grandmother's advice as to 'Think Twice before We Speak Once' – A maxim I shall practice whenever I am in Company with Mrs M† of H‡ an honour I shall never be ambitious of.

Monday October 31st   My Beloved wrote a Long Letter to the Barretts vindicating Mrs Kynaston and me from Mrs M's Tattling aspersion of our having laugh'd at their kinsfolks . . . At seven we walked before our door and in the shrubbery to see the Bonfires, which in Commemoration of a Victory gained over the English are annually lighted up on this night upon every Eminence in North Wales. From the Lawn on which We Stood saw nineteen Fires around us. One on the Eglwyseg, Pen-y-coed, Pengwern, Llantysilio, the Hill of the Empty Well, one large fire in the centre of Dinas Bran, three on the Berwyn, an immense one on the summit of Moel Mawr.

(The Journal)

1788

Friday October 3rd   Sunshine. Sweet concert of Birds. A person

---

* Life's too short to bother.
† Mytton.
‡ Halston.

in this village had lost some yarn last Wednesday. Yesterday he went to the Conjurer who lives in the Parish of Ruabon to discover who stole this yarn. The people of this valley attribute the violent storm which arose yesterday to the incantations the Conjurer made use of to raise the Infernal Prince.

Saturday October 4th · That little Dirty village quack sent in his Bill – Never paid money with more reluctance.

Expenses

Oct. 4 An Imposing Bill of the little Doctor £2.2.6.

Monday October 6th Reading. Writing. Received a note directed to the Ladies at the Hall House. 'The Comedians in Llangollen present their most respectful Duty to the Ladies at the Hall House, humbly beg leave to Sollicit the Honour of their encouragement for one night which they will ever bear in the Most Grateful remembrance.' There was a play Bill enclosed. 'By a Company of Comedians. At the Theatre in Llangollen will be a concert of vocal and instrumental Music. Between the Several parts of the Concert will be presented gratis a Comedy called "The Provoked Husband or Journey to London". The Characters to the best Advantage. Singing, and other entertainments, between the Acts, to which will be added a Farce called "The Devil to Pay".'

Tuesday October 7th Walked round the field before our Cottage. Spoke to the Joiner whom we met directing an old man comfortably drest, well mounted, with good stuffed saddle bags, who was going to Llansantffraid Glyn Ceirog . . . Blue mists ascending from the River and every Brook and rivulet freezing.

Thursday October 9th Mr Parry of the Ship sent in his bill previous to that most tiresome Chester Fair. Wrote an Excuse having paid away all the little money we had. Gloom and wind. The Habits which we returned to Donnes he sent by this days Coach, but altered in such a manner that we have returned them again, with their Petticoats.

Friday October 10th Thin blue transparent smoke curling and spiring up the mountain side through the Trees from the Village. Writing. The Joiner came to fasten the back board of the book case by Lady Anne Wesley's Picture . . . Artichokes coming up for the winter. Evans of Oswestry's man came previous to this most hateful Chester Fair. We had nothing to give him. Lord help us . . . Reading – working. My Beloved and I walked to the white gate – delicious calm warm dark evening. Met a little Boy coming down the field with a Basket of Potatoes on his head. We asked him his name. 'Peter Jones, son to Thomas the Lime Burner.' Where do you get these Potatoes? On the Bank, beyond yonder wood, they are my Father's. Shall we take one or two? Yes and welcome – I am very much obliged to you. For what, my good Boy? It is we who should thank you for your generosity. Indeed you are kindly welcome to the whole Basket. Will you come to our House and we will give you Something? No indeed I will not take anything, but you are welcome to the Basket and I am greatly obliged to you. We made him come with us, took 3 Potatoes and gave him a huge piece of Bread and Butter. We shall always reflect with pleasure on this instance of the kindness and generosity of this poor child.

Monday October 13th   Letter from Lady Frances Douglas dated Petersham September 24th introducing the Dowager Mrs Crewe and her Daughter . . . We instantly dresst – frizzled and powdered – My head splitting all the while – then walked down the Lane . . . we met Mrs Crewe, Miss Crewe, Miss Needham coming up. We let them in at the lower door, brought them into the House . . . Sat there two hours in the most delightful conversation. Mrs Crewe perfectly amusing. Mrs Hunt's description, 'Mrs Crewe at 79 years of age has all the vivacity of 35, an excellent understanding and a polished one, with the additional blessing of good Health and Strength to a wonderful degree'. It pains us beyond expression that we did not invite them to dinner and I shall always detest the Influenza for seizing me at this time . . . The minute they were gone I returned to bed – took an emetic which gave me some relief. My Sweet Love never quitted me for a single moment but read to me 'till I fell asleep.

Wednesday October 15th   Beautiful day – azure sky – Lilac and silver rocks – russet green and scarlet and gold valley.

Friday October 17th   Half-past three – our Old Chimney Sweeper with the little Prince of the Isles of Ebony was perceived coming down the field which occasioned a general joy throughout the whole

Household. Every hand was instantly employed in removing the Pictures, globes, Tables, China from the Library preparatory to this very necessary operation. Spoke to the Chimney Sweeper, an intelligent being – Lives in the Town of Corwen when he is at home, which is seldom – his time being principally employed in going round North Wales with his boys.

Saturday October 18th   My beloved and I visited our little Workman. A Consultation with the joiner and the large faced Carpenter. Mr Lloydde of Trevor's hounds on the summit of Dinas Bran in full cry. Sir Watkin Williams Wynn's game keeper rode through the field with Pointers, Spaniels, Terriers and water dogs following him.

Monday October 20th   That great worthless old Tyrant the Turkey Cock killed our beautiful Jersey spangled Cock who was the most perfect fowl for shape, size and plumage I ever beheld. A silver white with golden feathers.

Expenses

Oct. 20 Making 2 of our New Shifts 2s. Lost in a light Guinea* the 18th 10d. Do. the 20th 10d.

21 John Hughes Hedging the farm Yard 1s.2d. Do. repairing the Breeches made by Peggeen in Mrs Parke's Hedge, and cleaning the gutter 1s.

Wednesday October 22nd   Beauteous day. Hum of bees and Insects – sweet wild notes of birds – bleating of sheep – cackling of geese –

* Possibly a clipped coin. At all events, not up to weight.

songs and whistlings of farmers at their Plough – the only sounds to be heard in this lovely spot. Writing. Drawing. Another visit to the garden.

Thursday October 23rd   Letter from Hampton Court the 19th. On Wednesday the 15th poor Lady D* was taken up by four Bailliffs and carried to a Spunging House† and there remained some time 'till Lord Mornington and Lord Fairford released her. Poor Woman may the Almighty give her Strength and resignation to support her trouble in this advanced period of her life . . . My Beloved and I went the Home Circuit – very dark – inclined to mizzle. Carpenter at work – Mountain Peach nailed . . . The fig tree nailed . . . Edward Edwards the carpenter and his man hammering the boards. The joiner and his boy pitching the Posts. William Jones sinking holes for them.

Friday October 24th   The Thatcher came – a snuffy sauntering lazy creature. I am persuaded he is a vile workman. Double Mountain Peach nailed. Sent William Jones and the sauntering Thatcher to the Mountain for hazel rods to bind the Thatch.

Saturday October 25th   Think the Thatcher horrible. Told him so. Fought him . . . The large faced Carpenter made a frame for the pendant sides of the Shed. The little workman binds them with hazel – The Thatcher, who has nothing to recommend him as a workman but Simplicity, good humour and a good Complexion, went on clumsily with his job . . . A watchmaker from Wrexham (who I hope deals in the marvellous) related several sad disasters in the kitchen, which, he said, happened in the course of last week at Wrexham. In particular of a young Man who had been bit by a Mad Dog and in consequence of that bite seized with so dreadful a Hydrophobie that his friends gave him a Potion.‡ He was buried this day.

Monday October 27th   Made a plantation by the shed of Lilaks, Laburnums, Seringas, White Broom, Weeping Willow, Apple Trees, poplar . . . Staid with our Workmen 'till it was quite dark. The shed thatched – The Thatcher paid . . .

* Dungannon.
† A place of house arrest for debtors.
‡ Presumably to dispatch him.

Expenses

Oct. 27   Thatcher covering the Shed in the Farm Yd. 2 and a half
days 3s.3d.

Wednesday October 29th   The Barretts and Miss Davies came at
Twelve – the Barretts went away at Four, being under apprehension
if they staid later of meeting the Robber who infests the Wrexham
Road. When they were gone my beloved and I accompanied
Margaret* in the Home circuit – Sweet evening – Sat by the fire 'till
ten.

(The Journal)

Expenses

Oct.   Fires on the Hills 1s.

1789

Wednesday October 7th   Rose at four. Rain and wind. Set off in the
Lyon Chaise and four. The country on either side to Ellesmere wet,
rushy, spongy . . . Arrived at Ellesmere at eight. Stopped at the Oak
formerly kept by Rowlands now by a Widow Price. The house full
of people – tenants to the Duke of Bridgewater – paying their rent
to his Steward Mr Gilber. A Very pretty little boy by way of Waiter.
Sent for Gloves. A great fat Pudding boy brought some. Not fit to
wear. Sent to another shop. A dark sharp thin young man, crooked
and not of the English breed, brought some. Got a pair. When the
horses had baited† an hour set off from Ellesmere to Wem. The roads
bad, the country in many parts beautiful. Oteley Park – The different
meres fringed with venerable Oak – Little Hamlets with gardens and
Trees about them – Streams and Pools of water every hundred yards
– the harvest all brought home. In one of the Villages a new built
octagon Brick church – Not calculated I should imagine to inspire
devotion . . . From Wem to the village of Weston . . . Found Miss
Hill at her Harpsichord – Mrs Hill came in soon after – Expressed
great joy at seeing us. In the course of the conversation it appeared
she had not received our Letter. She got breakfast immediately.

* Miss Davies, not the cow!
† Rested and fed.

Expenses

Oct. 7 Turnpikes to and from Hawkestone 5s.1d. Edward's
Breakfast and Supper 2s.9d. Driver 6s. Gloves
3s.6d. Our Supper 3s. Waiter 1s.6d. Maid 6d.

Friday October 9th Set off in the Lyon Chaise. Met the post man
near the village. From Whittington we turned into Babbinswood.
The road excellent. Country on either side Wet and misty but
beautifully planted – clumps of fine oak and beech. We sat in the
chaise 'till the horses were baited. Many women rode by to the Salop
market, all well mounted, dressed in kidney coats, oilskin caps over
their hats – Bags under their saddles with geese on either side
peeping out ... Mountford Bridge terrific* – wants repairing.
Arrived at Underdale – Found that excellent Bell Pigott in the
parlour – rejoiced to see her. Then Miss Honor, Miss Anne, and
Miss Mary Pigott made their appearance ...

Tuesday October 13th An old woman came to enquire how we
were – Her name is Purcel. She lives at Borris† and is going to
London to see her son and grandson who are established there and
sent for her. She walks the entire way. Tho' old she is strong, stout
and hale.

Wednesday October 14th A box from Donnes with our cloaks
arrived a week too late. I regret it as they are admirably made – Are
of a deep and modest blue.

Tuesday October 20th The Barretts arrived at eleven and ordered
their horses and carriages to the Hand. We had presence of mind
sufficient to remember we were in our own house, therefore
determined that neither by look or word our Resentment at this
offence should transpire‡ ... Worked at the Tapestry chair covers.
Dined at three. At 5 the Barretts went away. My beloved and I talked
the matter over.

Wednesday October 28th Sweet and delicate day. We went again
to our bank – planted all with cowslips – primroses – violets – lily of
the Valley.

(The Journal)

* She means 'terrifying'.
† Eleanor's sister's home in Ireland.
‡ The Ladies had a vendetta with the Hand at this time.

1790

Friday October 1st   Saw a pretty young woman habited in close mourning coming towards us. Mrs Rogers, the Friend and Ally of Mrs Goddard, whom we had expected some days and hoped to have for our guest – but she travelled in the Stage Coach and therefore could not stay above three minutes to our great regret . . . We conducted her down the Lane where two hideous men, her companions in the Stage Coach, were waiting for her. One of them a formal wretch, like one of the Holy Brotherhood of the Inquisition, the other flat faced and vulgar. Returned to the Library – began to write . . . Brewed Four Swipes the second time – of J. Williams's Malt.

Monday October 4th   Mr Edwards of the Hand brought a note from Mr Wilberforce* written in the most Polite and flattering terms. We shall carefully preserve it, proud of this distinction from a character we so highly respect.

Thursday October 7th   How can I express the tenderness and anxiety of this Most Angelic of Friends. She never quitted me for a single instant 'till the pain was abated – She sat there and sketched beside me all the time of a deep and heavy sleep which I continued in 'till two o'clock when I awoke. My head ache so unsupportable that I thought I could not sustain it – her Agony and distress rouzed me. I took another Emetic which effectually removed all the pain and distress . . .

Monday October 11th   A letter without a signature, dated Shrewsbury the 9th – written in the handsomest terms and enclosing the most flattering Poem – evidently written from the heart.

Wednesday October 13th   It is precisely a year this day† since we received Mrs Barrett here. We have never had reason for a single instant's regret since we broke off with those false and perfidious Friends.‡ Au contraire – au contraire.

* William Wilberforce (1759–1833), the slavery abolitionist.
† In fact it was October 20th, 1789, when the Barretts visited.
‡ The poor Barretts were never really forgiven for innocently sending their horses to the Hand Inn.

Monday October 25th Arranging our Papers. Burning some. Agreeably surprised by the arrival of Lord Templetown who was speedily followed by his charming mother and sister. As we have forgiven the Hand Inn she ordered her Horses to be sent there.

Tuesday October 26th Mr Lloydde of Aston came for an hour. Showed us the Beautiful Prize sent by the Prince of Wales as a prize to be shot for by the Ladies of the Royal British Bowmen. Won by Lady Cunliffe.

Saturday October 30th Dark oppressive morning – No letters. The Wynnstay Wagon drawn by six Oxen which are going to Llantysilio for Timber, brought us from Mr Evans six beautiful Beech – one fine Laurel and a Bay Tree.

Sunday October 31st Note from a gentleman and two ladies attracted by the fame and Beauty of our cottage – desired permission to see it. Our Compliments – never permitted this Cottage to be seen by persons whose names we were unacquainted with. They very politely sent up theirs. General and Mrs Nelson and Miss Watson . . . Dinner. A Roasted Goose. Mutton and Turnips. Clear – Transparent crisp evening – Smoke issuing from the interstices of all the Vale preparatory to the fires on the Summits. Reading. When the fires were kindled my beloved and I walked to Pengwern to behold them. A glorious sight indeed – a sight the Gods might have stooped from Olympus to behold. The summit of every eminence was crowned with a large Bonfire around which crowds of people were Shouting and Dancing – Immense Volumes of smoke ascending and Distant Shouts evinced that many fires were kindled in sequestered regions. The night was pensive and still – Stars innumerable – Returned to our field – From the white gate we counted Eleven fires. Went to the shrubbery – the scene there glorious beyond description. From the Lane we counted above twenty fires, one in the ruins of Dinas Bran, and sixteen on the various swells of the eminence on which it is Erected. An immense one at the top of our quarry, the light and blaze of which gleamed thro' our Trees illuminated the entire shrubbery.

(The Journal)

1791

Expenses

Oct.   8   Beef for a wonder at 2 and a half pence the 1lb. 2s.8 and a
          half pence.
      10   Thomas Jones for solution of Opium 1s. A Coal Box 5s.3d.
      19   Foolish Beggar 1s.
      21   Workmen 4 days raising Potatoes 4s.8d.
      22   Years rent for 1791 to Mr Myddelton £1.
          Trevor Gardener with present of Wallnuts 3s.
      25   Carrier with Trees from Wynnstay 6s.
      26   Evan Williams for Permission to plant against the Wall 1s.
          Moses for Turning his Coat 6d.
          Baillis for repairing Kitchen fire Place 1s.

1793

October 25th . . . nothing could induce us ever to revisit Ireland,
except the Dowager Lady Ormonde, were to make it a point of duty
with My Better half to go for her last Blessing. which however, we
tremble but to think of . . . if the other Lady Ormonde* has inclination, She certainly has no right to expect We should go on her
account – for though She certainly has all the good qualities you
ascribe to her . . . she denies herself the pleasure of adding the Title
of Friend to that of Sister-in-law, by seeming to forget in her own
immense Opulence (and prosperous conditions) – Not the *Compar-
ative* but the *actual* trifle, which would gratify the utmost ambition
– of the *sole* Inheritrix of all the Ormonde Virtues† – She knows that
one hundred pounds would remove any present and future *pecuniary*
thorn from our Pillows – that one Syllable from her, would instantly
procure it, for my B has been besought to utter that Syllable in
vain . . . Alas! for the poor Queen of France! don't you think the end
of the world approaches?

(Sarah Ponsonby to Mrs Tighe)

* Eleanor's sister-in-law.
† Eleanor!

Receipts

A LAMB'S HEAD (an excellent Receipt)

When the Head is cut in two take the Black from the eyes, tongue and Brains – leave the Head to soak in Water 5 or 6 hours. Boil the Tongue Heart and lights. Skin the Tongue, and chop it with the Heart and lights – put them in a Stewpan with an ounce of fresh Butter – some Pepper and Salt – put them on the fire – when the Butter is melted add a Spoonful of Flour – Stir with a Spoon add a quarter of a pint of good Gravy – a quarter of a pint of good Cream – leave the Whole to Boil on a gentle fire for Half an hour – put the Head in a Stew pan – Boil it, when done serve it on the Sauce – when the Brains are Boiled they must be hashed and mixt with some Butter Sauce – some Parsley Boil'd and Chopt and Served on the Head – The Liver must be Broiled Cut in two and Served on the dish.

TO PRESERVE PLUMS

They must be used before they are quite ripe – and the Tails left on as in all Fruits which are preserved with the Stones in. Prick them with a Pin, and simmer them a moment in boiling Water – then drain very well, and boil them a moment in Sugar highly Clarified – skim it well, and let all rest together a Couple of days, then boil the Syrup well adding a little more raw Sugar to it – then Boil the Plums in it a few Minutes – the proportion is a pound of sugar to each pound of Fruit.

DESERT CAKES

Take some Double refin'd sugar – pound and sift it – Beat the white of 6 or 8 Eggs to a Strong froth then put in as many spoonfuls of sugar as there are whites of Eggs – Stir them together but not too much, for that will make the froth fall – You may put in the Rind of a fresh Lemon grated – Drop them upon Tins with writing paper under, put them in the oven after Bread and stop it Close – when they are Dry enough and of a good Colour Take them off the paper and if you Chuse it, you may put two Botoms together with Raspberry or appricott Jam Between – put them before the fire to

Dry – you must not Let them stand after they are mixt together, but put them in the oven immediately and dredge sifted Sugar over them.

1796

October 4th   Lady Eleanor Butler and Miss Ponsonby return the parishes of Whiteford and Holywell* – with many thanks for the Great amusement received from their perusal – Some of the French Mountain Spinach Seed, which Mrs Pennant wanted to have is likewise enclosed.

(Lady Eleanor Butler to Thomas Pennant Esq.)

1797

Lichfield Oct. 30th   Be, my beloved Miss Ponsonby and Lady Eleanor, assured, that I consider Llangollen as my little Elysium . . . on my road home, imagination gave back to me the image of good Mrs Roberts† in a tragi-comic situation . . . She always remains till near dinner time in her very pleasant bed-room on the ground floor; and there, in her tristful days, I used to behold her, the large Venetian sash lifted up to its utmost extent, sitting in an arm-chair before it, in broad attitude, with contracted lips, wide eyes and Ugolino brow, exactly opposite old Castel Dinas Bran, which, separated only by that narrow glen, stood staring upon her in rigid opposition – its dark mass unsoftened by distance, frowning like herself, in dun cogitation. O! there was no desiring better sympathy, or a more twin resemblance between a matron and a mountain.

(Anna Seward to Sarah Ponsonby)

Expenses

Oct. 30   Poor Tatters aged 18 buried this morning 1s.

* By Thomas Pennant – an early local history.

† Wife of Mr Roberts of Dinbren. Her memorial (a huge urn) can be seen in Llantysilio churchyard to this day.

1799

October 21st ... the Spirits of Sorrow – Huff – and Frettability have been raised by Your long silence ... Miss Seward gave us three days in the *close* of last month ...

> (Sarah Ponsonby to Mrs Tighe)

Expenses

Oct. 21 Man from Hardwick with a present of 91 fine Trees 3s.
    23 Drink Money to Simon and Moses Jones completing the beautiful plantation 1s.
    24 Simon for burning his leg and hand with boiling Cement for the Trees 1s.
    25 Simon and William completed the Abber railing 1s.
    29 Dick Morris driving Mary to and from Brynkinalt 2s.6d.
    31 Stamp for a Receipt of our Half Years rent to John Edwards which *He says* should be £12.5.9. therefore he *is* paid £12.5.9.*

1801

Lichfield October 3rd   Just as I finished the last sentence, Cousin Thomas White shouted in the gallery, 'Peace! Peace on earth, and good will towards men!' – and rushed breathless into my dressing room to confirm his annunciation ... In less than half an hour the bells in all our churches began to clash their sonorous tongue in exulting imitation of the cannon's thunder ...

Monday Oct. the 5th   Joy sits on every face! – even those, who warmly defended the infatuated contest ... I congratulate you both upon these blessed tidings; auspicious to the quiet of your hearts in a degree beyond that of an individual portion in this general good ...

> (Anna Seward to Lady Eleanor Butler and Sarah Ponsonby)

---

* This was the beginning of the battle with the new landlord to renew the lease of Plas Newydd.

1802

Lichfield Oct. 4th   Ah! dearest ladies, it is under the pressure of a severe cold, fierce cough, and inflamed lungs, that I address you. A duty so delightful had, but for this incapacitating malady, been earlier paid. I have to thank dear Miss Ponsonby for a manuscript of many verses, which she had the goodness to make for me in hours so engrossed, amid engagements so indispensable. I had the honour to receive it as I was stepping into the chaise which was to convey Mrs Smith and myself far from that Edenic region where we had recently passed so many happy hours; from those bowers in Llangollen Vale, whence the purest pleasures have so often flowed to my heart and mind, as from a full and overflowing fountain.

(Anna Seward to Lady Eleanor Butler and Sarah Ponsonby)

1805

Oct. 31st   It is shocking to send you such an unsightly scroll; but if you were to see how strangely I am obliged to place my paper, suspended on the left elbow of an high arm-chair, in which I may lean back and have my head supported! If I stoop my head in the least degree forward, dreadful dizziness instantly ensues . . .

(Anna Seward to Sarah Ponsonby)

1807

Thursday October 1st   Mr K called while we were at Breakfast about the sale of Pengwern which occasioned so much anxiety and distress in the minds of so many people.

Saturday October 10th   Extreme heat. Sultry wind. Miss Williams Wynn, then Sir Arthur Wellesley* 'till three.

Wednesday October 21st   My Better half and I rose at five. Went at six to Oswestry. Stopped at the Cross Keys . . . Went to Vaughans, then to Eddowes, then to two other filthy Booksellers shops. Then drove to the Council House. Did not alight. Went on to Berwick . . . Luncheon. Mr Jones powdered and dressed our hair . . . Dinner. At twelve Mrs R. Wingfield and we set out in darkness and rain. One

* Later the Duke of Wellington.

wheel flew off near Aston. Called to the Lodge near the gate. Terrified by the noise, and we made amends. Wheel right – we got to Oswestry. Sat in the parlour of the Cross Keys 'till the chaise which was to convey Mrs Wingfield to Porkington was ready. Got home at five in the morning.

(The Journal)

1811

October 29th   Company from Ten am to Ten pm . . .

(Sarah Ponsonby to Mrs Parker)

1812

October 7th   . . . to show You the sort of life we *sometimes* lead in our *Strict* retirement . . . [followed by an enormous list of visitors].

(Sarah Ponsonby to Mrs Parker)

1814

Llangollen Vale Tuesday October 9th   Dearest Mrs Piozzi, We trust you will hold yourself bound to make us Ample recompence for the Many and Cruel disappointments we have experienced in learning that you had so frequently Journied To and From Brynbella without bestowing a Single glance Upon us. Though we So repeatedly and so earnestly supplicated for even a few hours of Your *You Know* Singularly Charming Society. Dear Dear Mrs Piozzi – do indulge us with one Call en passant . . .*

(Sarah Ponsonby to Mrs Piozzi)

October [undated]   My dearest Miss Harriet – I verily believe the Demon of Procrastination Abides in My pen – the moment I attempt to employ it – You would be terrified to behold the Multitude of persons who are conjured up to prevent My Writing – persons of whose existence I had no idea – persons whom I thought had ceased to exist ages past – Sir John Cotterill and his three Most hideous

---

* A fair example of blackmailish wheedling!

Daughters came introduced by Lady Dungannon – Mr and Mrs Becker – he a German of immense Opulence – She built on a very large Scale with a Magnificent face in the Rubens stile – a Massish Beauty – Then we have had the Algernon Grevilles – we like them very Much – if he could be Convinced of how much More becoming it is to stand erect than to Lounge and Sweep the Carpet with his head – he would be very handsome Graceful and pleasing – it seems he is highly accomplished – Musical – dresses finely – in short *rempli de Talent* – would you believe it from his Manners and Appearance?

(Lady Eleanor Butler to Miss Pigott)

Llangollen October 29th   Let us hear from you perpetually and tell me how you like my dear dear France and all you see and all you hear there – Send me your Address – I wish I had known that you were staying with Mr Williams – I should have besought you to speak to him on My Behalf and gently hint of what essential – what incalculable service a little Money would do me – The trifle Lord Ormonde Could So *well* Spare would be Absolute Wealth to *poor* me – but you would have put all this in good words and find a *proper* moment for their utterance – My dear – My kind Miss Harriet – I well know that Zeal would not have been wanting on your part . . .

(Lady Eleanor Butler to Miss Harriet Bowdler)

1819

Thursday October Twenty one   Universal Snow.

(The Journal)

1820

Porkington October 24th   Well, I have seen them, heard them, touched them. The pets, 'the ladies' as they are called, dined here yesterday – Lady Eleanor Butler and Miss Ponsonby, the curiosities of Llangollen mentioned by Miss Seward in her letters, about the year 1760. I mentioned to you in a former letter the effect they produced upon me in public, but never shall I forget the first burst yesterday upon entering the drawing-room to find the dear ante-diluvian darlings attired for dinner in the same manified dress, with the Croix St. Louis, and other orders, and myriads of large brooches, with stones large enough for snuff-boxes, stuck into their starched neckcloths. I have not room to describe their most fascinating persons. I have an invitation from them which I much fear I cannot accept. They returned home last night fourteen miles, after twelve o'clock. They have not slept one night from home for above forty years.* I longed to put Lady Eleanor under a bell-glass and bring her to Highgate for you to look at.

(Charles Mathews to Mrs Mathews)

---

* This in fact was apocryphal, though it is still uttered in Llangollen to this day.

NOVEMBER

1784

Tuesday November 6th ... any little Book if you know of such, that gives directions for the Construction of Maps According to the Stereographic projection ... Map drawing being one of my favourite employments ...

(Sarah Ponsonby to Mrs Tighe)

November 29th I return you a thousand thanks my Dearest Friend for your kind Communications which have made me Completely Mistress of the Stereographic Projection of the Sphere.

(Sarah Ponsonby to Mrs Tighe)

Saturday November 5th Incessant rain. Violent Storm. Kitchen full of Smoke – Mary Raging at it. Bought Herrings. I finished my Manuscript this Morning.

Sunday November 6th I had a dreadful Head-ache all night – My Sweet Love all tenderness and anxiety – We did not rise 'till Ten . . . Showery Windy Morning. The Shoemaker from Chirk brought our Shoes. Very neatly Made – Present of a large Woodcock from the Lyon . . . My Beloved finished her Map* with a neatness and accuracy peculiar to herself. The Writing and Ornaments particularly Beautiful.

Monday November 7th Five gallons of Frontinac raisin wine in a small cask to Entertain our Barretts when they come here – From Five 'till Ten read Rousseau (finished the 7th tome) to My Sally. She made a Portfeuille of Parchment and White and Blue Satin for her B. to keep this Journal in.

Tuesday November 8th Rose at eight – a Charming morning – Put on our Good Habits – the others (Particularly Mine) being absolutely Worn to Rags . . . A Rumour in the kitchen that a Rat had been seen in the Fowl yard. John Thomas (the mason) sent for in haste to stop up the Holes and quiet the alarms of the quality.

Wednesday November 9th Before Breakfast the waiter of the Hand brought a Box which had arrived by the Chester Waggon from London. On opening found the Contents to be a Beautiful Bason or Vessel to contain water for the dogs. Mr Wedgwood's† new invention and we conclude a Souvenir from Him as there was no Letter . . . Mr Whalley showed us Paterson's Itinary which I am glad to have seen as it has effectually removed Every wish I formerly had of purchasing it – He gave my beloved Some drawing paper and duck Quill pens. At Nine Mr Thomas arrived to conduct us home. The finest night. Course of the Dee through the Valley Marked by a Blue Transparent Mist. The owls at the Abbey – Dinas Bran and Pengwern in Plaintive Concert . . . Four strikes of Malt. Three pounds of Hops – for Tomorrows Brewing.

* Of the World.
† Josiah Wedgwood (1730–95), the master potter and industrialist.

Thursday November 10th   Our Landlord, Richard Griffiths, and the Clerk ploughing, sowing, harrowing and limeing the Field before our Cottage. No words can describe the Sweetness, the Festivity of the Scene – the Brilliancy of the Day – the Beauty of the Country – The field so animated – The number of workmen – the various implements of Husbandry, as Carts, Plough, Harrow and Sacks of Corn, altogether formed a Picture of Rural Content and Simplicity that monarchs might behold with envy . . . We Brewed this morning and compleated our Winter provision of Beer . . . from Five 'till Six Sitting in the Library with My hearts darling 'in Converse Sweet' – Then walked about the gardens – the most glorious Moon – a Sweet Scene.

Friday November 11th   Rose at Eight – dark Still Morning. Our habits at length arrived by the Stage. Donnes has acquitted himself Very much to our Satisfaction. Mrs Thomas (who I perceive delights in the marvellous) gave a fearful account of the devastation the Rats had made in the Fowl house. My beloved and I went to examine it. Found one poor solitary hole – made Powell stop it up . . . Turner came and dress'd our Hair (Said to *me* he was sure I wou'd be very much pleased with young Mr Folliot's head of hair when I saw it!) We bought Ten measures of Potatoes from Francis for the Winter . . . High Wind – heavy Clouds. bright Moon. a Wild Night.

Saturday November 12th   My Beloved and I Consulted Mrs Jeffreys about the proper form of making our Wills – While she was Instructing us and we were Settling our affairs the Whalleys and their children Came in – Wished them at the Deuce for interrupting us – they staid but a few minutes . . . Twenty four yards of cloth from the Loom this day for Table Linen which our under Vestals spun last Winter.

Sunday November 13th   Rose at Eight, a calm grey day – at nine Walked to the Hand – breakfasted there. Then Sign'd and Seal'd our Last Wills and Testaments with the Codicils . . . deposited a Copy Sealed with Black Seals in the hand of Mrs Jeffreys.

Monday November 14th   My Beloved and I walked in the Shrubbery 'till the Village Clock told Twelve – the Loveliest Silent Night – light as day – every object diminish'd but perfectly distinct – an Idle day – When Shall We be Sweetly alone?

Wednesday November 16th   Rose at nine (Shamefully late to-day) after breakfast Went the Home Circuit. My Beloved return'd to the Library to draw her Map. I remained in the Shrubbery – Transplanting – Brought an green Oak – Horse Chestnut – Purple Beech, double flowering Cherry, Sumach, Lime and Honey-Suckle, which had been concealed in the little Wood – to the front of the Lawn and North Border. Planted Mrs Barker's rose Trees in the East Border . . . came in at Twelve – wrote 'till near two – My beloved still at her Map. (Letter from Miss H. Bowdler dated Bath the 9th. The Beautiful vessel for the dog's water a present from their generous Friend – What a mercy that we did not write to thank Wedgwood!) . . . Note from Mr and Mrs Fairfax desiring to see the House and Garden. Permitted. Mrs Fairfax said to Mary She hoped We might Long Enjoy our *Solitude* which she thought charming. After dinner My Beloved and I walked round the Shrubbery and Kitchen garden. My Sweet Sally kindly approved of all my Transplantations.

Thursday November 17th   John Jones Staid 'till Three – Provincial Politics how I hate them – Treated him to Butter Milk and New Brown Bread . . . I read 'till past Twelve – heard the Owls as distinctly as if they were in the room with us – at Eleven Miss Vent Rush'd Suddenly thro' the Valley in a Violent Bustle. I began *Les Oeuvres de Thomas* this Morning.

Friday November 18th   A man from Hodges and Lawrence. Paid them – thank Heaven. A Receipt in full one of the greatest Luxurys of Life . . . Present of Fish from the Lyon. I hate culinary presents . . . The moon rising as I write this – Shining full in front of the Middle Window – a day of Retirement of Sentiment and of *Tenderness* – which Increases with any Vexation . . .

Sunday November 20th   Talked over our affairs 'till Ten. Informed the Talbots of the measures I mean to pursue – Which they approve of – Mrs Talbot has a perfect recollection of the provision which was made for me in my Brother's Marriage Settlement. They agree in thinking I have been barbarously Cheated. I also acquainted them with my having sign'd sealed and delivered My Last Will and Testament That I might Secure all I am possess'd or Entitled to to the Beloved of My heart – They will See Justice done her when I am no more . . .

Monday November 21st   Frost. Snow. Sleet and Wind ... Mr Whalley came, staid half an hour – a tedious dissertation on Crimes and punishments. Wish'd him hanged for interrupting us ... When he Was gone My Beloved began to draw from Palladio – I read 'till Three ... after dinner Went the Home Circuit. Powell at Work in the Kitchen garden taking up Pea Sticks – digging and raking the ground on which they Stood. Rolling the Lawn. Wind abated – Sky red and Inflamed.

Tuesday November 22nd   Did not rise 'till nine – Shameful! White glittering Frost. Country magnificently beautiful. A Fair in the Village. What a picture might be drawn from our Parlour Window of the crowds descending the opposite mountain and passing through the Field before our Cottage. Some on horseback, many on Foot, all comfortably Clad, each bringing their different commodity to the Fair, as Cattle, Pigs, Poultry, eggs, Cheese, Woolen Cloth, Baskets, Wooden ware, Spinning wheels. The women knitting as they went along, the young People in their best apparel – health, content and Innocence illuminating every Countenance, all speeding with heartfelt Joy to Llangollen ... Mary in her Glory purchasing Beef for hanging, and exerting all her powers of Eloquence in bargaining with the Butchers.

Wednesday November 23rd   Our Landlord with his Team in the field before our Cottage. Went to him. Made him come in and warm himself in the kitchen. Gave him some Ale to drink ...

Thursday November 24th   Letter from Lady Dungannon with a present of a white Turkey cock and hen ... Order'd the Turkey Cock to be killed lest his company should be offensive to the old Tyrant here. Sent him the Hen for his seraglio.

24th November   We have found sleeping with the Head Dress'd excessively warm – with innumerable Night Caps – Very effectual both as a cure and preventative of Head achs and tooth achs – Do you practise it?

(Sarah Ponsonby to Mrs Tighe)

Saturday November 26th   Storm all night. Rose at Eight. dark. Windy. Wet morning. I read 'till Breakfast ... Simon still at Work Stopping up all the Rat holes with Mortar and powdered Glass. *Cette*

Maudite Engeance will be disappointed of the Luxury with which they used to revel and Spend their Winter in the Fowl yard.

Tuesday November 29th   Powell at Work in the New garden – digging among the Strawberries and Raspberries and planting out 140 little rose trees which We have raised from Berries of Our Garden Saved in the year 1783 – Penetrating Cold Hurricane. Wild light and Shadow flitting about the Mountains.

Wednesday November 30th   Bought four Cheeses Weighing 106lb for the Family* from Parry the Farmer at Llangollen.

(The Journal)

1788

Tuesday November 4th   My beloved and I went to our Farmyard and round the field . . . When we came in ran to the Kitchen to warm ourselves – The evening being bitter cold. The Kitchen fire excellent. Heard the gate open – ran to the window – our good Friend Ned Tighe . . . We accompanied him through very dirty streets and drops of rain to the Hand. Mrs E. Tighe soon made her appearance . . . They dined, drank coffee, and then the Moon and the stars shining bright we all walked up here. The streets horribly dirty. Saw an odd looking man and woman in the Churchyard who frightened us. Observed Peter our Smith standing there – called him – he ran for a Lanthorn and conducted us safely to our little abode.

*As people did then, Eleanor speaks of the servants as 'family'.

Found the candles lighted and excellent fires in each room. The Tighes delighted at the cheerful and comfortable appearance they exhibited . . .

Wednesday November 5th   Reading. Drawing. My beloved and I walked to the White gate. The finest Night. Pensive – Steady Moon over the center of the field – pale blue faint sky – constellations – stars – planets – mists rising and gradually ascending the mountains from the Rivers, Brooks and Streams. One large Bonfire on the green. Bells ringing in Commemoration of the Revolution.*

Friday November 7th   The Vicar's large Dog went mad last night and was shot this morning. There must be some mysterious cause of all these large dogs in the country going mad. I suspect it originates from Potions administered to them by the numerous Vagabonds with which the roads and Villages Swarm, under the appearance of maim'd Sailors, servants out of place, Pedlars etc. who meditate an attack upon the house and thus remove the incorruptible guardians from them.

Sunday November 9th   No letters from Wrexham. Fearful accounts of mad Dogs about Wrexham – Overton. Sir Watkin Williams Wynne has ordered his game keeper and people to go about Wynnstay, Ruabon and the Coal Works and shoot every dog they meet. The same orders have been issued by the Justices at Wrexham and are to be put in Execution to-morrow.

Saturday November 15th   *St James' Chronicle* accounts of His Majesty as bad as possible. They are received with universal Terror and Consternation. Gloomy and bitter cold – Writing – Reading. When we heard the Stage Coach come into the village from Oswestry, Sent to enquire of the Passengers from London what account they brought of his Majesty – very ill if alive, which we most sincerely lament, not from interested motives solely but concern for loss of a Good Man. A King's Messenger went through the village for Ireland. The King alive yesterday but without hope of recovery – How sorry we are!

Sunday November 16th   Prayers offered up at church this day for the King's recovery. I hope they may be heard.

* The Bloodless Revolution of 1688.

Monday November 17th   The universal and unfeigned sorrow for the King's illness – *St James' Chronicle* . . . Letter from Mr Chambre – pension not to be paid for two months. The Lord help the poor Creatures who have nothing to subsist on but the Royal bounty. I am far from implying any reflection on his *Majesty* but on his *Money* which his Ministers receive and will not pay – as we miserably experience.

Monday November 24th   The tax gatherer came. Paid him £4.1.6. Evaded the stamp.

Tuesday November 25th   Sent for Mrs Pryce* who with her husband came from Oswestry. Conversed with them about Lady Dungannon. So amazingly unfeeling after the fearful adventure with the Bailiffs who under the pretence of bringing her a letter enter'd her apartment, then conducted her to a Chaise which with two other Bailiffs and six Marshal Men were in the Court waiting for her. They stop'd at Twickenham to Dine, then brought her to a Spunging house!, whither Mr Cavendish and his mistress had just before been conducted. Lady Dungannon in high conversation with *La Pucelle* when Lord Fairford and Lord Mornington made their appearance. They brought her to Lady Morningtons. She dined and conversed with the greatest unconcern. Lady Mornington who was entirely overset with grief, horror, and apprehension, conveyed her to Hampton Court, where she lay that night and returned to Town next morning. Shocked and provoked by her mother's want of feeling or shame. Lord Dungannon's goodness – so little known, his tenderness – his generosity – his continual attention to his grandmother, whose want of economy has involved him and all her family in Trouble and anxiety.

(The Journal)

1789

Tuesday November 3rd   The civilest of all trades-people Woolham called here this evening. Alas, to no purpose. He mentioned the great alteration the absence of so many families who have deserted the neighbourhood has occasioned at Wrexham. Mr York of Erddig coming only for a month to Erdigg. The present Sir W. W. Wynne

* Servant to Lady Dungannon.

not come to Wynnstay till he is of age. Bryn-y-pys empty. Mr Wynne leaving the Country and settling in Hampstead. Sir Foster Cunliffe to spend the winter in Scotland.

Sunday November 15th   Fearful hurricane. Reading. Drawing. Loud rap at the Door. Lady Templeton's Servant, soon followed by that charming woman herself, and her sweet Daughter. Such mutual joy at meeting – on our part so unexpected. Got tea and coffee instantly – Cake, brown and white bread and butter – toast and butter – an excellent bright fire – Shutters closed – Curtain let down. She exclaimed with surprise and admiration of the beauty and comfort of our little abode. The latter greatly enhanced by the fearful Storm which raged and howled about the Mountains.

Tuesday November 17th   Carts in the field. John Edwards and his Hinds at work spreading Soil over the field, preparatory to sowing Wheat.

Saturday November 21st   Our poor Landlord came to ask us how the broth we ordered for his wife was to be made. His tears – his regret for her illness – his recapitulation of her goodness, and the happy life they had led together these fifty years affected us and called forth our Tears. Reading. Writing. Saw the burial of a little girl coming thro' the Field. Enquired the reason of its being attended by such a multitude of children. The person of whom we enquired said it was the Custom here when a Child died that all its companions and playmates of the same age attended the funeral and Bore the Coffin to the Grave.

November 23rd   How apt should we some Years since have been to exclaim against any Lady who had declared that She Could not Afford to live upon £800 per Annum! I know of many who live Handsomely upon half that income – and whose charity contributes to the Comfort if not Support of numbers besides . . .

> (Sarah Ponsonby to Mrs Tighe,
> currently in financial difficulties)

Receipts

November 23rd.   Received of Mr Chambre £16.16s. in pt. of *another* Quarter of our Pensions paid up to July. Long Live the King.

Friday November 27th Sweet day under clouds. Soft sunshine dissolving the hoar frost on the eves of the house. Patches of blue sky. Writing. Note from the Comte de Jarnac who has just arrived at the Lyon Inn. Sent to invite him up ... M. de Jarnac related all the horrid particulars of the King's* capture at which he was Present. It originated from a report being Maliciously circulated at Paris that there was neither Corn nor Flour and consequently there would be no Bread. The next Morning all the Fish women, all the common prostitutes, assembled and, armed with canes, to the ends of which they fixed sharp spikes, proceeded two by two to Versailles. They drew with them two pieces of cannon and every Woman or Lady they met they forced to accompany them in this procession. They were followed by 600 Banditti armed with heavy Triangular pieces of wood with sharp Long Nails fastened at each end. These Banditti were followed by nearly twenty-two Thousand of the National Troops, sixteen pieces of cannon, headed by the Marquis de la Fayette. They set out from Paris at 9 in the morning, and at 8 at night they all reached Versailles, twelve miles from Paris. The first Outrage was the Fish women who desired and obtained admittance. They harangued him† as usual on their knees – demanded Bread, which he ordered should be given to them. They retired and went to the Assembly of the States – demanded male deputies, and returned to the Palace. The Garde de Corps would not admit them, and, on their attempting to force in, they fired, on which these demons seized Mons. de Valincourt and Mons. Launay, cut off their Heads – sent them to Paris – but first had the hair powdered and dressed of these unfortunate victims of their Barbarity . . . By this time the Banditti were arrived and dispersed themselves quickly all over the town. At eight o'clock the discharge of six field pieces announced the arrival of Mons. de la Fayette and his twenty two Thousand troops. He immediately demanded audience of the King – was admitted – appeared grave and sorrowful – expressed his regret for coming in this manner, but excused himself by saying he must have been hanged had he refused – that he was deputed by the National troops to request his Majesty would put himself and Royal Person under the care of his Loyal and Faithful Subjects and dismiss the Garde de Corps who had proved traitors to their Countrymen.

* Louis XVI.

† The King.

In this deplorable situation the King was obliged to comply. Mons. de la Fayette then placed guards on all the Avenues at the Palace and answered for the safety of the Persons of the Royal Family. The Queen received private information that there was a design against her life and advised her to pass the Night in the King's Apartment. She replied if her life was to be attacked should she be the person to Conduct the Danger towards the King? No – she said – she committed herself to the Care of Providence and was determined to await the event with resolution, and receive it with resignation. Two hundred of the faithful Garde du Corps dispersed themselves about the Palace. The Queen's footman sat up in the Ante-Chamber and she retired to rest. At 5 o'c. the six hundred Banditti rushed in the Palace, killed 16 of the Garde du Corps in one room, and rushed about like so many demoniacs in Search of the Queen's Apartment. The footman instantly rapt at her Door to apprize her of her Danger and bid her fly to the King's Apartment. She had but just time to put on her shoes, stockings and one petticoat. The other she had not time to tye on. When she heard them coming she ran to the room of one of her women – threw on a wrapper and ran to the King whose door was locked but it was instantly opened to her. She and the King went down to the Dauphin's Apartment, and brought him and his Sister up in their arms. The Marquis de la Fayette entered and appeared in great consternation, for by this time the troops, the Women, the Banditti were all assembled about the palace to the number of above 40 thousand. They were firing shots in at all the Windows and calling for the Royal family to appear at the windows. They all came to the Balcony – When they had stood there some time they retired – Then the Mob clamoured violently that the Queen should come to the Balcony and come alone. Everyone present suspected their design, when she, with infinite presence of Mind seized the Arm of that Traitor, La Fayette, saying 'Allons Monsieur' and made him accompany her. When she had stood there some moments they applauded then dismissed her. In a short time they renewed their demands that the Court should abandon Versailles and reside with them in Paris. They had no longer the power of refusal, therefore consented . . . They were eight hours moving from Versailles to Paris, which as I said above is no more than 12 miles . . . After some hours' deliberation they were brought to the Thuilleries which, from not having been inhabited from the time of the minority of Louis XV, was wholly destitute of every Convenience. Therefore, when the Royal Family arrived, they found the floors covered with Wool etc. and people at work making beds and mattresses for their use, nothing having been brought from Versailles for that purpose . . .

(The Journal)

1790

Monday November 15th   Roses and Lilies secured from frost by Muck.

Tuesday November 23rd   Sent for the man of the Hand – Paid him – Then sent him to the Village for the man with the Bear – The man brought it – A tame huge animal – female I suppose – by the Master calling it Nancy. We fed it with Bread and Mutton. It drank Small Beer. It was exhibited in the field before our Cottage.

(The Journal)

Expenses

Nov. 23   For seeing Miss Nancy a very aimiable Bear 1s.

1795

Expenses

Nov. 2   Poor People 2s. Half Hundred and more baking Apples 3s.
    6   Watchmaker a not unconsiderable Bill 16s.6d.
       Our Cow's Starved Summer to Mrs Parkes £2.2.0.
  11   Simon and Molly attending Our poor greatly aged Landlord 1s.
  26   Sandford the Shrewsbury Bookseller in full and for ever £11.2.2.
  30   Cooper's Bill in full £4.8.9.

1798

Lichfield November 15th   I see with the deepest concern and the most desponding fears for the result, the success of this country's renewed incendiarisms on the continent. Ah, Heaven! is it thus the English nation shews its gratitude to thee for the signal, the glorious victories, with which thou has blest our fleets! How much more worthy a wise, a humane, a Christian nation ... to have said to France – 'Let the exterminating sword be sheathed. Meet us with reasonable terms of reconcilement, and we will find our noblest pride in shewing you, and the whole world, that our naval victories have not shut our hearts to compassion for the miseries our continued warfare must produce to both nations.'

(Anna Seward to Sarah Ponsonby)

November [*undated*]

Accompanying the Present of an Alderney Cow

From Alderney's far distant shore
Encircled by the stormy main
I come that pity to implore
Which misery asks *not here* in vain.

Oh gentle Ladies of the vale
Receive a young and friendless guest
Indulgent hear my artless tale
And give a weary wanderer rest.

(Harriet Bowdler to the Ladies)

Expenses

Nov. 30   To the Man who brought the Dear little Linda 5s.

[*December 7th*   ... gentle as a lamb, tame as a lapdog.

(Sarah Ponsonby to Mrs Tighe)]

1802

Lichfield November 9th   Naughty brook, for having behaved out-rageously again! That little stream of the mountain is a true spoiled child, whom we love the better for its faults, and for all the trouble and alarm they occasion. You see I presume to involve myself, as if, in some sort, the interesting little virago belonged to me. Certainly it is my peculiar pet amongst your scenic children, dear to my taste, as they are beautiful to my heart, as being yours.

> (Anna Seward to Sarah Ponsonby,
> on the Cufflymen bursting its banks)

Receipts

TO PICKLE BEEF

Take part of the Plate or Brisket of Beef and rub it with Salt – get some of the commonest Brown Sugar, an equal quantity of Salt Petre and Sal Prunalle pounded and dried. Mix them together and make them Hot, then rub your Beef well with it. Let it lie for three Days and then repeat it again. Make a Pickle beat in an Egg. Boil it and let it stand for three Days. Pour it on Your Beef and Cover it close. It is fit for boiling in nine or ten days.

APPLE PUDDING

Pare and Core 12 middling Apples – boil them tender and pulp them through a Sieve – put to them half a pound of Sugar, the peel of a Lemon Grated, and Squeeze in the juice. The yolks of Six Eggs and whites of three, mix them with your Apples and Sugar, melt two ounces of butter, thicken and mix it with the rest, put thin paste under and round the edge of the dish – half an hour Bakes it.

CHOCOLATE

Simmer the Chocolate on a slow fire in the proportion of two Ounces to each Cup: stir it about a good deal with a Chocolate Mill, and when it is properly thickened add the White of an Egg in the proportion of One to every four Cups. Beat it equally, throwing the first Froth away – mix it first with a little of the Chocolate which add to the rest and Mill it together – this will make it of a proper Consistence and a better froth – it is best made a day before Using.

1806

November 5th   Will you believe it my dearest friend, here is the 5th November arrived – our loyal village bells ringing for joy of King

James I's escape from the gunpowder treason, its annual bonfire to which Mary always contributes about a soup ladle full of coals and then expects the children to shour applauses of her generosity . . .

(Sarah Ponsonby to Mrs Tighe)

1807

Monday November 2nd   Poor Mrs Parry shut up her shop this day, which we are very sorry for . . .

Sunday November 22nd   The same fearful depth of snow. Intense frost. Azure sky.

Monday November 23rd   Deep, deep and universal snow. Deeper than was ever remembered – Snowing large flakes. The son of Jones, poor Mrs Parry's creditor with her – thank God – little Bill of £1.11.0.

Thursday November 26th   The road open to Travellers once more.

Friday November 27th   Universal deep snow. Such weather never remembered by the oldest person.

Sunday November 29th   Atmosphere too heavy and opaque to admit of our seeing the Eclipse. Impenetrable mist. All stillness and silence.

(The Journal)

1818

Llangollen Vale, Llangollen, 11th November   Lady Eleanor Butler and Miss Ponsonby in Consequence of Mr Bouchier's wish for a Continuance of their Custom – request he will send them the following Articles – As they hope he has such Candles as will suit them some time ready made, as they always burn so much better than Newly made Ones – they will not pretend to give any other directions besides begging that they may be Very Handsome to look at – free from Tallowish Smell – and burn brightly and clearly – And hope the late advance in the price of Tallow is by this time Moderated.

Five Dozen Pounds very best *Wax* – *Wicked* Mould Candles – *Four* to the pound.

Five Dozen Ditto Ditto *Three* to the Pound.
One Dozen Pound best Wax Candles *Four* to the pound.
One Dozen Pounds Do. Do. *Three* to the pound.
Half a Dozen pounds D.D. *Two* to the Pound.
Three pounds best Carriage Do.
Three pounds best purified and perfumed Windsor Soap.

All to be Carefully packed in a Box and forwarded as usual by Shrewsbury Waggon – for Lady E Butler and Miss Ponsonby, Llangollen.
P.S. Mr Bouchier will please to send a letter when the Box is despatched from London.

DECEMBER

1784

Sunday December 11th Discharged John Addington for his *Sins* and Baseness and Ingratitude. *Mem* (a Methodist). Ill of an Headach...

Monday December 19th *Mem* no letter from the Barretts. This to be remembered when those Ladies perhaps wish to forget it.

(Eleanor Butler's Pocket Book)

1785

Friday December 1st At eight o Clock Moved all the Pictures and Furniture out of the Parlour and Library preparatory to the Chimnies being swept. Sent Mr Thomas and Mlle Babet* each to their

* Two of their cats.

respective apartment. My Beloved and I sat in the Kitchen beside a clear Chearful Fire and Clean Hearth looking over the Multitude of Prints in the *Physica Sacra*. Imagine it to be a Treatise of Sacred Natural History – some of the Prints a Confused Rhapsody like a Sick Mans dream – Strange – Foolish representation of the devil.

Saturday December 2nd   At Two o'clock this Morning the Chimney Sweeper came. Mary got up . . . at Eleven everything was in the most perfect order and neatness – I kept my bed all day with one of My dreadful Headaches My Sally – My Tender, My Sweet Love lay beside me holding and Supporting My Head till one o'clock when I by Much entreaty prevail'd with her to rise and get her Breakfast. She never left me for half a Moment the entire day Except at Two o'Clock when she perceived Mr Whalley and little Richard coming down the Field. She ran out to prevent his rapping at the door and to borrow the 1st Volume of the *Tab. de la Suisse* which she knew I was pining for – at four o'Clock old Joesy from Brynkinalt came. Letter from Poor Lady Dungannon with a pressing invitation for Monday which We are too much attach'd to our dear Cottage to accept of. At Five the delightful Book arrived from Tower. My Beloved Sat by My Bed Side reading it to me for near Two Hours – I wou'd not permit her to Continue – lest it shou'd impare her precious Health . . . Mrs Tatters uneasy that we did not come down stairs at the usual hour Scratched at our Door for admittance, came on the bed to me and lay there till Ten o'clock at night Purring all the Time – a day of Tenderness and Sensibility. My Sally How can I acknowledge the grateful Sense My Heart labours under of your Tenderness, anxiety and uncessant attention to your B.

Sunday December 3rd   Seventeen rainbows this Morning . . . Margaret this night put into her stable for the Winter with her own old Hay and her favourite cow to keep her Company as it was known she could not exist without society.

Monday December 4th   Mild Night – Sent the Family to their Apartments for the night. My Hearts darling and I sat by the Kitchen Fire talking of our Poverty. My Sally's affecting Exclamation! – retired at Twelve.

Wednesday December 6th   Rose at eight after a tedious night Spent in coughing and with a most dreadful head ache. My dearest, My

Kindest Love did not sleep even for one moment the entire night but lay beside me watching and lamenting my illness and soothing by her tenderness the distressing pain of My Head.

Thursday December 7th   The Wind howling for Entrance into the Vale, behind Cefnuche and Sounding like a distant raging Sea. From two 'till Three I read *Tab. de la Suisse*. My beloved at her map. Spent the evening without candles, by the light of the Fire and faint glimmering of a pale Moon, talking over our affairs. My Sweet Love. A Silent Pensive day.

Friday December 8th   My Sweet Love Settled her Drawers Transcribed the Weeks Account into her large Book and began a Plan of a House for young Blighe.

Sunday December 10th   Rose at Eight – dark morning. 2 quire glazed paper from Sandford – Wax – Wafers – Raven Quills – almanacks and Calendar from Do. kept a Repository and The atlas. My Sally gave me the Repository – I gave her an Atlas ... Mr Lloydde's Hounds on the Mountains opposite the Windows – from the Stillness of the air particularly melodious.

Monday December 11th   Little Pryce came with newspapers from Mrs Jones and to show us his new green Coat – all the Mountains Covered with Snow. Cold Wind. Snow and Sleet – after dinner My Sally and I ran the Home Circuit. Piercing Wind. Snow and Sleet. Shut the Shutters got Candles. Made a Blazing Fire. drew the Table near it and Enjoyed the Tempest that Thunder'd around us.

Tuesday December 12th   Letter by the Oswestry Post from my Friend Boissiere Enclosing a pattern of paper – a Vignette avec Envelope done by a Protegée of His – Some poor tawdry French Creature – who like a Cameleon lives upon air in some garret in London. *Mem* to write to Mrs Simpson and recommend her to her protection and oblige my Friend Boissiere ... after dinner went round the Gardens. Cold beyond Imagination. the Library as Exquisitely Warm and Comfortable ...

Wednesday December 13th   Black Scowling Wind in Violent Squalls. Three Strikes of Wheat ... the Penecoed Woman returned at Eight from Wrexham. No letters – She brought 24lb large and Small candles – Tea and Raisins for Mince pies ...

December

Thursday December 14th . . . a parcel by the Stage Coach Containing Sixty Raspberry Trees and Twelve plants of Black Strawberry – a present from poor Mrs Whalley which She Wrote for to her Sister Wickham in Somersetshire – The Tax gatherers came – paid them . . . The Sweetest Evening and most Splendid Majestic Moon – all traces of Snow entirely Wash'd away. Powell nailing the Fruit Trees in the Melon ground. from Seven 'till nine – Looking over Correcting and Binding this Journal – from Ten 'till Twelve I read Sterne – an agreeable Morning – an Evening of Sweet retirement peace and Delight.

(The Journal)

1788

Wednesday December 3rd Mr Edwards of the Hand brought us a present of fine partridges. Stormy night. Very cold. Reading. Writing. Letter by the Bath Carrier from Mrs Hunt, Chester, dated Tuesday, December 2nd: 'I doubt not your receiving every account of our poor King and his malady that transpires, tho' I am informed no one but those essentially necessary see him. All accounts agree in saying there is no Danger of his Death, nor any probability of his returning reason. Hard to pronounce positively, I think, in an Event that is much beyond the Power of Mortal Skill. This unfortunate malady has certainly been coming on him for some time – Cheltenham waters I do believe repeated his scrofulous complaint which probably might be attended by dangerous consequences to his mind. From a General officer that had attended every Levée since his return from Cheltenham it appears that all he said to his Courtiers (till the last Levée) was Silly and insane to a Strange Degree – but at the last where he stayed only 6 minutes he appeared quite an idiot, spoke to nobody, looked shockingly like one, and so departed out of the Drawing Room. The poor Queen is more to be pitied than any of her Subjects in the Meanest Line. The last Drawing Room at which she was to have appeared was put off on the King's having set fire to the Bed Curtains after she was in bed, and by her struggling to get the Candle from him one side of her Cap was burnt. This occasioned Violent Hysteric fits, which disabled her (as is natural to suppose) from appearing in Public.' – With the highest respect for Mrs Hunt's Veracity I give very little credit to this

Provincial intelligence, and cannot forgo my hope that his Majesty will yet be restored to the prayers of his Nation.

Friday December 5th   Turned into the kitchen where there was a most excellent bright fire. The young woman from Dinbrenisaf, the picture of health and cleanliness, standing with her good crock of Butter by the window. Asked how her Mother did. Much the better for the receipt we sent her. Asked her how old her Landlord, Roberts of Dinbren is? Fourscore and eleven, rides and walks about his lands every day and in all weather, his sight not so perfect as it was, but his hearing as acute as ever. His wife who is fourscore and two manages the family, attends her Dairy of twelve cows, makes butter and cheese for sale, is as active and notable as a person of forty.

Monday December 8th   Present by the Post of a turkey, of a roasting pig, from the Cross Keys. Writing. Reading. At twelve our dear Barretts and Margaret* came. Sweet day. When we had sat some time went the home circuit with them. They admired the new plantation in the new garden . . . After dinner the Barretts and our Dear Miss Davies went away. With tender and most sincere regret did we bid her adieu, as she leaves Oswestry next Wednesday. Accounts of the King: so very outrageous that he almost strangled the Duke of York, who lay senseless for a considerable time after. The Prince of Wales galloped to Town to consult with the Chancellor what methods might be made use of. This is Pigott's intelligence, to which I never give credit.

Thursday December 11th   My Beloved and I went the Farm circuit. Lovely day, rather cold. Somebody, I suspect that vile woman of Penycoed, has stolen our poor faithful hen whom we have fed and cherished so long, for whom we were going to erect a wall in order to enclose her precincts and secure her from annoyance of Dogs and Fowl. But she is gone. My beloved and I went to feed her with oats when we missed her. Sent to search every field, dingle, the banks of every stream, the Penycoed mountain. But this fell Inhabitant whose cottage we were the means of securing has made this grateful return . . . As my beloved and I were going to see the soil and sod which came in the Pengwern cart from the mountain we were assaulted by the Weaver's Bull Dog. Went down to his House,

* Not their cow, but their friend Miss Margaret Davies!

threatened him if he did not Shoot it or send it away this Very Night, he and his Dog should take the Consequence. He was saucy. We were determined and acted as I think and hope became us. Our poor hen is certainly gone. We fear destroyed by a Fitchet at an hour when we were not near to protect her. I daresay she thought of, perhaps called on us, but we Alas! heard her not.

Friday December 12th   Very gloomy, wet, cold. The Irish woman, whom we sent to Trevor with a letter to Mr Pleydell about the Bull Dog whom the weaver kept in defiance of us, returned with a Letter from Pleydell which we shall ever consider as an obligation. He also sent his gardener to summon the Weaver and his dog to Trevor Hall, and in every respect behaved as became the *Magistrate* upon whom we called, and the *Gentleman* to whom we applied. Reading. Writing. The Bird is dead that we made so much on. Robert the Weaver (our old neighbour) found her headless body under an old wall by the brookside where a Fitchet had brought and destroyed her – Poor Thing. This Fitchet is an old offender, the hatred and terror of all the Cottagers possessed of fowls, it inhabits an impenetrable fastness beside the Cyflymen. Reading. Drawing. Splendid heavenly glittering day. The Poor woman from whom we got our Hen, hearing of her dismal end came (with a kindness, a degree of feeling and sentiment which belongs to this country) with the present of a Hen which she hoped would be acceptable as we were so fond of the old Hen. This was a daughter of hers, rear'd from an egg of her own

Hatching. We were grateful for the Intention, sent the Hen to the fowlyard, but did not nor ever shall behold her as the successor of one who has left no Equal.

Saturday December 13th   Letter from Miss H. Bowdler dated Bath the 8th. Sir Henry Englefield says we shall not see the Comet long as it has paid its Visit to the sun and is going further from us every day. It is to be seen at 6 o'c. in the morning blazing in the East. The accounts of the poor King grow worse and worse: they have taken him from the place he loved and he has been much worse since. Those who love him must wish him in Heaven.

Monday December 15th   An old nailer in this village who goes every week to Wrexham says yesterday morning he came and went on an eminence near Wrexham on purpose to see the Comet, which he discovered blazing in the East. He described it as resembling a Hauberk, with a tail a yard long. The diameter of the Comet half the size of the Moon. As the sun rose it became dim and was at length gradually concealed by a circle of mist which enclosed it.

Monday December 22nd   Dr Willis has no doubt of the King's recovery as he never knew an instance of incurable Insanity which had not been preceded by melancholy.

December 25th   Three Dinner. Boiled Neck of Mutton and Turnips. Roast Goose. plum Pudding. Minced Pye. Christmas Day – My Beloved and I went to the field before our cottage. Farm Yard and etc. Very Misty – the village lights and the fire and Candles in our Kitchen gleaming. Thro them Stars Shining dimly – a distant pipe. Rush of the Mill Water fall.

(The Journal)

Expenses for Christmas Week

Dec. 17   Poor Mary Green 1s. a Wild Duck 1s.
    18   Post 2s.
    20   Moses Jones Weeks Wages 10s.
        Post 3s. Market 15s. poor Woman 1s.
        Paid the Cooper for mending a Table 6s.
        Making 2 more of our new Shifts 2s.
        Sundries 2s.

21 A little Water Glass 6d.
22 Turkey and Sausages etc. 5s.
25 Postman's Christmas Box 5s. Sundries 4s.6d.
    Letters 11d.
    Dinbren for Butter and Cheese etc £1.16s.
    Edward Evans for Coal Carriage £1.8s.
    Edward Parry's Quarter's Wages £2.7.3.

Receipts

RECIPE FOR PARTRIDGE WITH CABBAGE

Cut a large Cabbage into Quarters, scald it first then put it to boil or rather to stew with about half a pound of Pickled Pork Broth a paquet of sweet Herbs – Pepper, a little Salt and two or three Cloves – when almost done put in the Partridges, if they have been done before – let them stew some time, when done drain the Partridges and the Cabbage, put the Birds into a Deep Dish, the Cabbage round or between, and the Pickled Pork upon them.

MRS WORRALLS POUND CAKE

Take two pound of Good fresh Butter, work it with your hand to a Cream, then put two pound of good Lump Sugar in, well beat, dry'd and sifted, then work it well together for half an hour, then put in two pounds of fine Flour, then add Sixteen Eggs that have been well beat in a vessel by themselves with a whisk for an hour, then add a little Brandy, some sweet Almonds, a little pounded Citron and preserved Orange shred – and two pounds of Currents well cleaned – the Sugar and Flour must be sifted and put before the fire to dry for some time before you begin to make your Cake, and the other things got ready, and never take your hand out till you put it in the pan you bake it in, but keep beating it all the time for a full hour, take care your Oven is not very hot, it will take three hours and half baking in a moderate Oven.

1789

Thursday December 3rd   My beloved and I went the Home Circuit: walks all swept, borders raked, etc. Lovely day. Mrs Parry of Ruabon came – not with her Bill. We received her not as a Creditor but as the person whom for Eleven years we have dealt with and who for Eleven years had treated us with honesty, punctuality and the greatest attention.

Monday December 7th   While we were at dinner saw a gentleman and Lady in Mourning, a very tall young man in Blue, a Very little Woman also in Blue. Each of the Ladies a violent profusion of hair. Walked up and down the field. Enquired who they were? The Bishop of Llandaff, was the reply. Impossible. It must be that swaggering Lord Llandaff with his Tall Son and Daughter of a former Marriage. My Beloved and I went the Home Circuit. Reading. It was not Lord Llandaff but the new Bishop of Cork and half a hundred Fosters who walked up our field. A day of such Sweet Retirement.

Tuesday December 8th   Mrs Phyllis* so very condescending that we thought it advisable to lock her up. The last time she was confined she had a companion whom we shall ever regret.

Sunday December 13th   Thought the Library appeared unusually comfortable. The prospect from it magnificent. Rocks dark and gloomy. Mountains brown and withered, trees leafless.

Saturday December 19th   Reading. Working. My beloved finished the White Satin Letter Case with the Cyphers etc. in gold with a border of Shades of Blue and gold, the Quilting White Silk, the whole lined and bound with Pale Blue.

Friday December 25th   A tall thin old man came to the Door and Sung a Christmas Carol in a Melodious, solemn Voice. Listened to it with pleasure. Three Dinner. Roast Beef, mince pies.

Expenses for Christmas Week

Dec. 17   Postman for Sundries. Letters.
Fish Kettle etc. 12s. 6d.
Fowl and Sundries 5s.
Kitchen Chimney Swept 8d. Smoke Jacks cleaned 2s. 6d.

* Lady Dungannon's 'little yellow spaniel'.

18 Poor Mary Green 3s.
19 Sundries 3s.
  Edward Parry's Quarter's Wages £2.12.6.
  Beef 7s.6d. Mutton 5s.3d. Bakehouse 1s.8d.
  Richard Griffiths for Sundries 5s.2d.
  Mrs Parkes for Fish 3s.9d.
  Moses Jones Weeks Wages 10s.
  Poor Woman 4s.
20 Lodwick the Carrier from Wrexham 1s.6d.
22 Coal Carriage 1s.8d.
24 Christmas Eve. Market 17s. Poor Woman 4s. Sundries 6s.
  Moses Jones 10s. Postman 1s.
25 Clogmaker 1s. Carol Singer 6d.

Saturday December 26th Sweet, calm, still day. We dined early as on this day our Landlord and his family dine in the kitchen. At half past two our Landlord John, his wife, their son, and little Maudy our Landlord's Granddaughter, came in their best clothes, so respectable, so primitive, so simple. Our poor Landlady was afraid to venture out. Reading. Drawing.

Thursday December 31st Soaking rain, snow on the mountains. A parcel by the Stage Coach from the Head which had been sent from Shrewsbury and carried by Mistake to Holyhead. It contained almanaks from that civil Sandford. Kept an Atlas, a Repository with a Tuck, a Ladies new Royal Pocket Companion, a Housekeepers Accompt Book, a Royal Kalendar for the year '90.

(The Journal)

1790

Saturday December 25th Dinner Roast Beef. Plum Pudding. Soft mild evening. Reading. My Beloved and I got a lantern visited our Dear Margaret in her stable.

December 27th Our Landlord and Landlady their grand Daughter (Maudy) John and his wife their Two sons. Mr and Mrs Edwards of the Hand, Anne Jones and her Grand daughter dined in the kitchen According to Annual Custom.

(The Journal)

Total Expenses for 1790 – £568.19.3.

In which many debts were paid which We trust will never occur again – and a foundation laid for living in future Upon if not Within Our income – Praise be to God this 31st December 1790.

(The Account Book)

1791

December 27th   In his sermon he spoke of the *right* of the poor to relief, and that the power of bestowing it was the most valuable privilege of the rich . . .

(Harriet Bowdler, at Bath, to Sarah Ponsonby)

1794

December 5th   I remember that the wind was particularly tremendous on Saturday, but nothing like what you describe. I once or twice thought I distinguished thunder, but it was not so loud as the wind, and little did I imagine the violence wth wch it fell on the spot for wch I am most tenderly interested, and for wch I most fervently beg the protection of Providence.

(Harriet Bowdler to Sarah Ponsonby)

1795

December 9th   Before I speak to you, dearest Lady Eleanor, of the contents of your thrice-gratifying, thrice-beautiful letter, suffer me to present my thanks for a bounteous present of fruit trees. They will be the pride of my garden, and I shall watch their growth with solicitude, as the pledges of an highly-prized friendship.

(Anna Seward to Lady Eleanor Butler)

1796

December 11th   We have now got a nice snow and hard frost which will I hope keep us a good while alone and allow us to amuse ourselves.

(Sarah Ponsonby to Mrs Tighe)

1798

December 7th . . . a present of the most beautiful, the most amiable, the most valuable little cow I believe in the world. It appeared quite unexpectedly at our door having travelled all the way from Bristol, some verses hanging by a riband to its horn and enclosed in an envelope to us . . . The pretty little thing was terribly footsore after her long journey but is now quite well, gives abundance of milk like cream, is in calf, gentle as a lamb, tame as a lapdog.

(Sarah Ponsonby to Mrs Tighe)

1800

Expenses for Christmas Week

Dec. 12   to Edward Evans in payment for a quart of Ale 7d.
             to a Wonderful little Boy in Mrs Parry's Shop 6d.

      13   Mutton 7s. 6d.
             John Jones from Chirk brought Cabbage Plants 6d.
             Partridge 1s. 6d.

      15   Edward Evans for Carriage of Coals 16s. 6d.

      18   Postboy for 2 Glasses and himself 2s. 6d.

      19   Molly's Mother Boiling Goose 2s.

      20   Mutton from J. Roberts 9s. Beef 5s. 2d.
             Due to Mary Williams for a Goose 4s. Do. for Butter 6s. all paid this day.
             Simon's Weeks Wages 9s.

      24   to Dr Conway his most reasonable charge for Jane's medicine, he refusing any for attendance. We gave him 2s. 6d. extra as a present for his children.

      25   Our offering at Llantysilio – and half Crown to the Church 12s. 6d.

      27   Bakehouse for 16 loaves of Bread Christmas Day 4s.
             Peggeen for five days work when Jane was ill 2s. 6d.
             The Post Boy for a Christmas Box 2s. 6d.

1806

[*Undated*] Lady Powys has three rooms at Walcot filled with stuffed Birds in Glass Cases – Among them the Argus Pheasant –

and the King Bird of Paradise – they require the incessant attention of One Person to preserve them from Damp or they would melt away – there are not only fires – but stoves in all the rooms.

'Paris is now a Second Sodom and Gomorrah' declares Dr Glass. 'No, I am sure they were much stricter in those days!' [ripostes Eleanor]

(Lady Eleanor's Day Book, in which subjects for conversation were recorded and, once used, meticulously ticked)

1807

Friday December 4th   Lovely spring day. At nine set off for Brynkinalt. Staid an hour. Then proceeded to Aston. Staid two hours. Company Lady Louisa, two Miss Harveys, Mr Grosvenor. Brought Lady Louisa to Porkington. Dinner. Company Mr and Mrs Parker, Miss Ormsby, Mr and Mrs Bedingfield, Mr Charles, and Miss Wingfield, Miss Gore, Mr Edward Hunt, Mr and Mrs Kenyon, Mr and Mrs Lloyd, Mr Charles Lloyd, Miss Pigott. After coffee went up stairs. Saw *The Force of Love*. Descended to tea, then reascended to the farce of *The Devil to Pay*, admirably, most admirably performed. We did not stay to supper. Returned home. Night fine but windy. Arrived at our peaceful mansion at midnight.

Receipt

A PREVENTATIVE GARGLE

One Table Spoonful of Cayenne pepper, and One Tea Spoonful of Common Salt – put them into Six Table Spoonfuls of distilled Vinegar and Six Table Spoonfuls of boiling Water.

Saturday December 12th   Lovely enchanting spring day. Emerald valley, amethyst mountains. Evening fine. Bat fluttering about as in summer.

Sunday December 20th   Intense frost, air so rarefied that the little cracked Bell of Llantysilio church was as distinctly heard at our door as the village bells. Sun rayless, white, round, and not to be known except from its place in the heavens from the moon.

Wednesday December 23rd   Intense frost. At noon my Better half and I set out for Oswestry. Road hard but not slippery. Brilliant sun and azure sky. Shopped at Oswestry. Went to the Silversmiths, nothing but old and broken articles in his shop. Next to Edwards the Booksellers. Got some things there. Spoke to the Butcher's wife. Great Market. Went on to Porkington. In the Library Miss Ormsby, Miss Gore, Mr and Mrs Wingfield, with Miss Wingfield, Miss Mytton, Miss Pigott. We went with Miss Ormsby in her carriage to Aston. At Aston found Admiral and Lady Louisa Harvey. Staid an hour. Delightfully agreeable day.

(The Journal)

1817

December 2nd　Two dozen very finest Old Red Port.
(Lady Eleanor Butler to Mr Hesketh, their wine merchant)

1818

December 18th　My Better Half contented herself with Opening the Box – giving it one look – and having it laid by very Carefully – being her customary mode of treating almost all prescriptions.

(Sarah Ponsonby to Mrs Parker, thanking her for a prescription)

1819

December 25th　Beautiful French perfumes from Nightingale Shrewsbury – the gift of My Beloved.*

(The Journal)

* The recipient was now eighty!

Index

MORE ABOUT PENGUINS, PELICANS,
PEREGRINES AND PUFFINS

For further information about books available from Penguins please write to Dept EP, Penguin Books Ltd, Harmondsworth, Middlesex UB7 0DA.

In the U.S.A.: For a complete list of books available from Penguins in the United States write to Dept DG, Penguin Books, 299 Murray Hill Parkway, East Rutherford, New Jersey 07073.

In Canada: For a complete list of books available from Penguins in Canada write to Penguin Books Canada Ltd, 2801 John Street, Markham, Ontario L3R 1B4.

In Australia: For a complete list of books available from Penguins in Australia write to the Marketing Department, Penguin Books Australia Ltd, P.O. Box 257, Ringwood, Victoria 3134.

In New Zealand: For a complete list of books available from Penguins in New Zealand write to the Marketing Department, Penguin Books (N.Z.) Ltd, Private Bag, Takapuna, Auckland 9.

In India: For a complete list of books available from Penguins in India write to Penguin Overseas Ltd, 706 Eros Apartments, 56 Nehru Place, New Delhi 110019.